D0330174

Profile of Terror

Alexa Grace

Cover design by Christy Carlyle of Gilded Heart Design

ISBN-13: 978-0-9855939-6-4

DEDICATION

This book is dedicated to my angel team of physicians, nurses, technicians, friends, family and readers who blessed me with their expertise, kindness, prayers and support during my cancer journey.

CONTENTS

ACKNOWLEDGMENTS

I extend a special thank you to Lt. Adrian Youngblood of the Seminole County Sheriff's Office, who generously gave his time to answer my questions and review the book for law enforcement accuracy.

Thank you also to Nate Kitts, who helped me stay accurate in the facts of computer technology. Any mistakes here are entirely mine.

My gratitude goes to my editors and friends Vicki Braun and Ally Robertson.

My appreciation goes to my dear friend, Nancy Carlson, who approved the use of her name for the character Judge Carlson.

I am very grateful for the hard work of the *Profile of Terror* Beta Reader Team, which devoted personal time to review each page of this book: Nancy Carlson, Gail Goodenough, Barrie MacLaughlin, Sandra Galloway, Lisa Jackson, Tammy Richardson, Kimberly Stripling, Mona Kekstadt, Anna Coy, Debbie Dumke, Sylvia Smith, Mary Hesselgesser-Wright, Debbie Perry, Teresa Stirewalt, Cindy Rossetti and Catherine Scott.

Finally, I want to express my appreciation to my daughter, Melissa, my family, friends, readers and Street Team. Without their encouragement and support, this book would not have been possible.

CHAPTER ONE

At one in the morning, the dark sky was illuminated by a full moon as they drove on a country road, trees hanging overhead like skeletal arms, nearly touching their vehicle. Driving slowly, they made periodic stops, for only the perfect place would do.

Approaching a bridge over a deep ravine with a wide creek, the van stopped. Both got out and circled to the back of the white utility van, where they pulled out a young woman's body, already stiffening with rigor mortis. They carried her to the edge of the road, where they set down her corpse, gave it a push, and sent it rolling down the ravine until it landed on the rocky creek bed below. Hands on hips, they waited and watched the body at rest, as if they expected it to magically come to life and run away.

"I wonder how long it will take the cops to find this one." The driver chuckled as he followed his passenger to the back of the van.

"Good question. The one last winter wasn't found

until the spring thaw." He flipped through a stack of magnetic business signs he'd collected in the back of the vehicle. Choosing one, he slapped it on the side of the van and climbed inside.

"So how many magnetic signs do we have now?"

"Fifteen or so. We've got signs for plumbing, locksmithing, house painting, and general repair businesses. Think we need more?"

"No." He shook his head. "You did a good job stealing those. Even if we have an eye witness tonight, they'll describe a business truck, complete with a name and phone number the cops will use to try to track down their suspects. Too bad it will be a dead end. Any time we can toy with the cops is a good time."

"Agreed," he said, as a slow, evil smile spread across his handsome face.

Devan Roth glanced at his twin brother, Evan, sitting in the passenger seat, and thought about how much Evan craved his praise. He'd used that need to his advantage their entire lives. It wasn't that Devan didn't love his twin. He did, but he loved manipulating him more. Although Evan had a higher intelligence level than Devan ever dreamed of reaching, Evan's adoration for his twin was his weak spot. And if there was anything that Devan could identify from a mile away, it was someone else's weakness. That's what made Devan the leader.

From early childhood, he could get Evan to do absolutely anything he wanted. Devan invented the "Double Dare" game when the twins were twelve; he double-dared Evan to jump off the second-story roof. Evan leaped, and broke both his legs. But he never told their parents that Devan had dared him to do it. His loyalty to his twin outweighed the pain he suffered that summer.

The Double Dare game continued. Early on, they stole and killed their neighbors' pets, and then moved on to peeping in windows in the neighborhood and videotaping the event so they could relive the thrill later. Now they were abducting and killing prostitutes, then disposing of their bodies in remote areas surrounding Indianapolis.

Devan complained, "I'm getting tired of prostitutes. As prey, they're too easy. Where's the challenge? I'm ready to step up the game a notch or two."

"What do you have in mind?"

Devan did a U-turn to head back to town. "I've been reading a series of articles about a serial killer they caught in Shawnee County."

"Are you talking about the guy who used the Internet to hook up with preteen girls so he could torture and murder them?" Evan asked.

"That's the one. Jim Ryder is his name."

"Why are you interested in him?"

"It's not him I'm interested in. It's the Shawnee County Sheriff Office."

"I'm not following."

"Ryder killed girls over a four to five-year period before they caught him."

"No kidding?"

"Here's the clincher. Ryder was a deputy for Shawnee County," Devan said with a grin. "I mean, you got to see the humor in it. For years, the serial killer the sheriff's team was searching for was one of their own. He was right there working with them the whole time."

"So you're thinking of moving the game to Shawnee County?"

"Definitely. It'd be fun to play with Sheriff Brody Chase and his band of idiots."

"Are we changing the rules of the game?" asked Evan.

"Yes. I was talking to this computer geek in my math class the other day. He taught me a way to locate people through their digital photos on social media sites like Twitter, Google+, YouTube, Facebook, and Foursquare. "

"I don't get it. What does that have to do with our game?"

"Evan, sometimes you can be so fucking dense," Devan barked. "We can look for victims on these social media sites and get their addresses from the embedded EXIF data. In other words, if they've used a cell phone or high-end digital camera with built-in GPS to take the photo they post, we can determine our victims' exact addresses and follow them until the right time to snatch them."

Evan nodded. "So if we aren't going for prostitutes, who are we looking for?"

"Our new game victims, or should we say targets, are beautiful, smart, and popular coeds from Shawnee County," Devan announced. "They'll be the kind of victims who get residents all riled up and focusing their wrath on the Shawnee County Sheriff Office."

"Right. It hasn't been that long since they had to deal with Jim Ryder's murders, and now we'll give them a brand-new nightmare. I like it. Game on," Evan said excitedly.

City lights sparkled ahead of them. "Pull up the hood of your sweatshirt. Make sure it covers most of your face."

"We better hurry if we don't want Mom and Dad to discover we're out after curfew again."

CHAPTER TWO

It was early August in Indiana, sunny with temperatures in the low eighties. A light breeze whistled through the tall trees surrounding the huge yard and sparkling blue lake on the Chase property. Balloons and streamers adorned the outside living area, and a banner reading "Happy Birthday, Carly" hung above the stone fireplace. Three long tables with crisp white tablecloths displayed real china and glassware from the catering team.

Gabe Chase inspected the decorations and grinned with pleasure. He and his oldest brother, Brody, had done a good job planning the party.

As a child, Gabe had always envied his friends who had big family gatherings to celebrate life events like graduations, Thanksgiving or Christmas. His two brothers were his only family, and until now, they'd never had a large get-together at their home. He hadn't known how good it would feel to have family and friends together to celebrate a special event.

As planned, Jennifer Brennan-Stone, Frankie Douglas-

Hansen, Megan Brennan, and Anne Mason-Brandt had whisked Carly Stone away for a day at the spa and shopping, not mentioning they knew it was Carly's birthday. At six o'clock, the women would return for the surprise party and dinner.

Their husbands, Blake Stone, Lane Hansen, Tim Brennan, and Michael Brandt, were spending the afternoon playing with a Wiffle ball and plastic bat with five kids, and making a valiant effort to keep them out of the lake.

"Don't you and your brothers know anyone but cops?" Gabe's date, Abby Reece, asked with her hands on her hips.

"Why?"

"Look around. Every man here is a cop. This party is a cop convention."

Gabe lifted his eyebrows over the tops of his sunglasses as he scanned the crowd. "Not true. See that big guy in the yellow shirt over there, helping the little boy with the Wiffle ball?"

Abby nodded.

"That's Michael Brandt. He's a county prosecutor."

"Oh, excuse me," Abby said sarcastically. "This party is more like a *Law and Order* episode."

"That's very funny, Abby," Gabe said, without smiling. "How about using your inside voice for those kinds of remarks?"

For at least the tenth time that day, Gabe Chase realized what a mistake it was to invite his current girlfriend to Carly's surprise birthday party. What was he thinking?

Although he'd told Abby the party was a family event, when he picked her up at her apartment, the petite blonde wore a red knit, strapless dress that was so short and tight she could barely walk. Add to the getup a pair of four-inch heeled sandals. She was a good candidate for a *What Not to Wear* television episode featuring outfits to avoid wearing to an outing kids and parents would attend. Typical Abby. Her motto was strut-your-stuff and show-what-you've-got. An attitude he used to find a turn-on, but now found downright embarrassing, especially when he saw Brody's look of disapproval. Brody was the county sheriff, and appearances were important to him. Obviously, he was not impressed with Abby's appearance.

"Where did you say the wives and girlfriends are?" she inquired.

"They took Carly out for a spa day — facials, pedicures, and shopping."

"Why didn't I get invited?" Abby's lips formed an exaggerated pout.

"I told you before, I forgot about it until we arrived. I'm really sorry, Abby. I'll make it up to you."

"Oh, that's for sure, hot stuff," Abby grazed her hand over his zipper in a blatantly sexual way. "I'm making a list."

That was the thing with Abby. It was all about sex. She was the most overtly sexual woman he'd ever met. When it came to bedroom Olympics, Abby was gold medal contender. Early in their relationship, Gabe more than appreciated her skills in bed. The woman was unbelievably inventive. A gymnast in high school, she had moves that Cirque de Soleil would envy.

Lately, he'd found her one-track mind a little insulting. Was his body her only interest? Dissatisfaction was setting in, and he knew the time was nearing when he'd break up with her.

Gabe and Abby had been dating for four weeks, a record for him. In the past, he'd go out with a girl just a couple of times before he moved on. Brody wasn't entirely incorrect when he once referred to one of Gabe's dates as the flavor of the week. He'd leave the relationship soon, and it wasn't because Abby wasn't pretty, intelligent or sexy enough.

Gabe would leave the relationship because it wasn't a relationship, nor would it ever be. Abby had made it abundantly clear she was in it for the heart-stopping, world-shaking, five-alarm-fire, multiple-orgasms kind of sex, and not much else. This was okay in the beginning, but he'd changed, and it was no longer enough. Gabe wanted to make love to a woman to express how deeply he felt about her, and Abby would never be the woman to appreciate that. Not in a million years.

If someone had told Gabe a couple of years ago that he'd tire of fast cars and hot women, he would have laughed in his or her face. But that was exactly what had happened. Call it maturing or growing up, whatever it was, Gabe Chase had changed. He wanted more than sex from a woman. He wanted the kind of relationship Brody had with Carly.

Watching Brody and Carly interact the past couple of months made him realize what he was missing. They'd become best friends and lovers. Gabe rarely saw one without the other, whether it was fishing in the lake, going for a run, or taking walks through the woods. He envied their closeness. It was something he'd never had with a woman.

When Brody brought the profiler from Florida to Indiana a year ago, no one could have predicted Carly Stone would make such a positive impact to their sex predator investigation, or to his brother's life. The two had been inseparable ever since, and Gabe was delighted to see his brother so happy.

"What did Brody get Carly for her birthday?" Abby asked, twirling a lock of hair between two fingers.

"He turned one of the guest rooms in the Honeymoon

Cottage into an office for her. The furniture arrived this morning, and then I set up her new computer equipment."

"An office? That's an odd gift. Not very romantic."

"Actually, it's the perfect gift. Carly is a profiler and has her own consulting business. She's never complained about working in the dining or living room with her laptop, but Brody wanted her to have a professional home office. She's going to love it!"

"No big, sparkling engagement ring?"

"Not yet," Gabe said quietly.

He wished that Carly would agree to marry Brody, but she wanted more time. Brody accepted that, and so did he. But it didn't stop him from wishing. He'd never had a sister, but if he had, he'd want her to be just like Carly. Unlike his two brothers, Carly never gave him a hard time about how he lived his life. She respected him and sought his advice about computer technology. Best of all, she was fun, easy to talk to, and unlike Brody, she wasn't judgmental. Although Gabe was twenty-seven-years-old, Brody still parented him like he did when they lost their dad and mom years ago.

"So what's going on with Cameron?" Abby wanted to know.

"Why do you ask?" Gabe scanned the backyard until he discovered his brother, Cameron, sitting on a picnic table alone near the lake.

"He's been sulking all afternoon."

"Cam has a couple of tough cases he's investigating. They're probably on his mind today." Gabe rarely told a lie, but he made his response an exception.

A few months earlier, Cameron had found the love of his life holding his brother, Brody, in her arms in his hospital bed as she planted kisses on his face. The fact that his brother was barely conscious from a surgery didn't make it any better. That was the day Cameron cut things off with Mollie Adams.

Mollie and Brody had been an item in high school, but their relationship ended when their sheriff mom was shot by a drug dealer she'd stopped for a traffic violation. He had no time for a relationship with Mollie or any other woman. Brody spent years dividing his energies between graduating from the police academy, attending college, and caring for his two younger brothers. Mollie moved on, got pregnant, married, and then became a widow. Cameron never left her side, giving her his friendship and support. But last year, something happened between the two of them, and Gabe knew Cameron was hopelessly in love with Mollie. Seeing her holding his brother was something Cameron couldn't deal with, especially since he'd asked Mollie repeatedly about her feelings for Brody. She'd violated his brother's trust, and Gabe knew earning it back would be next to impossible.

Lane Hansen shouted, "Just got a call from Frankie.

The girls are five minutes away!" Scooping up his four-year-old daughter, Ashley, he put her on his shoulders and moved toward the house.

With eight-month-old Mylee strapped to his chest in her baby carrier, Blake Stone grasped his son Shawn's hand and did the same. They were followed closely by Michael Brandt and his twins, Melissa and Michael, Jr. The group gathered in the outdoor living area until the birthday girl's arrival.

Soon they heard the van coming down the driveway and stopping in front of the house. The vehicle's doors opened, and there was a lot of giggling and chatting as the women got out.

"Carly, let's sit in the outdoor living space," suggested Frankie Hansen, who was eight months pregnant and had a big baby bump stretching the front of her yellow sundress to prove it.

"Great idea," said Carly. "That's my favorite part of the house."

Walking to the side of the house, Jennifer, Frankie, and Megan slowed to see Carly's reaction. Finally, she looked up and noticed the balloons, streamers, and banner.

"Oh, my God. I don't believe it!" Carly was clearly astonished, her jaw dropping in disbelief. "This is the best surprise ever. I don't think I've had a birthday party since grade school."

"You haven't!" her brother, Blake, chimed in as the entire group of men applauded.

"Thank you so much, everyone. I don't know whether to laugh or cry!" Carly said as she did both.

Brody rushed across the lawn, threw his arms around her, and kissed her soundly. "Happy birthday, baby."

"Did you arrange all this?" Carly asked.

"Nope. Gabe was a big help."

While the other women greeted their husbands and children, Brody held Carly out at arm's length and scanned her body from head to toe. "Wow, if that is a new dress, I like it."

Carly pulled out the full skirt of her vintage rose printed strapless dress and curtsied. "Frankie urged me to buy it. She said she was tired of seeing me in my usual conservative suits with buttoned-up white blouses."

"Remind me to thank Frankie later." Brody kissed her again and picked up her shopping bags. "Victoria's Secret? My favorite ex-federal agent shopped at Victoria's Secret? Sweet! Do I get a fashion show later? I'm getting turned on just thinking about it."

"Down, boy. We've got guests and a birthday to celebrate, but I'm sure I can arrange something for you later."

At the dinner table, Carly stood and tapped her wine glass with her fork. "I just want to thank all of you for what is my best birthday ever."

To Gabe, she said, "Brody tells me how hard you worked to arrange all this. I can't thank you enough."

Blushing, Gabe smiled as he laid a huge platter of barbequed ribs on the table and gave Carly a birthday hug. "My pleasure. Happy birthday."

"And to the rest of you, let's eat this incredible food and enjoy being with each other."

The caterer appeared with all of Carly's favorite foods: potato salad, slaw, fresh corn on the cob, green bean casserole, and homemade yeast rolls.

At the children's table, Shawn, the Brandt twins, Michael Jr. and Melissa, along with Ashley Hansen, waited patiently for their parents to fill their plates. Nearby in her high chair next to Shawn, Mylee munched on crackers until Jennifer had a chance to get her baby food.

At the grown-up table, Gabe sat down next to Abby, just in time to see her stroke Blake's bicep.

"Do you work out, Blake? Your biceps are amazing," Abby cooed.

Blake shifted uncomfortably in his seat and continued eating, saying nothing until he saw the small white card with a phone number written on it that Abby placed on his thigh.

Blake leaned close to Abby and in a low whisper said, "See that beautiful woman over there feeding the baby? That's my wife and I love her more than life itself. I don't need or want your phone number." He slipped the card under her plate.

Abby just smiled, flipped her hair, and continued eating.

Gabe reddened with embarrassment and anger. He couldn't get Abby home soon enough. Breaking up with someone was something Gabe always dreaded, although in Abby's case, he would make an exception.

Noting the exchange, Carly said to Megan, "I hear you may have an exciting announcement."

Megan smiled. "The large space we added to the back of the house is a reading and playroom for the kids and turned out beautifully. Tim put the finishing touches on the playground equipment yesterday. Megan's Child Care is open for business."

"She already has customers," said Frankie. "Michael Jr., Melissa, Shawn and Mylee Stone, as well as our Ashley, now have a fun place to go when their parents are working. The kids love spending time with Megan, as well as with each other. I've had a couple of days when Ashley has told me she wasn't ready to go home. She was having too much fun."

Michael turned to Brody. "I hate to bring up shoptalk, but have you heard anything new regarding the Jim Ryder trial? I'm hearing rumors that his defense attorney is asking for a change of venue."

"To where? Mars?" Brody shook his head in disbelief. "That's about the only place where the case hasn't been discussed. Jacob Lohman is the prosecuting attorney. I talked to him the other day about how the media might impact his case."

"Brody's right," Carly said. "All the news networks have broadcasted about Ryder's crimes, including HLN and CNN."

Evan rushed into his brother's room at what their pretentious mother referred to as the "Mansion of Morel." The twins detested living at the so-called mansion with their mother and father. But the flow of money from their father into their pockets was dependent on his control of them. One of his conditions was that they live at home until they went to college. As seniors in high school, that meant another year of misery.

Devan, hunched over his computer, was so engrossed with what he was doing, he didn't even hear Evan enter the room.

"Earth to Devan, what are you doing?"

Shooting him a glare, he snapped, "What have I told you about knocking?"

"Whatever. If you were doing something you're not supposed to be doing, you would have locked the door."

"Shut the door," Devan said, and then looked back at his laptop display. "I'm identifying our first target on Facebook. Have a look."

"She's definitely hard-on worthy. What's not to like about a blonde with those kind of assets? Who is she?"

"She's a Purdue student. Check out her photo albums. They look like a Playboy spread. Here she's on her bed, lying on her stomach, wearing only a white lacy thong. In this one, she's coming out of the pool in the tiniest bikini I've ever seen. There are dozens like these. The bitch is asking for it."

"Were you able to get her name and address?"

"Yes, her name is Abby Reece. Later tonight we'll stake out her apartment in West Lafayette to get an idea of her schedule. When the time is right, she'll be all ours."

The drive to Abby's apartment was forty-five minutes. Tonight, it seemed to Gabe as if it were forty-five hours. Abby sullenly peered out the passenger door window. They hadn't said a word to each other since entering his truck. Finally, Gabe turned into the alleyway that led to the small parking area in the back of Abby's apartment building.

As soon as he stopped the vehicle, he turned to Abby. "We have to talk."

"Sounds serious. You should know by now, I don't do serious." She gazed out the passenger door window.

"You're going to have to make an exception tonight, Abby."

Twisting in her seat to face him, her eyes were blazing. "So let's hear it, Gabe. What's so important?"

"This relationship is not working for me."

"Who said we have a relationship? That's something I'm allergic to, and I let you know that early on. I don't want to be tied down to one guy. I like men. I like sex, and I want as many sexual adventures as I can arrange."

"I've changed, Abby. I want to be in a solid relationship with a woman who wants only me. I'm looking for someone who is my best friend and my lover, a woman who isn't afraid to make a lifetime commitment."

Abby glared at him. "Sounds like your goal is the stereotypical picket fence, two kids and a puppy. That's the last thing I want. So I guess what we're saying is that we're over."

"Yes, Abby. I'm sorry," Gabe said solemnly.

Abby grabbed her purse and got out of the truck, slamming the door behind her. By the time she rounded the front of the vehicle, Gabe was out of the truck and standing in front of her. "You can go straight to hell, Gabe Chase. I was getting tired of you anyway," she shouted.

"Abby, calm down. I don't want it to end like this." He lightly touched her arm.

"Don't touch me. In fact, don't contact me in any way. I never want to see or hear from you again. You're dead to me." She marched across the gravel parking lot, entered the back of her apartment building, and disappeared.

Gabe got back in his vehicle and waited for the light to come on in her upstairs apartment. When it did, he fired up his truck and headed home, thinking about how much he hated break-ups. He vowed not to get involved again unless he found someone he cared for enough to create a long-term relationship.

Outside Abby's apartment building from the shadows, Devan and Evan headed back to their white van to review what they'd just witnessed.

"Interesting. It seems our Abby no longer has a boyfriend."

"Evan, is that all you noticed?" asked Devan coldly.

"Why? What did you see?"

"Abby's now ex-boyfriend is Gabriel Chase, the youngest brother of Sheriff Brody Chase. Saw an article about him in the newspaper. Our game just got that much more interesting."

"How do you figure that?"

"There is nothing that means more to Sheriff Chase than his brothers, and we're going to stir up a world of trouble for his youngest."

"I'm not sure I get it." Evan frowned.

"The ex-boyfriend or ex-husband is the first person cops consider when a woman goes missing or is murdered. So when we snatch Abby Reece, the first one they'll suspect for her disappearance is Mr. Gabriel Chase."

September began with a solid week of rain and thunderstorms, and temperatures dipped into the mid-fifties. So much rain caused flooding near the Wabash River, and homes nearby had to be evacuated. There was a chill in the air, but it wasn't cold enough to make the leaves turn to autumn shades of yellow, gold and red.

In a small conference room at the Sheriff's Office, Gabe and Cameron busily organized the physical evidence to prepare for the Jim Ryder trial. Gabe itemized the computer forensics and prepared to testify. It was his first time to testify at a trial, and he wanted his testimony to be effective. He was as determined as his brothers to do all he could to make sure Jim Ryder was found guilty for the nightmare he'd created in Shawnee County. Ryder's victims and families weighed heavily on his mind.

Brody appeared, leaned against the door frame, and watched them work. Gabe noticed him first. His usually expressive face was downright somber.

"Brody, what's wrong?" Gabe asked.

"I was just notified that Jacob Lohman won't be prosecuting the Ryder case. He had a heart attack last night and he might need surgery."

"Heart attack? He's only in his forties." Cameron let out a disbelieving groan, stunned at the news.

Gabe said, "I'm sorry to hear that, but if he can't prosecute Jim Ryder, then who will?"

"He's appointed Michael Brandt as a special prosecutor to handle Ryder's case."

Cameron nodded. "Brandt is an excellent prosecuting

attorney, so Jacob appointed the right guy for the case. If anyone is going to nail Ryder, it's him."

"I think so, too," said Brody. "I just talked to him about temporarily relocating closer to the courthouse. There's an empty office on the second floor he can use until the trial ends. Brandt's moving in before the end of the week. In addition, he's setting up a meeting with both of you to go through the evidence we've collected. He'll get with Carly to discuss Ryder's profile."

"Excellent." Gabe labeled an evidence bag and put it in a box. "We'll give him any help he needs to prosecute the bastard. There's no way Ryder can go free after all the damage he's done."

Brody asked Cameron, "Are we sure that Alison Brown is still willing to testify?"

"Yes. In fact, I talked to her yesterday. She wants to do it, not only for what he did to her, but for killing his last victim, Jasmine, the young girl from West Lafayette. Alison and Jasmine were held captive together in Ryder's basement and became close. Alison was there when Ryder beat Jasmine. She was also there when Jasmine died."

"You mean second-to-last, right? Didn't Ryder shoot his sister the day after he killed Jasmine?" Gabe noted.

"Right. I wonder what happened to make him kill Erin. I mean without her, would he have been able to do all the things he did?" Cameron said. "Remember the surveillance we saw of Alison at the bus station? Alison is a smart girl. There is no way she would have left with Ryder, if he'd been the one to meet her instead of Erin."

"Why isn't Erin Ryder added to the seven counts of murder Brandt will prosecute Ryder for?" Gabe wondered aloud.

"We've got the bullet casing that matches his handgun, but no witness or anything else. It was just the two of them in that basement when it happened. Jacob didn't think he had enough to prove Ryder was the killer," said Brody before he headed back to his office.

Cameron leaned toward Gabe, propping his elbows on the conference table. "How much sympathy could any prosecutor get from a jury for someone like Erin Ryder? She was just as evil as her brother."

A week later, Gabe spotted a rare parking space in front of the Sheriff's Office and maneuvered his truck to park. It was weeks before the trial would begin, yet media vans, campers, and tents dotted a small tract of land near the Sheriff's Office, a couple of blocks from the Shawnee County Courthouse in the downtown square.

A crowd of reporters peppered him with questions as he headed toward the front door.

"Who are you?"

"Are you working on the Jim Ryder murder case?"

"What can you tell us about Jim Ryder? Did you know him?"

"Do you think his conviction is a slam dunk?"

"No comment," Gabe responded as he pushed forward, turning his head away from the cameras when he could.

Gabe knew Brody scheduled a press conference for the afternoon and he didn't envy him. Brody could only predict so many of the questions he'd be asked. Inevitably, he'd be asked how he could not have known one of his deputies was a serial killer.

Deputy Gail Sawyer greeted him at the door. "Well, if it isn't my favorite private investigator."

"Hi, Gail. Is Cam in his office?"

"No, he was on his way to work when he responded to a call for backup about thirty minutes ago. Deputy Arnold stopped a truck near Veedersburg for an expired license plate. He noticed the two men inside were acting squirrelly, really nervous, and wouldn't make eye contact. Coincidentally, the deputy had a K-9 with him, who alerted to presence of drugs in the vehicle."

"No kidding?"

"Wish I was." Gail paused to open the door for a dispatcher arriving for work, and then continued, "The deputy waited for Detective Chase to arrive, and then put the suspects in the squad car before they searched the truck. In the back seat was a bottle of muriatic acid and camp fuel."

"Two ingredients used to make meth," Gabe interrupted.

"Right."

"No wonder they were nervous when they got stopped."

"Oh, there's more. Inside a backpack, they found coffee filters, drain opener, ice packs, a plastic hose, and funnel, along with two syringes that had trace amounts of methamphetamine."

"Mobile meth lab," Gabe stated with disgust. He had no understanding why anyone would put meth in their bodies. It was a self-inflicted death sentence. "What about the two men?"

"The driver admitted to owning the backpack and knowing what was inside. The other guy had a small baggie in his back pocket with trace amounts of meth in it. My kind of bust. I guess the K-9 nearly ripped off the back pocket of his jeans before the deputy could stop him and put him back in his car."

"Do you have any idea when Cam will be here? We

have a meeting at nine."

"He should arrive in thirty minutes," Gail began. "Are you talking about that meeting Michael Brandt scheduled?"

"Yes. Besides Detective Chase, Brody and Carly are attending, too."

"They're both in their offices."

"Good. If no one is in the conference room, I'll work in there on my laptop until Cam gets here."

Gabe started to walk away, but Gail called him back.

"Gabe, if your meeting goes until noon, how about grabbing some lunch with me?"

"Sorry, Gail, I have to run back to my office after the meeting. I have a pile of work waiting for me."

Noting her disappointed expression, Gabe headed toward the conference room. He'd known for months that Gail was attracted to him, but felt nothing in return. That was the thing about chemistry. It was there or it wasn't. Gail was a good woman, intelligent, and with a great sense of humor. Why he couldn't be attracted to someone like Gail instead of women like Abby Reece was a mystery, and a habit he was determined to break.

When Michael Brandt entered the conference room, it was the first time Gabe had seen him since Carly's birthday party the previous month. He was a big man, six feet and five inches, with around two hundred and thirty pounds of hard muscle. His expression dead-serious, his voice held little humor as he greeted the group and lowered himself to sit at the head of the long conference table.

"I'm depending on all of you to help me convict Jim Ryder for seven counts of murder. I'm going for the death penalty. If anyone deserves the needle, it's Ryder. If we're going to win, our evidence has to be rock-solid." Michael spoke with conviction, branding them with the importance of information and evidence each had to offer.

"For any DNA evidence, we need an expert to explain it to the jury in simple terms. I don't want a repeat of the Casey Anthony case in Orlando, where it's suspected the jury members didn't understand what the DNA expert was talking about. Casey Anthony walked. Jim Ryder will not. Not on my watch, he won't." Michael paused, glancing at the overstuffed files before each of them.

Directing the question to Carly, he asked, "I know you have an FBI background as an agent. Do you have any contacts who are DNA experts we could get to testify?"

"I do, but I'm not sure they would make the complex DNA information easier. Their expertise is to understand the complexities, but not necessarily to explain in layman's terms so the average person can understand. That's not their focus," Carly explained. "I think the best expert for the job is Dr. Pittman, our coroner here in Shawnee County. I've discussed autopsy results with him, and he is gifted in explaining the complex with absolute clarity, in the simplest language."

Carly's cell phone vibrated on the table. Glancing at the display and discovering the caller's name, she rose from her seat, her expression tense. "I have to take this. Excuse me." Rushing from the room, she answered the phone and began speaking with the caller.

"I haven't met Pittman, but it sounds like he's our guy," said Michael.

"I'll arrange a meeting for you to talk to Bryan. He's one of my oldest friends. Why don't we do lunch soon?" Brody offered.

"Sounds like a plan."

"Which victims do you want to discuss first?" Brody asked, eager for his team to discuss the evidence they'd painstakingly collected.

"Tell me what you have for all of them, including the four victims found in the shallow graves at the Johnson farm, the two in the burning car, and Jasmine Norris." Michael flipped back a page to write on his legal pad.

Brody gave Cameron a nod, signaling him to present first. "Jasmine Norris was beaten to death. The remaining six victims were shot execution-style, at point-blank range through the back of the skull. No bullet casings were found at the shallow graves or the burning car crime scene, but at autopsy, judging from the size of the hole in the skulls, Bryan believes the bullet was a nine millimeter."

His expression filled with doubt, Michael said, "I'm not sure that's going to help much at trial without tangible evidence that backs him up."

Cameron nodded in agreement. "We've got the backup. Nine millimeter casings were found in Ryder's backyard, where we think the six girls were executed."

"How do we link that to Ryder, besides the location?"

"In addition to his department-issued nine millimeter Sig Sauer Pro, Ryder had a nine millimeter Glock taped on the underside of a kitchen drawer. ATF tested the Glock and it produced the same type of striations on the bullets we found on Ryder's property."

"Good work, Detective."

Carly appeared in the doorway and motioned for Brody to join her in the hallway.

"Brody, my call was from Alison's mother."

"What's wrong?"

"A man calling himself Jim Ryder phoned Alison last night on her home's landline and threatened to kill her if she testified."

Brody's face reddened with anger. "How the hell could Ryder call her from the county jail? He doesn't have a cell phone, nor does he have phone privileges. He's in solitary so we can keep the other inmates away from him."

"We don't know if it was actually Ryder who called. But Mrs. Brown is hysterical. They just moved into a new house after she got a job at the hospital in Evansville. She's afraid if the caller found their phone number, which is unlisted, he'll find their house. Alison is terrified."

"Give me some time to call the jail to see what's going on with Ryder." Brody headed toward his office with Carly by his side. "If we have to, we'll move them back into another safe house."

In the evidence meeting, Michael asked, "Anything else?"

Gabe spoke up. "We discovered items in Ryder's basement that belonged to each of the victims."

It wasn't Gabe's job to search Ryder's basement. He was a relatively inexperienced computer forensics professional when Cameron asked for his help. Gabe sensed his brother was offering a learning experience, and he'd eagerly accepted.

The day they searched the basement, it was dark, except for sunlight leaking through a small dirty window. It smelled of mold, mildew and human waste. Gabe had forced himself to focus on the search for evidence, instead of the depressing, sickening visuals in his head of how the young girls were caged, raped and tortured at the hands of a deputy he'd shared coffee and donuts with.

"What did you find?" Michael asked.

Gabe noticed a glint of approval in his brother's eyes. "We found laptops and cell phones belonging to six of the victims, and Samantha Grey's e-reader, cell, and leather purse, which contained her library card."

"We also found dog collars hanging on hooks on one wall of the basement. There was one for each victim."

"How can you tell which item belongs to which victim?" Michael asked, clearly confused.

Cameron interjected, "The victim's DNA and fingerprints were found on each item, as were Ryder's."

"Do you mean that there's evidence that Ryder handled each item?"

"Absolutely," said Gabe. He pulled out a photo of the basement area where a tall stack of boxes were found, and handed the picture to Michael. "He may have just handled the items as he stored them in the cardboard boxes where we found them in the basement. Whatever the case, his fingerprints and DNA are on each item, along with the whip he used to beat them."

"Excellent!" Michael did a high-five with Gabe, as Cameron smiled with pride.

"Did you forensically examine each of the laptops?" asked Michael. "If so, tell me what you found."

"After subpoenaing each Internet Service Provider or ISP, I got copies of each victim's email that was downloaded on the ISP's server. I discovered all seven girls frequently communicated on Teen Chat, as did Jim Ryder. After we served a subpoena to Teen Chat, they provided transcripts of each conversation between Ryder and the victims."

"Yes!" Michael did a fist pump. "What else do we have?"

"Ryder's sperm and DNA were discovered on Jasmine Norris during her autopsy. His fingerprints and DNA are on the dog collar found on her neck, on the leather restraints hanging from the ceiling, and in both of the dog crates."

"Anything else?" The prosecutor asked, as he wrote down the information.

A smile creased Cameron's face. "We're saving the best for last, counselor."

Puzzled, Michael looked at him.

"There was a plastic bin in Ryder's basement filled with

DVDs. The bastard filmed his torture of the girls so he could relive the sick thrill later. There is a DVD for each victim, including his vicious attack on Jasmine Norris and the rape of Alison Brown."

"There is no way Ryder's defense attorney will want these DVDs admitted to evidence, and he'll fight it. It will be in the judge's hands to allow them or not," said Michael. "But if I can show the jury even one of these DVDs, we've got Ryder. There's no way a jury won't convict him."

"What about cell phone records?" Michael inquired.

Gabe tapped on a stuffed folder. "We got a court order for each cell phone carrier and they all cooperated, providing records that tell us each time a victim and Ryder communicated on the cell phone."

"That's helpful. What about GPS information that puts Ryder and the victims in the same location?"

"Sorry, that info, I don't have. We think Ryder instructed the girls to turn off their cell phones or take out the batteries prior to reaching Shawnee County."

"He was a deputy sheriff. Unfortunately, one of ours," said Cameron with disgust. "He knew this was one way to keep law enforcement from finding the girls once they went missing."

"Do we know how he lured the victims to Morel?"

"Yes. Carly was right in the profile she wrote before we had any idea Jim Ryder was our killer. Ryder targeted preteen girls who were having problems at school or at home. The guy knew exactly what to say to these girls to earn their trust. He was patient enough to build the relationships to the point he could persuade them to meet him in person in Shawnee County."

"I've seen Ryder. He's nothing to look at. How did he attract these young girls in the first place?"

"He didn't use his own photo," Gabe said angrily. "He used a photo of me that was taken when I was in high school. I found out the night I walked into Alison Brown's hospital room. She screamed and called me 'Anthony,' which was the online name Ryder was using."

"He's a devious bastard. That's for sure." Michael quickly jotted down the information. "He thought of everything he needed to do to bait and trap his victims."

Brody and Carly entered the room and returned to their seats at the table.

Brody scrubbed his hands tiredly over his face. "Sorry to interrupt, but I have some news."

"I can tell it isn't good," said Michael. "Let's hear it."

"Ryder, or someone he's hired, threatened to kill Alison Brown last night if she testifies."

"You have got to be kidding me." Michael shook his head in disbelief.

"Wish I was."

"I thought you had him in solitary. How could he hire anyone to do this?"

"We're kidding ourselves if we think that inmates don't talk to each other. Hell, they smuggle in cell phones all the time. They also pass notes. I don't know how Ryder did it, but he managed to terrify both Alison and her mother."

"Can't you move them to a safe house until after the trial?"

"That's what I'm trying to do, but Alison and her mother are pushing back. Mrs. Brown has a new job and Alison just started school. They both moved into their new house two weeks ago. They don't want their new lives disrupted."

"I get that," Michael replied. "But Alison is my only witness. I'm not sure I can get a conviction without her. In addition, we can't keep them safe if they don't cooperate."

"I agree. Let's give them the night to think about it, and I'll try again tomorrow."

Carly leaned toward Brody. "Let me try tomorrow. I have a good relationship with Alison and her mom. Maybe I can persuade them both."

CHAPTER THREE

"Devan, wake up!" Evan punched his brother on the arm. "She's on the move." He slipped the key in the ignition of the van to turn on the motor.

"On the move? You've been watching too many cop shows,"

"Whatever." Evan gazed at the silhouette of Abby Reece, who was sitting in her car, her cell phone pressed against her ear, the interior illuminated by the garage light that spilled across the parking area. He and Devan had been following Abby since September, after school and on the weekends, and Evan was tired of all the stalking. He wanted some action and hoped tonight was the night they grabbed her.

"What time is it?" asked Devan.

"Eight-forty-five."

"Think she might be meeting someone at nine?"

"Let's find out."

Hanging back a couple of cars so she wouldn't notice them, they followed Abby to the Hoosier Sports Bar and Grill. Since the place was brimming with the Friday night crowd, Evan had to circle the lot twice before finding a parking place. As was his habit, Devan pulled down the cosmetic mirror to primp and comb his hair. Though they were identical twins, Evan had always thought Devan was more pretty than handsome, with cropped blonde hair, chiseled jaw bones, and startling light blue eyes under a shield of thick lashes. The girls at school thought he was hot and vied for his attention, making Devan egotistical and vain. Evan pitied any female who developed feelings for Devan, for they would never be returned. The only time Devan felt anything for a female was when he was choking the life out of her. Satisfied with his look, Devan handed the comb to his brother.

Once inside, they eased up to the bar, ordered a couple of beers with fake driver's licenses, and then casually scanned the room, searching for their target.

Abby Reece wasn't hard to find. She was gyrating on the dance floor with a group of people, wearing a body-hugging cherry-red wrap dress that threatened to unwrap itself as she danced. With her arms up high, she wiggled and flipped her hair as she sought the attention of the men on the dance floor.

Devan and Evan moved to a table, ordered more

drinks and appetizers, and watched the impromptu show on the dance floor, starring Abby Reece. They joined her, dancing until a little after one o'clock, when Abby appeared to be winding down. They took the opportunity to pay their bill and depart. After waiting in their van for thirty minutes for Abby to leave the bar, they decided it might be smarter to wait at her apartment.

At Abby's apartment building, Devan backed the van under a large oak tree, while Evan used a baseball bat to break a flood light mounted on the garage. With the exception of a sliver of moonlight, the area was quite dark, the way they wanted it.

In the back of the van, Devan covered the floor with a thick sheet of plastic. He planned to abduct her, not kill her, at least not yet, but wanted to be prepared for the unexpected. He'd learned that lesson the hard way when a prostitute they'd kidnapped pulled a small knife out of her purse and stabbed Evan in the arm before Devan could snap her neck. It was a superficial cut, but blood spattered everywhere, and it took forever for them to scrub the van with bleach.

Evan pulled out a duffle bag that held duct tape, two syringes, a box of surgical gloves, two ski masks, handcuffs, trash bags, a coil of rope, two stun guns, a couple of knives, and a roll of paper towels. Tucking one of the stun guns into his back pocket, he handed the other to Devan. Using a stun gun was the most effective way to subdue their target. It instantly disabled a victim's muscles so she could not run away or fight back.

The crunch of gravel under tires and the appearance of headlights caught their attention. Abby had returned.

Devan turned off the internal lights of their vehicle, and both men climbed out. By the time they reached Abby, she was leaning into her car, reaching for her purse on the passenger seat. When she straightened and closed the door, Evan jabbed her in the neck with his stun gun, and she crumpled to the ground as if her muscles had melted. Devan flung her over his shoulder and carried her fireman-style to the van, laying her limp body on the sheet of plastic in the back.

Evan quickly bound her wrists and legs with duct tape, then covered her mouth with more tape. Closing the van doors, he stayed in the back of the vehicle with Abby, while Devan drove quickly through the quiet neighborhood into the night. The game had begun.

Abby Reece lay motionless next to Evan. The effects of the stun gun would wear off soon, and her muscles would slowly come to life. Evan lightly brushed her blonde hair out of the way so he could better see her face. With porcelain skin and delicate, high cheek bones, she was exquisite, with long, dark eyelashes that slightly fluttered now. Abby Reece was prettier than any of the girls at his school. Evan yearned to stroke her skin but alarm tensed his body.

His eyes flew to the rearview mirror in the front of the vehicle to see if Devan was watching the road or him. Abby was a target for the game. Touching a target was not allowed, and he would suffer serious consequences from Devan if he even suspected Evan's attraction to her. Thankfully, Devan's eyes were on the road. They were almost out of the city limits.

"Did you remember the roofies?" asked Devan, as he glanced back at Evan through the rear view mirror.

"Don't I always? I'm not the village idiot you seem to think I am."

Devan's face flushed as he glared at him through the mirror. Finally he said, "Don't get testy, and just answer the fucking question, Evan."

"Yes, I remembered the Rohypnol. I filled a couple of syringes with it and put them in the duffle bag. I'll give her one in a few minutes to keep her quiet."

Satisfied with that answer, Devan returned his attention to the road, and Evan turned his to Abby. Her delicate features reminded him of one of the sleeping princesses in a fairy tale one of their nannies used to read to them.

Abby groaned as she tried to move her bound legs and wrists. Why did she feel so exhausted? It was such an effort to even try to move her arms and legs. Why couldn't she move?

Her eyes flew open with alarm, and she scanned her surroundings and recognized the interior of a van. Where in the hell was she? Was this real? Was this a nightmare? Wasn't this one of the guys she danced with at the bar, hovering over her, his face inches from her own? Panic like she'd never known welled in her throat.

His laptop secured under his arm, Gabe pushed up the Shawnee County Courthouse stairs to the second floor, where Jim Ryder's trial would finally reconvene at one o'clock in courtroom number four. Ryder's defense attorney had successfully pushed back his trial date to October 10 from October 1, and Gabe was impatient for it to get started. It was his first time to testify as an expert witness, and butterflies were dancing in his stomach. At the same time, a fierce determination drove him to make sure the jury understood how each piece of incriminating evidence he'd uncovered pointed to Ryder's guilt.

After meeting with Michael the previous day, he'd spent the night going over his evidence, imagining how he'd present it to the jury, and wondering which piece of evidence would inspire Ryder's defense attorney to voice an objection. As far as Gabe was concerned, he could object all he wanted. The evidence was a solid demonstration of Ryder's involvement with the victims.

Cameron had testified in the morning regarding the bullet casings, restraints and dog collars, as well as anything else they found in the basement, except for the laptops and cell phones, which Gabe would present. After Cameron, Dr. Bryan Pittman testified, explaining in the simplest terms the DNA, as well as the results of the autopsies.

Both men said the jurors listened intently, occasionally stealing glances at Jim Ryder, who sat stoically next to his attorney, drawing on a legal pad.

Someone slammed into Gabe, shoving him against the stair railing and knocking his laptop out of his grip. It tumbled down the stairs with a metallic thud on each step.

"What the hell?" Gabe cursed aloud, as he watched a light-haired teenager wearing a Morel High School athletic jacket race down the rest of the steps. Picking up the laptop, he prayed his hard drive was intact.

"So sorry, Mr. Chase." The kid said without looking back, his voice laced with sarcasm.

Gabe bolted down the stairs to catch him, but couldn't spot him in the crowd entering the courthouse. Cursing to himself, he was convinced the teen bumped into him on purpose. Why? Who was he? How did he know his name?

Reaching the top of the staircase, Gabe waded through the overcrowded hallway outside courtroom four. He'd heard on the news that the entire state of Indiana, as well as the surrounding states, wanted a seat in the courtroom to witness the trial. So many people were vying for seats that a lottery system had to be set up.

He spotted Alison Brown waiting on a bench outside the courtroom, flanked by her mother on one side and Carly Stone on the other. Alison and her mother had finally agreed to move into the safe house, and a deputy assigned to them stood nearby. Gabe quietly settled down next to Carly. So he didn't appear to be eavesdropping on their conversation, he opened his laptop to assess it for damage. Luckily, some scrapes on the case were the only things he found. The content on his hard drive appeared to be intact.

Periodically, he scanned the hallway for signs of the jerk who slammed into him on the staircase. Still angry, Gabe wanted to kick his ass, and then ask some relevant questions, starting with 'how did he know his name?'

"Are you okay?" her mother asked, as she smoothed Alison's hair and kissed her cheek.

"Mom, please don't fuss."

To Carly, Mrs. Brown said, "I hate that she has to go through this. Hasn't she been through enough? Why does she have to relive the way that monster caged her in his basement and tortured her?"

"I understand how you feel. But she has to testify. She's the only living witness — the only one who can stop Jim Ryder's reign of terror."

"Stop it, Mom," Alison interjected. "We discussed this. No matter how scary it is to face him in the courtroom, I have to do it for Jasmine and the other girls he killed."

Carly turned to the young girl. "Do you feel prepared, Alison? Did Mr. Brandt and I help at all in easing your fear of testifying?"

"Do I have to look at him?" Alison asked fearfully.

"No, you don't have to look at him. Because he wore the ski mask, you were only able to identify his voice, so neither of the attorneys will ask you to point him out in court."

"Then why am I testifying at all? The jury may not believe anything I say because I can't identify his face."

"Alison, remember we talked about this. Mr. Brandt is going to show the jury a short excerpt from the DVD Ryder made when he beat you. That will eliminate any doubt in their minds of your connection to Jim Ryder."

"He's not going to show the one of him raping me, is he? He promised me that he wouldn't show them that DVD."

"No, he won't. Mr. Brandt keeps his promises. Don't worry about that." Carly squeezed Alison's hand. "Just concentrate on answering Mr. Brandt's questions to the best of your ability."

"Are Jasmine's parents here?"

"Yes, honey, they're seated in the second row behind the prosecutor's table."

"They won't see that DVD he made of him beating Jasmine, will they?"

"No, they won't. Mr. Brandt will ask the Victim Advocate sitting next to them to take Reverend and Mrs. Norris out of the courtroom when he shows that DVD," Carly paused for a moment, then continued. "Mr. Brandt wished he didn't have to show the filming at all. But it's one of the only times when Ryder's ski mask slipped, exposing his face. The jury has to see that."

"Will you be in the courtroom?"

"Yes," Carly responded. "And your mom will be there, too. Just look at one of us if you feel frightened, or need to feel how much we support what you're doing. We can't let Jim Ryder get away with what he did to you, Jasmine, and the rest of the victims."

<><><>

After the first day of testimony, Carly, Brody and Michael met in the bar at the Sugar Creek Inn, a historic hotel on the square across from the courthouse.

"How do you think it went today?" Brody asked Michael.

"Hard to say," Michael began. "The jurors were very attentive to the testimony. That's a good sign. But Ryder's defense attorney, Brett Newson, got several of his objections sustained. But he succeeded in shaking up Alison Brown so much she started crying, and the judge called a recess so we could calm her down. I watched the jurors' expressions. They felt sorry for her and looked at Newson like they were pissed he was bullying her. All in all, Alison did an amazing job in reaching the jurors. Several had tears in their eyes once she finished."

"Poor kid," remarked Carly.

"More like brave kid," Brody returned. "How many teenagers who have gone through what she has would have the guts to get in front of a packed courtroom to testify about it?"

Carly squeezed Brody's hand under the table. "I agree."

"By the way, Gabe did an excellent job testifying. He even had a couple of PowerPoint slides showing jurors the actual emails Ryder had exchanged with the victims," said

Michael. "I plan to use him as a consultant for a couple of cases I have coming up."

"He did a good job," Brody said with pride. "He'll appreciate the work."

To Carly, Michael said, "Tell me about Ryder. What makes him tick? Give me some information I can use in final arguments."

"Ryder is a sexual sadist who only gets turned on when his victims are helpless and vulnerable. Their suffering is the most important thing to him. He rapes them to exert his power over his victims, not for any kind of sexual satisfaction. He gets off by reliving the attacks later. That's why the box of DVDs and photographs were found."

"Do you think he will insist on testifying on his own behalf?"

"It's a safe bet he's pressuring his attorney to let him testify," said Carly. "He's an arrogant man and a prolific liar. Ryder's convinced he's far more intelligent than law enforcement, and certainly smarter than any juror. He'll want to tell his version of events. In his mind, the girls came to him willingly and asked for what they got."

"If Brett Newson is as smart as I think he is, he'll keep Ryder off the stand because he knows I'll tear him apart."

"I'd want to be there for that," said Brody.

Two days later, thanks to a surveillance job in Indianapolis, Gabe hadn't gotten home until three in the morning. So when he awoke to loud pounding on his bedroom door two hours later, he was anything but overjoyed.

"What the hell?" Gabe grumbled as he rolled out of bed, flicked his lamp on, and opened the door to find his brother, Cameron, who shoved a mug of hot, dark coffee into his hand.

"Wake up, Gabe. I have to tell you something," Cameron pushed past him and sat in a chair near the desk.

"Can't this wait?" After nearly stumbling over one of his shoes, Gabe made it to his bed and sat down. Sipping the hot coffee, he squinted at Cameron. "What's happened?"

When his brother didn't immediately answer, Gabe took a good look at him and noticed worry pinched between his dark brows. Cameron was a laid-back, Type B, and it took a lot to get him upset. So whatever he had to tell him was not going to be good news.

"Spill it," Gabe demanded.

"A Purdue University student was reported missing this morning in West Lafayette."

"So why do I need to know this?" Gabe asked, rubbing

his eyes. "Which Purdue student?"

"Abby Reece."

Gabe felt the blood drain from his face. "No way. Abby can't be missing. She's probably off somewhere with her latest conquest."

"No one's seen her for four days."

A wave of apprehension swept through Gabe. He was momentarily speechless: Abby was missing.

"I'll find her," Gabe declared, determination etched in his facial features.

"Stay out of it," Cameron insisted.

"Cam, if it were you, would you stay out of it?"

Cameron ignored the question. "You have to distance yourself, Gabe. You've been dating her for how many weeks?"

"Four, but we broke up."

"When?"

"The night of Carly's birthday party."

"That wasn't even two months ago."

"So what's your point?"

"If I were investigating a young woman's disappearance, the first person I'd want to talk to is the current or ex-boyfriend, because he's usually the doer."

"Whatever, Cam. I'm talking to the police. If Abby is missing, I want to help if I can," Gabe said. "Which police agency has the case?"

"Since she lives off campus, the West Lafayette police have it."

Gabe's visit to the West Lafayette Police Department was interesting but predictable. They already had his name listed as one of Abby's boyfriends. They wanted to know when he'd seen her last, why they broke up, the date of the breakup, and if he knew anyone who would want to hurt her. These were the same questions he'd ask if he were investigating a disappearance, but it was odd to hear them directed at him. He still hadn't completely accepted that Abby was actually missing.

Fingering the key she'd given him, he decided to visit Abby's apartment off-campus, near North Chauncey Avenue. Parking in front, Gabe remembered how he'd urged Abby to install surveillance cameras, or at least an alarm, but she'd just laughed at him.

Abby's apartment was one of two upstairs in an older house that could use a new roof, a fresh coat of paint, and a dozen repairs or more. She rented from a seventy-five-year-old retired anthropology professor, Dr. Ramsey, who lived on the first floor. Noticing the professor's car was not parked in the driveway, Gabe parked at the rear entrance and immediately saw that Abby's 1998 white BMW roadster was parked near the building. Did that mean she was upstairs in her apartment?

Once inside, he returned her key to his pocket and slipped on a pair of latex gloves so he wouldn't add his fingerprints or DNA to the crime scene, if the apartment should become one. The first thing he noticed was how clean and neat the place was, everything in its place. That was typical Abby Reece. Her personal life might be a mess, but her apartment was always pristine.

Gabe did a quick sweep of each room and didn't notice anything unusual, except Abby's ivory Coach purse and new iPhone were not in their place on her desk next to her laptop. Two items she'd wouldn't be without. Where was she?

Gabe opened Abby's laptop and found it to be on. Slipping an external drive from his pocket, he quickly connected it, and then copied each of her Outlook email folders so he could study them later in his office. Checking her Outlook Calendar, he discovered that Abby used it extensively, but found nothing other than class reminders and appointments. Nothing suspicious, but he copied the current and past three months anyway.

Next, he searched her Internet browser files and made

a copy of temporary files onto the external drive. These files would enable him to see Abby's browsing history with the websites the browser had visited. Later, he would go to the sites to see if Abby had any recent communications that might help him locate her. Gabe copied the contents of the laptop's hard drive. Without her iPhone, he would have to use his contact at the phone company to get a record of her calls.

Pulling out the external drive, he slipped it into his jeans pocket and went through the apartment again. There were absolutely no signs a struggle had occurred here. If Abby had been abducted, it did not occur inside her apartment.

Hearing a car motor and the crunch of gravel beneath the tires, Gabe rushed to Abby's window to see that Dr. Ramsey had arrived. He raced down the back stairs and then up the driveway, and met the older woman at her car in front of the house.

Gabe didn't hesitate to ask Dr. Ramsey his first question, "When was the last time you saw Abby?"

"That's just what the policeman asked when I reported her missing. I saw Abby last Friday. We had lemonade and a nice chat on the porch when she returned from one of her classes." She paused. "I did hear her go out later that night, must have been around nine o'clock or so."

Recording the information in a small notebook, he asked, "When you talked to her, did Abby seem worried or upset about anything?"

Dr. Ramsey considered the question, and then said, "No. She was in a good mood. She'd just gotten an A on an essay she'd written for her English class."

"What about visitors?"

"Abby has always had her share of male visitors. No one that stands out, but then I don't really notice much of what goes on at the back of the building where Abby's entrance is located. My living space is in front," said Dr. Ramsey, and then added. "But I do remember you. You came around more than the others. I was hoping you were the one for her."

Ignoring her statement, Gabe fished a business card out of his pocket and handed it to her. "If you think of anything that might help me find Abby, give me a call."

"You're a private investigator? Did Abby's mother hire you?"

"No, I've never met Abby's mother."

"You might want to give her a call. She could use help from someone like you."

Gabe's cell phone alerted he'd received a text. Excusing himself, he headed for his truck in the back of the building. The text was from Michael Brandt. Ryder's verdict was in and the court would reconvene within the hour.

As quietly as she could, Kaitlyn Reece opened the louvered doors to her sister's closet and stepped into the room. Taking a deep breath, she moved to the window and watched the man who had just been in Abby's apartment talking with her sister's landlord downstairs. Who was he and why did he have a key to Abby's apartment? Answering her own questions, she concluded he was probably one of Abby's many boyfriends. The most important question was what did he have to do with her disappearance? Why did he copy the contents of her laptop?

Kaitlyn had almost finished her search of the apartment when she'd heard the metal key in the lock that inspired her to hide in the bedroom closet.

She'd already looked everywhere in the apartment for anything that would tell her where her sister was. Kaitlyn found Abby's suitcases tucked away in the bottom of the pantry in the kitchen, so she ruled out an impromptu trip out of town. Her sister's purse and iPhone were gone, but her car was still parked behind the building. Kaitlyn had a terrible feeling that wherever Abby was, she did not go there willingly.

There was one more thing on her list to search for. It was something that Abby would never willingly leave behind. Moving into the bedroom, she lifted the mattress and discovered a small, blue journal. Quick tears trembled on her eyelids as she held the journal close to her chest and sat down on the bed. There was no denying now that her sister's disappearance was not her choice. Abby had recorded her thoughts in her journal since elementary school, and never missed a day. If she were going away, she would never leave it behind.

Kaitlyn retrieved her purse from the closet, tucked the journal inside, and headed toward the back stairs. Once she reached the exit door, she noticed the man she saw in Abby's apartment talking on his cell phone in a black Dodge Ram Sport. Finally, he finished his conversation and pulled out of the parking lot.

Gabe made the drive from West Lafayette to Morel in record time and rushed up the steps to the courtroom. Reporters and those who hadn't won a courtroom seat in the daily lottery jam-packed the hallway, and it was difficult for him to wade through the crowd. Once inside the courtroom, he spotted his two brothers along with Carly, who was saving a seat for him on the long bench closest to the prosecutor's wooden table. Michael Brandt stood talking with his wife, Anne, at the opposite end of the bench. Ryder's defense attorney leafed through papers in a file before him. The jury, judge, and Ryder had not entered yet.

Settling down next to Carly, Gabe greeted his brothers and looked around the room. The only people seated behind the defense table were reporters who chatted with each other, predicting the jury's decision and Ryder's fate.

Gabe's stomach clenched as he thought about his search of Abby's apartment, and his brain wouldn't let go of the suspicion that she'd been abducted from the parking lot. If he were right, time was of the essence. She'd been missing for four days. If he was going to find Abby alive, time was running out.

"What's wrong?" Carly whispered.

He glanced at her, noting Cameron and Brody deep in conversation about the trial. "Abby Reece is missing."

"Wasn't she your date at . . ."

"Yes," Gabe interrupted.

Abruptly, a hush covered the room like a thick fog when a door at the right opened and Jim Ryder entered the room, accompanied by two deputies. Ryder, wearing a navy suit and tie, walked into the crowded room as if he were making an entrance to a party held in his honor. Smiling confidently at reporters aiming cameras, he walked to the defense table, where a deputy unlocked his handcuffs.

"The bastard's enjoying this," Gabe said.

"He probably thinks he's getting a 'Not Guilty' verdict," Carly replied.

The bailiff, an older man, who looked close to retirement, called out, "All rise."

All rose from their seats as Judge Carlson entered the room. The door leading to the jury room opened and the twelve jurors, two men and ten women, took their seats in the jury box.

The judge asked if the jury had reached a verdict. The jury foreman, a small nervous man, stood up and cleared his throat before speaking. "Yes, Your Honor, we have."

His hand shook so badly the white piece of paper he was holding looked like a surrender flag. It seemed the entire courtroom held its collective breath. Fearfully, glancing at Jim Ryder, he said, "Guilty!"

Once the guilty verdict was read, chaos ensued. The victims' families alternately cheered or sobbed, and reporters ran from the room to communicate the verdict. A small congratulatory crowd surrounded Michael Brandt, including his wife, and Judge Carlson pounded her gavel in an attempt to create order in the courtroom.

Ryder jumped to his feet, bumped against one of his

guards, and snatched the man's gun out of its holster. A second guard grabbed for Ryder unsuccessfully, just as a shot went off, grazing Carly's arm. A trail of blood ran down her arm, staining her white sleeve crimson, as she sank to the floor. A second shot caught a deputy in the chest, and a third bullet disabled the second deputy, who tumbled to the floor. The bailiff rushed the judge into her chambers; terrified screams were deafening as people panicked, pushing each other to escape the room.

On the floor, Brody radioed for back up and covered Carly with his body like a shield. Cameron jerked out his gun as Gabe leapt over the wooden railing and tackled Ryder, slamming him to the floor, and struggled to grab the gun. Gabe clamped his hand around Ryder's wrist and slammed it against the oak floor until the criminal howled with pain and released the weapon. Cameron kicked the gun several feet away, out of Ryder's reach. Ryder cursed and wildly bucked as he thrashed to get Gabe off him.

Pointing his gun at Ryder, Cameron said, "Move an inch and I'll blow your head off."

Two deputies rushed into the room and gave handcuffs to Gabe, who quickly secured Ryder's wrists behind his back. Jerking the man to his feet, Gabe handed him over to the deputies, who pushed Ryder toward the door leading to the cell block in the basement.

In a dark rage, Ryder struggled with the deputies and

screamed, "You Chase brothers are going down. If it's the last thing I do, I'll kill all of you, and your profiling bitch gets hers first. This is her fault. She and that Alison Brown bitch set me up! This isn't over! Not by a long shot!"

Gabe waited with Cameron outside the emergency department at the Morel Hospital for three hours. Finally Brody emerged to announce that the bullet had grazed Carly's arm and she'd received some stitches to close the wound. Thankfully he'd soon be able to take her home.

Back at his office, Gabe retrieved the external drive where he'd stored Abby's laptop information, and connected it to his computer's USB port. First he searched Abby's recent emails to see if she'd communicated about any plans she may have had on Friday. There was nothing.

Next, he opened her Internet browsing history and discovered she visited Facebook a couple of times per day, so he opened the site, then quickly found Abby's page. Gabe didn't use Facebook, so he'd never visited her page. Her banner at the top of the page was a horizontal photo of Abby lying on a beach in the tiniest of string bikinis. When he clicked on her photo albums, he found they were filled with nude or partially nude photos of Abby in various positions. Anger swept through him. He could care less that Abby had these photographs of herself, but that she posted them in a place easily accessed by an Internet filled with countless predators was crazy. What was she thinking? Why didn't she just paint an online target on her back?

Just last year, he was contacted by a distraught mother who'd discovered a man in his forties was sending sexually explicit messages and photos to her fourteen-year-old daughter. The woman brought the girl's cell phone to Gabe, and he was able to use the man's photos to trace the phone number they came from and identify the sender. Right-clicking on each photo, he looked for evidence of an EXIF date, or data about the camera that took the photo, and the exact location and time the photo was taken. Since the geotagging feature was enabled on the suspect's phone, each image had a latitude and longitude of exactly where the man was when the image was taken. When Gabe handed the case over to Cameron, he was able to provide the man's name and address, and the date each photo was taken.

Unfortunately, people like Abby didn't know that when they posted photos on the web on social media sites like Facebook, with the geotagging feature enabled, they were sharing their names and locations to tech-savvy sexual predators, who use the data to track them to their doorsteps.

Gabe examined Abby's photos. Most were taken at Abby's apartment. Each revealed her full name and apartment address. This added a new element in his search for Abby. Was she targeted and abducted by a sexual predator? Was his rich imagination working overtime, fueled by fear that Abby may be in danger?

Reading the messages on her Facebook home page, he noticed the last message from Abby was written at five o'clock last Friday. In it she shared her elation on getting an 'A' in English. A Facebook friend named Emily Smith commented with the message: "That's great. Let's go out tonight to celebrate." To which Abby responded, "You're on."

Gabe knew Emily Smith was Abby's former dorm roommate. He slipped his cell phone out of his jeans pocket and called her.

"Emily, this is Gabe Chase. I'm looking for Abby—"

"Oh my God, I can't believe she's missing. I've been upset about it since the police were here," she interrupted.

"I visited Abby's Facebook page and noticed that last Friday you and Abby may have been making plans to go out that night. Did you?"

"We were supposed to meet up, but as I was leaving my apartment, I ran into my boyfriend and spent the night with him. I texted Abby a couple of times to tell her I couldn't make it, but she never texted me back."

"Where were you supposed to meet?"

"Hoosier Sports Bar and Grill."

Fishing Abby's photo out of his pocket, Gabe slid it across the bar to the Hoosier Sports Bar and Grill owner, Cliff Olsen.

"This woman was in your bar on the twelfth of October. Do you remember seeing her?"

"Sure, that's Abby Reece. She's here most Friday nights. Why do you want to know?"

"Abby is missing. I'm a private investigator, and I'm trying to find her," Gabe responded. It wasn't the whole story, but Gabe didn't think his dating Abby was anyone's business, least of all this bar owner.

"Abby was here alright. She had a couple of drinks at the bar. She was waiting for someone. Didn't say who. But once the band started, she was on the dance floor until she left around closing," Olsen replied.

"What time do you close the bar?"

"Two in the morning."

"Was there anyone here who seemed to pay a lot of attention to Abby?"

"Are you serious?" Olsen asked incredulously. "First of all, she had on a red dress that fit like a second skin. Secondly, her moves on the dance floor are the sexiest I've ever seen. Who in his right mind *wouldn't* pay a lot of attention to Abby Reece?"

"Did you see her leave?"

"Yeah. We said good night."

"Did anyone leave after her?"

"No, I think she was the last one out the door before I closed up."

"What kind of surveillance do you have? I noticed the camera outside facing the parking lot.

"The front and back door and the parking lot are the only surveillance taping we do."

"Any chance you have a copy of the surveillance tape for that night?"

"I'll check. It's there unless we taped over it." Olsen headed toward the back of the bar, and returned with a DVD that he handed to Gabe. "Here it is. Knock yourself out. Hope you find her."

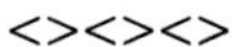

Parking his truck outside his office building the next day, Gabe grabbed his briefcase and got out of the truck. Glancing at his office window on the second floor, he noticed the blinds were open and the lights were on. What the hell?

Reaching back into his truck to his glove compartment, he pulled out his Glock and slipped it in his waistband. If someone had broken into his office and was still there, he wanted to be prepared.

Entering the building, he held his briefcase in his left hand, and pulled out his gun with his right. Leaning toward his right, his hip skimmed the railing as he crept up the stairs to the second floor. Once on the landing, he leaned against the wall and peeked down the hallway. His office door was open, and the scent of hot coffee wafted in the air.

Within seconds, he was standing in his office door frame, watching a woman he'd never seen before pour dark coffee into a mug.

"It's about time you got here," she said, once she noticed him leaning against the door frame. "Don't you keep regular office hours? I've been waiting since eight o'clock. Do you take cream and sugar in your coffee?" Gabe shook his head, and watched her pour coffee into a second mug. She took a seat on one of his guest chairs, crossing her mile-long legs. Sipping her coffee, she seemed to be waiting for him to say something.

Taking a second to size her up, Gabe decided she looked familiar, yet he was certain they'd never met. She was a dead-ringer for actress Jennifer Aniston, with silvery-blonde hair tumbling to her shoulders, full, lush lips, and a mischievous twinkle in her ocean-blue eyes. No, he definitely didn't know her. This woman, he would have remembered. Yet, he couldn't let go of how familiar she seemed.

Depositing his briefcase on the floor, Gabe slipped his gun into a desk drawer, pulled out his office chair and sat down as he rolled up the sleeves of his crisp white shirt.

Leaning across his desk, he said, "I don't want to seem rude, but who are you and how did you get into my office?"

"I'll ask the questions, Mr. Chase," she began. "Why did you illegally enter my sister's apartment yesterday and copy the contents of her laptop? Better yet, where's Abby?"

Gabe didn't know what surprised him more: That Abby had a sister, or that she was hiding in Abby's apartment and saw what he did. Hadn't he done a sweep of the apartment before he downloaded the information on her laptop? It was then he realized he hadn't checked the coat closet in the living room or the bedroom closet. *Great detective work.*

He took a shot at distracting her. "Who are you? Abby doesn't have a sister. So it sounds like you're the one who indulged in a little breaking and entering."

"Good try. Don't try to sidetrack me. It won't work. You're a private investigator. Did someone hire you to find Abby?"

Gabe scrubbed his hands over his face. "No one hired me to find Abby. We used to date, and I had a key to her apartment. When I heard she was reported missing, I talked to the police, and then I went to her place to check out things for myself."

"What did you find out?"

"For one thing, her purse containing her wallet, credit cards and iPhone weren't there."

"I noticed that, too," she said quietly. "She never goes anywhere without her designer purse. It's attached to her like Velcro."

Gazing at her for a moment, he stretched out his hand to her. "Can we start over with introductions? I'm Gabe Chase."

Clasping his hand, she responded, "I'm Kaitlyn Reece."

<><><>

Sipping her coffee, Kaitlyn let her eyes move over him. His jet-black hair curled over his ears and the collar of his white shirt. Long and lean, with broad shoulders and a wide chest, he was handsome as the devil, with a few days growth on his sculpted jaw. And why he seemed familiar to her was a mystery.

It was the muscles rippling under his white shirt that quickened her pulse as he leaned across the desk, dangerously close to her. Kaitlyn decided Gabe Chase was too good-looking for his own good. No, she corrected herself, he was drop-dead gorgeous. That her sister dated him was no surprise. To Abby, a man like Gabe would be another notch on her bedpost until she tired of him and threw him away like an old toy.

If that was what happened, she empathized with him. She knew from personal experience that getting dumped was no picnic.

"I'm not surprised Abby didn't tell you she had a sister," Kaitlyn said softly.

"Why is that?"

"We aren't close by any stretch of the imagination. Abby and I have polar-opposite personalities. I'm the responsible, older daughter who has life goals, and Abby is the younger wild-child who's been giving my mother ulcers since she was fourteen-years-old. If our father had stuck around, I'm sure she would have driven him to distraction, too."

"How did you find me, Kaitlyn?" Gabe asked, with a long, searching look.

"After you left the apartment yesterday, I watched you talk with Abby's landlady. Once you left, I had a talk with Dr. Ramsey myself. She told me who you were and gave me your business card. Later in the evening, I parked outside your building. I saw you pull up in your truck. So I waited until you entered the building, opened your office blinds, and turned on the lights. Then I slipped into the lobby to check the mailboxes — Gabriel Chase, Private

Investigations, Suite 201."

"That doesn't explain how you got in my locked office."

Kaitlyn shot him a sly, secretive smile and said, "I have my ways."

"Besides accusing me of breaking and entering, why are you here?" he asked sarcastically, wanting to put all the pieces together.

"I want to hire you to find Abby." Kaitlyn raised her eyes to his expectantly.

"I'm not sure I want to work for someone who accuses me of criminal acts." His response was curt, delivered in a cool, distant tone. Gabe was determined to find Abby, but wasn't at all sure he wanted to work for anyone but himself to do it.

Kaitlyn angrily pushed out of her chair and hissed, "Then I'll find her myself. I found you, didn't I?"

"That would be a dangerous and stupid move on your part."

"That's for me to judge," she returned.

When she stood to leave, Gabe grasped her arm, his touch sending a shiver down her spine. "I'll find her, Kaitlyn."

"You will?" Kaitlyn sat back down. "We haven't

discussed the money part. How much is your fee?"

"This one is on the house on one condition."

"What's that?"

"You leave the investigative footwork to me. You don't have the training I have. Asking questions of the wrong people can get you hurt." Gabe paused, and then continued, "There are some other ways you can help."

"Good. I'll do anything." For the first time, Kaitlyn felt a sense of relief, and just a little hope. It wasn't that she wanted to help, she had to. If she wasn't doing something to find her sister, she'd go crazy.

"Since we didn't find her purse, I hope you can answer a couple of questions."

"Sure, what are they?"

"Where does Abby bank?"

Kaitlyn thought for a second, and then said, "I think she uses Purdue Credit Union like I do."

Gabe made a note. "Does she have gas cards or credit cards?"

"Yes, Chevron for the gas card, and she has a VISA credit card."

"That's helpful, Kaitlyn. It gives me enough information to do some online research into when and where Abby last used her accounts. I'm also going to call one of my contacts to get a ping on her iPhone to see when it was last used," Gabe said. "In the meantime, there are some more things you can do to help, if you have time."

"Yes, of course."

"Follow me," Gabe said, as he led Kaitlyn to double pocket doors she hadn't noticed. He slid them open to reveal a living area with a black leather sofa and chair, and an oval ebony coffee table. Mounted on the wall opposite the furniture was a large, flat screen television. There was also a small kitchen. The flooring was oak throughout, save for an ivory shag rug under the coffee table.

"What a great space," she said as she scanned the room.

"All my computer equipment is here in my office to work on computer forensics cases. On nights when I work especially late, I just stay here instead of driving home," Gabe said. "I figured you can work in here, while I'm doing computer research in my office."

"Okay. What do you want me to do?"

"Make a list of Abby's friends, and call each one to find out the last time she was seen. We need the when and where."

"Sure. I can do that. But keep in mind, I don't know all of her friends." A pang of guilt shot through her. She should know her sister's friends. She would have if she'd done more to make amends with Abby. Maybe if she had. . .

"Call the ones you know. After you get those calls made, you can make a missing person flyer. I'll bring in a laptop for you. After you create it, we'll have copies made."

"Good idea. While I'm talking with Abby's friends, I'll ask them if they'll help distribute and post the missing flyers."

Gabe left the room to retrieve one of his laptops for her to use. When he returned, she was settled on the sofa, making a list on a yellow pad of paper she'd found on his coffee table. Once he set up the laptop for her, he returned to the computer in his office and immediately typed in her name for a Google search. The first piece of information he found about Kaitlyn Reece was an engagement announcement, with a photo of Kaitlyn and a man named Mitch Bargo standing together in a park. According to the article, Kaitlyn and Mitch were to be married in September of last year. This seemed curious to Gabe. There was no wedding ring on Kaitlyn's finger. Not that it was any of his business, but he wondered what had happened to prevent the wedding. Or maybe she was one of those women who didn't wear her wedding ring.

On the LinkedIn website, he discovered Kaitlyn was a Purdue University graduate in elementary education, with honors. On Facebook and Twitter, she was an infrequent user and had posted no messages since the year before.

He watched Kaitlyn in the next room pacing back and forth in front of his entertainment center as she talked on her cell phone to one of Abby's friends. Making the call was obviously hard for her. Her voice fragile and shaking, she wiped away a tear as she asked Abby's friend for help.

Gabe used the clearance he'd gotten from Brody last year to get information from Abby's gas cards, credit cards, and bank. He discovered that none of the accounts had been accessed since her disappearance. Not a good sign.

Gabe got out the surveillance DVD that the Hoosier Sports Bar and Grill owner had given him and slipped it in his computer. He fast-forwarded through hours of Friday's surveillance camera recording until he reached the segment showing people leaving the bar, just prior to closing. Finally he saw Abby as she headed toward her car, which was the only one parked in front. She got into her car and drove away without incident.

This bar was the last place that Abby was seen. His gut told him he was missing something. Gabe ran his fingers through his hair and started the recording from the beginning, fast-forwarded until he reached ten o'clock, then hit pause. From that point, he moved frame-to-frame and closely examined each person who left the bar. He saw nothing unusual until one in the morning, when two men walked from the bar to their white van, parked in the lot. The men sat in the van for a good thirty minutes until they drove away.

Maybe it was the white van that made Gabe suspicious. He knew from experience that windowless white vans were often involved in crimes, whether they were driven by child molesters, kidnappers, or murderers. And there were so many white vans out there, it was a nightmare for law enforcement to track them.

Searching for a mysterious white van had sent the investigators of the 2002 sniper attacks in the Washington, D.C, area in a tail spin, wasting valuable hours searching for the wrong vehicle, until John Allen Muhammad and Lee Boyd Malvo were arrested, driving a blue 1990 Chevrolet Caprice. Hell, Carly told him that even Ted Bundy used a white van when he abducted and murdered his last victim, Kimberly Leach.

Gabe backed up the recording and watched the two men leave the bar, walk across the parking lot, and enter the white van one more time. What in the hell were they doing sitting in the van for thirty additional minutes? If they were waiting for someone to leave the bar after them, why didn't they wait until closing?

In the kitchen, Gabe pulled out some containers of food. "Kaitlyn, are you hungry?"

"Starved. No breakfast."

"How about a ham or turkey sandwich with some chips?"

"Sounds great. Where is your bathroom? I'd like to wash my hands."

"It's the second room down the hallway." Gabe pulled out sandwich ingredients from the refrigerator. Hearing his office phone ring from the other room, Gabe raced toward it, hit his knee on the coffee table, and sent Kaitlyn's purse airborne. Its contents glided across the floor.

"Oh, shit!" He rubbed his knee, cursing the coffee table, along with his office phone, which had stopped ringing. If there was one thing that made him uncomfortable, it was a woman's purse. This uneasiness probably stemmed from the time he was caught searching his mom's purse for a piece of gum. He'd gotten a tongue-lashing from that event, along with ten minutes in the timeout corner. His mom had emphasized that there might be highly personal items in a woman's purse that would embarrass the heck out of him, along with the owner of the purse. That was enough to make him steer clear — until now.

Rushing to the purse, he located a wallet and lipstick which he slipped back into the purse.

"Is doing an inventory of my purse part of your investigative plan to find my sister?"

He looked up to see Kaitlyn, who wore an unmistakably annoyed expression on her face, standing with her arms crossed. Her foot tapped on the floor, much like his mother's had years ago.

Gabe held up his hands in defense. "Hey, this isn't how it looks. I tripped over the coffee table on the way to my office to answer the phone."

Resting down on the sofa, her arms still crossed, with just the hint of a grin tugging at the corners of her mouth. "Is that the story you're going with?"

Gabe plucked an odd-looking pink metal silhouette of a dog from the floor. "What's this?"

"That's my Attack Dog," she replied, as he handed it to her. "You put two fingers through the Attack Dog eye holes and the sharp tips of his ears can be used to defend yourself against an attacker, like this." Kaitlyn demonstrated jabbing an invisible attacker with the device.

He picked up another pink object. "Is this what I think it is?"

"Ah, the Blaster stun gun, a girl's best friend. Actually, it's one of my favorites. Notice it's dual-purpose, with the built-in rechargeable flashlight," Kaitlyn began. "The Blaster may look pink and girlish, but that baby delivers a powerful punch of 19 million volts. Just firing it into the air should be enough to stop any attacker with half a brain. It makes a scary electrical popping sound as the blinding electric current pulsates between the test prongs. One touch and the Blaster is guaranteed to bring a would-be assailant to his knees. Very cool."

Gabe shook his head and grinned. "I don't know whether to think you're a modern-day female avenger or a sales rep for self-defense weapons."

"Neither. I just happened to be a woman who is trained to defend herself."

Handing the purse to her, Gabe sat on the coffee table and watched Kaitlyn rummage through it. She was undoubtedly one of the most beautiful women he'd ever laid eyes on, *and* one of the most armed.

Finding what she was looking for, Kaitlyn held up a pink lipstick case. What was it with this girl and the color pink? "Are you thinking I'm about to touch up my lipstick?"

"Not sure."

Opening the case, she whipped out a small pink canister of pepper spray.

"You're a regular 007," Gabe said as he admired the resourceful woman.

"Frankie says it can make an attacker cry like a baby so you can kick him where it hurts and run like hell."

"Did you say Frankie?"

"Yes."

"Frankie Douglas?"

"She goes by her married name now. Frankie Douglas-Hansen."

"Small world. I know Frankie. She's one of my best friends. How do you know her?"

"Frankie teaches my self-defense class, plus she's my role model and hero."

He realized there was only one thing missing from her arsenal. "Where's your handgun, Kaitlyn?"

"Oh, it's in the glove box in my car. Want to see it? Before you ask, I do have a concealed weapon permit."

"Don't tell me. Let me guess. Frankie trained you to shoot it."

"Yes." She headed for the kitchen. Opening the mayonnaise jar, she laid out four slices of bread, then coated each with the creamy sauce."

Gabe joined her and pulled out two glasses and liter of Coke. Gazing at Kaitlyn, he wondered why she felt she had to have a self-defense collection. "May I ask you a personal question?"

She eyed him skeptically. "I think so."

"What are you so afraid of?"

"Nothing now."

"What were you afraid of *before* Frankie's training, and purchase of your self-defense collection?"

Kaitlyn squeezed her eyes closed for a second, as if a painful memory had crossed her mind. "I took a night class my last semester at Purdue. It was a long walk back to my apartment, so I always cut through an alley that ran between a campus bar and a pizza place. One night after class, I was walking through the alley and this guy jumped out at me from behind a dumpster and grabbed me. He clamped his hand over my mouth so I couldn't scream, and kicked my legs from under me so I fell flat on my back. I was so terrified that I froze. He yanked my panties down. He was unzipping his jeans, when my brain restarted, and I kicked him between the legs. As he howled with pain, I kicked him until I was sure he couldn't chase me when I ran."

"I'm glad you escaped unharmed."

"After that, I realized I didn't like feeling helpless, with no control over what happened to me. That's when I enrolled in Frankie's class. She helped me to believe in myself, and to always consider my options when threatened."

A mixture of interest and respect flowed through Gabe as he gazed at her. Some women would have been traumatized for life if they'd had an experience like Kaitlyn had. Her resilience and determination attracted him as no woman ever had.

As she prepared to leave Gabe's office, Kaitlyn glanced back at him. He was so engrossed with whatever he'd discovered on his computer that she had to clear her throat to get his attention. Finally, he looked up and shot her a seductive smile, and her hormones did an unwanted happy dance.

"I'm going to the Campus Printing in West Lafayette to get copies of Abby's missing flyers. I'll be back tomorrow morning."

Going down the stairs, Kaitlyn felt a little ball of need that burst to life in the pit of her stomach that could only mean one thing — she was physically attracted to Gabriel Chase, Private Investigator. Seriously? She gave herself a little shake. No way. She could *not* be attracted to this man. Sure, the man was hotter than hot, and had a body designed purely to give a woman hours and hours of female pleasure. But if he dated her sister, like Dr. Ramsey told her, he must be operating on less than half his brain power, and have no sexual scruples. Why? Because that was Abby's kind of man — eye candy on her arm on campus, no pressure from him for a real relationship, and like her, only in it for the sex.

Gabriel Chase was an amazing specimen of masculinity,

who could undoubtedly get any woman he wanted. She wanted a man who only had eyes for her. And if he were the least bit attracted to her, it was probably for a one-night-stand. And if there was one thing Kaitlyn didn't want, it was a fling. She wanted to settle down with a man who was both a lover and a best friend — someone who was in it for the long haul. She wanted happily ever after.

Compared to her sister, Kaitlyn was a Girl Scout with a badge in chastity. Okay, she wasn't completely chaste, thanks to Mitch Bargo, her no-good ex-fiancé, who'd turned her world upside down. And not in a good way. Just the thought of Mitch sent her stomach swirling and her teeth gritting.

Kaitlyn got into her car, plopping down in the driver's seat, slamming the door, and then locking it. As she turned the ignition on, a thought sizzled through her brain. Knowing Abby as well as she did, she was convinced that Abby dumped Gabe. As if she enjoyed it, her sister always had to be the one who broke up the non-relationship. Abby didn't have relationships. She hated the thought of being with any man more than a couple of weeks. So if Dr. Ramsey was correct and Abby dated Gabe for a month, it was highly unusual. For Abby, boredom always set in, and it was time to say good-bye. Abby had a way of breaking up with a man that didn't include sensitivity or empathy. The harder they took the break-up, the more she enjoyed it.

Her mind raced with all the possibilities, and one of them went on repeat. She couldn't get rid of the thought, fear, or whatever it was. What if Abby used her typical lack of finesse to break up with Gabe and she angered him so much that he made her disappear? If a private investigator specialized in finding people, he could be a master in knowing how to make people vanish. Right?

CHAPTER FOUR

Sitting cross-legged on her bed, Kaitlyn turned on her bedside lamp and pulled out Abby's journal. The first ten pages were about Abby's classes and about a professor named Ted Foster who gave Abby the creeps.

Professor Foster asked me to dinner again today. He waited until all the other students left the classroom before he handed me my test. He'd given me an "A." But did I really earn it? He appraised my breasts as he moved closer, until he was almost touching me. "I've given you another "A," Abby. Won't you reward me by having dinner with me tonight?"

I told him I had plans and raced out of there like my butt was on fire. Last Tuesday evening, just before dark, I saw him walk past my apartment. He stood under a street light for a while, and then walked down the alley that leads to the parking lot in back. God, he freaks me out. Every time he gets near me, a pervert alert goes off inside my brain. I'd like nothing better than to plant a hard kick to his groin. Perhaps I will someday. Something to look forward to.

When was the last time this creep saw Abby? Did he

hurt her because she rejected his advances one time too many?

She kept reading as she reached the middle of the journal. Abby wrote about the man Kaitlyn referred to as their ex-father.

I tried to find Daddy through the Internet tonight, and found many men named Robert Elliott Reece, but none of them was Daddy. I won't stop looking until I find him. I need him.

I wish I could wash the day he left out of my mind. From my bedroom, I could hear Daddy and Mommy arguing in the kitchen. I ran down the stairs and into the kitchen and begged for them to stop. I was crying and Daddy picked me up and hugged me. "Everything will be okay, Princess." But over his shoulders, I saw his suitcases near the back door and I knew he was leaving us. I remember crying hysterically and begging him not to go. He'd promised he'd be with me forever, and now he was leaving. Daddy put me down and told me to go to my room. I refused. "I'll send a check each month," he said to Mommy. "Don't try to find me. I'm not coming back." He picked up his suitcases and opened the back door. Mommy grabbed my wrist and I struggled to get free. I wanted to go with Daddy. I want to find him. After all these years, I still miss him. How could he have left me? I was his princess. How could he leave like that and never return?

Tears burning the back of her throat, Kaitlyn closed the journal and held it close to her chest. Poor Abby. She was still mourning for a father who didn't give a shit about his family and what his leaving did to them. As if the monthly child support checks would erase the pain. She was surprised Abby didn't write about blaming her. Kaitlyn still believed it was her fault their father left. He couldn't deal with her surgery, the slow healing afterwards, and the way her mother obsessed about caring for her, to the extent of ignoring her younger daughter and needy husband. It was too much responsibility for a man who yearned for his freedom and the arms of other women. Daddy was not the hero to Kaitlyn as he was to Abby. Though it seemed important for Abby to see him again, that was the farthest thing from Kaitlyn's mind. Her ex-father would remain just that.

Pulling open the journal, she scanned through pages of Abby's assessments of her sexual conquests, and how each man reacted when she dumped him. It was as if Abby got great gratification if the man was hurt and begged her to reconsider. Perhaps it was the power that turned Abby on. Kaitlyn didn't have to be a psychologist to realize her sister was leaving the men just like their father had left them. Abby wanted them to experience the pain she had.

Turning to the last page, the name "Gabe" jumped out

at her. But instead of the sexual assessment Kaitlyn expected, the entry mentioned her.

I dumped Gabe tonight. Okay, I'll be honest, at least, with myself. I broke up with Gabe before he could break up with me. He was too good a man for me. I don't deserve anyone like him. But Kaitlyn does. She's worthy of a man who will genuinely care for her and wants her for the long run. I'm not. What she didn't deserve was what that bastard Mitch did to her. Why wouldn't she listen to me when I tried to warn her? Mitch hit on me more times than I can count. Not that I would ever tell my big sister. Hurting Kaitlyn was never in my game plan, though I know I've caused her pain many times. I should have been at her rehearsal dinner when that pregnant bitch made her big announcement and Kaitlyn's world burst wide-open. I would have kicked Mitch's ass and then escorted his pregnant friend to her car. No one hurts my sister and gets away with it.

There are so many things about Gabe Chase that remind me of Kaitlyn, including the way he loves kids and wants to settle down with a forever love. He's exactly the kind of man Kaitlyn deserves. If there is any way to get them together, I'll do it. Of course, it would help if Kaitlyn and I were still speaking. Why we can't get along is beyond me. But I plan to make more of an effort. I love her so much. She matters so much to me, even more than Mom.

It was Abby's last entry in her journal. Tears flooded down Kaitlyn's cheeks with their heat and quiet power. Abby loved her. She wouldn't have guessed that in a million years. In fact, she always believed the opposite. What younger sister wouldn't resent the attention and affection her older and ill sister had received from their mother?

Finding Abby was even more important now. Kaitlyn had to make things right between them. Enough time had been wasted.

Wearing a body-hugging navy tee with a flirty, flared skirt and matching three-inch pumps, Kaitlyn Reece strode into the Hoosier Sports Bar and Grill like she owned the place — even though this was her first visit alone to any bar — ever. The place was jam-packed with no empty table in sight. A fleeting urge to bolt from the bar rushed through her, but she took a cleansing breath and headed toward the bar. Her mission was to find her sister, and turning back was not an option.

Sliding onto a bar stool, she laid her small white purse on the bar and motioned for the bartender.

Quickly scanning his name tag, Kaitlyn said, "Hi, Keith. I'll have a strawberry margarita," she said. If she wanted information, she needed to buy a drink and make friends with the bartender. "By the way, I'm Kaitlyn."

"Want the umbrella, too, Kaitlyn?" he teased, as his eyes appeared to be undressing her.

"Why not?" she answered.

A moment later, Keith returned with her drink, placed it before her, and accepted the money she slid back. Slipping the bills in his apron pocket, he leaned on the bar with his elbows. "I haven't seen you in here before."

Thirsty and nervous, she lifted her glass, nearly emptying it, and choked when the alcohol hit her throat. *That's what I get for ordering an alcoholic beverage when I rarely drink.*

"Another strawberry margarita, please."

"Coming right up." Keith turned his back to her to mix the drink. A short time later, he placed another drink before her, shot her his version of a sexy smile, and repeated, "I don't think I've seen you in here before."

"No, you haven't." She slipped Abby's photo out of her purse and slipped it across the bar to him. "What about her? Have you seen her?"

Holding the photo between two fingers, he said, "It looks like Abby."

"When is the last time you saw her?"

"Are you a cop?" he asked, as he looked at her with

distrust.

"No, I'm her sister," Kaitlyn said, sipping her drink, already feeling a little light-headed. "When is the last time you saw her?"

"About a week ago. On a Friday. It was late and she came in by herself, but she wasn't alone long. These two guys honed in on her, and before you know it, she's on the dance floor with both of them."

"How long did she stay? Did she leave with these two guys?"

"Abby stayed until closing. I think they left thirty or so minutes before she did."

They were interrupted by a young man who brushed against Kaitlyn as he sat on the barstool next to her. The bartender quickly took his order and left. Sliding his hand down her back, he whispered, "If I told you that you had a great body, would you hold it against me?"

Kaitlyn stiffened and said, "Seriously, that line is older than you are." He was in his twenties with over-moussed, slicked-back hair that made him look like a seventies mob boss. "You'd be wise to remove your hand from my butt before things get ugly."

For a Wednesday night, the Hoosier Sports Bar and

Grill was hopping. The parking lot was filled when Gabe arrived at nine o'clock, and he had to park his truck alongside the road. He'd decided to visit the popular bar at night and pass around Abby's photo to see if anyone had been there the night she disappeared. He was almost to the front door when he spotted a blue metallic Volkswagen Beetle. Moving to the back of the vehicle, he noted the license plate number. Kaitlyn Reece was here, and she better not be here doing the same thing he was. Not after he specifically told her not to. Mentally counting to ten, he clenched his jaw in an effort to cool his annoyance. If Kaitlyn was here playing amateur P.I., he had a thing or two to discuss with her about their agreement.

Spotting Kaitlyn as soon as he entered the bar, he strode toward her. As he grew closer, he realized she was sharing a heated conversation with the guy on the bar stool next to her. Kaitlyn had her hand on the guy's upper thigh in a claw grip and he was squealing in soprano.

"Hi, honey. The babysitter finally arrived. Have you been waiting long?" Gabe kissed Kaitlyn's cheek and hugged her hard enough to loosen her grip on the squealer's thigh.

Surprised, Kaitlyn turned to see Gabe Chase standing behind her, wearing a green long-sleeved T-shirt that stretched across his powerful chest, under a black leather jacket, along with a pair of black jeans. He looked hotter than any man had a right to look, except for the angry, scowling expression on his face.

To the bartender, Gabe said, "Would you please find us a table?"

Slipping Abby's photo into her purse, Kaitlyn, still feeling light headed, swiveled around on her barstool, and then moved next to Gabe, who had wrapped his arm around her waist to brace her. The seventies-mob-boss-wannabe took the opportunity to limp to a far corner of the bar, as far away from Kaitlyn as he could manage.

Kaitlyn shouldn't be this glad to see Gabe. After all, she was caught doing exactly what he asked her not to do — investigate her sister's disappearance on her own. She wasn't looking forward to the tongue-lashing he was sure to deliver.

A slow, romantic Michael Bublé song sounded from the loud speakers. The DJ announced it was a ladies choice dance, and Kaitlyn took the opportunity to distract Gabe.

"May I have this dance?" she asked, flashing her most persuasive smile at him.

Gabe squinted suspiciously down at her, making Kaitlyn certain he was about to turn her down. To her surprise, he pressed a large hand against the small of her back and led her to the dance floor.

Moving into the circle of his arms, Kaitlyn found her head fit perfectly in the hollow between his shoulders and neck. She settled in, enjoying the feel of his powerful arms around her, his large hand pressed against the base of her spine.

"How much have you had to drink?" Gabe asked.

"I'm on my second drink," she slurred.

"Second drink too many."

"I'm not used to drinking, and I couldn't very well ask the bartender any questions without ordering something," said Kaitlyn. "Have I told you how good you look tonight?"

Slipping her hands inside his jacket and around to his muscular back, she looked up at him, admiring the rugged angles, sharp planes, and high cheekbones of his recklessly handsome features.

Gabe glared down at her. "Kaitlyn, I appreciate this little seduction thing you've got going, but it's not distracting me, nor is it going to manipulate me."

Her eyebrows arched mischievously as she said, "I don't know what you're talking about."

Ignoring her remark, he said, "We need to have a talk. Do you want to do it here, or out in my truck?"

"That depends. On a scale of one to ten, how angry are you with me?"

"Between an eight and nine," Gabe responded, as he shot her a glare.

"Your truck sounds good."

Leading Kaitlyn, wobbly on her three-inch heels, to his truck proved to be a challenge, and Gabe sighed in relief once he had her in the passenger seat. Closing her door, he rounded the vehicle and climbed into the driver's seat.

"God, I'm dizzy."

Ignoring her statement, Gabe scowled at her. "I thought we agreed that you'd leave the investigative work to me?"

"I don't see why I can't help. In fact, I may have learned a couple of things already."

"Kaitlyn, you are not a cop or private investigator," Gabe interrupted. "Asking questions of the wrong people can get you hurt or killed. Don't do it again." Dark and hot, eyes narrowed, his gaze locked on her face. "I'm very serious about this."

"I might not be a cop or private investigator, but I may have found out something important from the bartender."

"Like what?"

"The last time he saw Abby was last Friday night. She was in the bar alone. The bartender said there were these two guys who paid a lot of attention to her. Abby danced with the two men, but didn't leave with them. He said the men left about thirty minutes before Abby."

"Interesting."

"So I'm not so bad at investigative work after all?"

"Oh, hell no. I didn't say that. You promised you would leave the private investigation to me."

"Okay, I won't do it again," Kaitlyn whispered.

Gabe softened a little and said, "I'll get your information to Cam."

"Who's Cam?"

"Cam is my brother. He heads the detective team for the county sheriff, who is also my brother."

Turning on the ignition, Gabe threw the truck into gear and entered the highway.

"Where are we going?"

"You're in no condition to be behind the wheel of a car. I'm taking you home. Where do you live?"

"Please don't take me home. I can't be alone tonight. Please." Kaitlyn's face reddened and a hot tear rolled down her cheek.

If there was one thing that Gabe couldn't take, it was a woman crying. "What's wrong? Why can't you go home?"

"I just can't talk about it. I can't be alone. Please, Gabe."

Grasping her hand, Gabe said, "Okay, we can go to my

office, but only if you'll tell me what's wrong."

"I will. I promise."

By the time they reached his office downtown, the world was spinning in her head, and she had to hold onto Gabe in order to stay upright in her three-inch heels. Feeling like a complete idiot, she asked herself, what twenty-four-year-old woman drinks a couple of margaritas and turns to Jell-O? It was too embarrassing. And did she really ask Gabe if she could stay with him? Unreal.

Upstairs, Gabe planted her on his sofa, and headed toward the kitchen to make some coffee. Kaitlyn melted into the cushions, slipping down until she rested her head on the sofa arm.

Soon Gabe hovered over her. "Kaitlyn, are you okay?"

"Just peachy."

"You don't look peachy. You look like you're going to be sick. Are you?" With a panicked look on his face, Gabe was ready to whisk her off the couch and into the bathroom.

"No. I'm just dizzy and embarrassed," she began. "You must think I'm a complete moron. Kaitlyn Reece, amateur detective, searching for the truth about her sister's disappearance by visiting one of Abby's favorite bars, only to become intoxicated after two drinks. What a sleuth."

"You're too hard on yourself," Gabe replied, then added sternly, "That said, don't even think of doing anything like that again." He sat down on the sofa near her.

She pulled herself to an upright position. "I had to do something, even if it meant breaking a promise to you. The longer my sister is missing, the less chance she will be found alive. It's eating me up inside. The last time I saw Abby, we had a terrible fight. I may never get to tell her I'm sorry."

"She'll be found, Kaitlyn." Immediately, Gabe realized he shouldn't have given her that assurance. It probably wasn't true. Every member of law enforcement knew that as more time passed, the likelihood of finding the missing alive diminished. The sad and frightened look on Kaitlyn's face tugged at his heart. He could only imagine how he'd feel if one of his brothers were missing.

Gabe got to his feet before he said something else he shouldn't and headed toward the kitchen. "I'll get you some hot coffee. It will make you feel better."

Returning to the living area, he handed Kaitlyn a mug of hot coffee and sat down in the chair next to the sofa.

"Is your concern about your sister the reason you don't want to be alone tonight?"

Kaitlyn took a deep breath and said, "That's the most important reason."

"What's the other reason?"

"A year ago today was supposed to be my wedding day, and I'm a selfish bitch for thinking about that while my sister is missing."

"What happened?"

Kaitlyn remembered what had occurred as clearly as if it had happened yesterday. Why wouldn't she? Her mind had done an instant replay of the events at least a million times.

"I met Mitch during my freshman year, and we were inseparable until we both graduated. It seemed inevitable we'd get married, so we got engaged and set a date. My mom was over-the-moon happy that one of her daughters was getting married, and planned a festive rehearsal dinner." She paused as Gabe moved from his chair to sit next to her on the sofa. Kaitlyn swallowed hard over the sudden lump of sadness in her throat.

"Guests were taking turns to extend toasts, and one of my bridesmaids, Barbie Denton, rose from her seat to say, 'I wish I could join all of you in toasting the happy couple, but my toast is to Mitch alone, who will become a father to our baby in seven months.' I looked at Mitch and knew instantly by his guilty expression that she was telling the truth. Every eye in the room was on me." She wiped at a tear that had slipped down her cheek, and felt Gabe squeeze her hand.

"What did you do?"

"I dumped my plate of prime rib, baked potato, and green beans in his lap and ran out of the room. I drove for hours until I checked into a Hampton Inn, and stayed the weekend in my room ordering room service and wondering why a man would screw his fiancée's friend behind her back, along with why said-friend would want to be a bridesmaid in my wedding. If Mitch wanted out of the engagement, just telling me would have been fine."

An urge to protect her from any more hurt washed over Gabe, and he pulled Kaitlyn into his arms. Wishing he could lift some of the burden from her slender shoulders, he pressed her head against his chest and kissed the top of her head. A pang of longing shot through Gabe. He wanted to hold her in his arms, soothe her and kiss away her pain. And that was such a monumentally bad idea. She was Abby's sister and now a client. It was beyond inappropriate. So why did it feel so right?

Kaitlyn tilted her head back and gazed at him for a long moment. Then she pressed her soft lips against his, making him tense once he realized what she was doing. He'd been fantasizing about kissing her since he discovered her in his office, but the reality was a trillion times better. Moving his mouth over hers, he devoured her softness, until finally he raised his head and gazed into her eyes. She was Abby's sister *and* his client. Besides the fact she was intoxicated. No matter how much he wanted her, he was taking advantage.

"Kaitlyn, we can't do this."

"I am so sorry, Gabe. I don't know what came over me."

"Don't apologize. I wanted it as much as you did. That's why I have to take you home."

Later, Gabe tossed and turned in his bed. He was having the dream again, the same dream that had haunted his sleep for years. He jerked awake, sat up, and looked at the clock — 5:20 in the morning. Pushing back against the headboard, he wondered why he relived in a dream events that happened twenty years ago.

He was seven-years-old and watched as a girl emerged from the school building. Her eyes scanned the playground until they landed on him, and then her smile widened in recognition as she ran toward him like she did every school recess. Her silvery-blond hair was long, nearly reaching her waist, and whipped in the wind as she approached him.

He called her "Cat" because her family owned several cats that spent their time in the front windows of her house. She'd become his best friend the year before in the middle of first grade, when her family moved to Morel to live in a big house on Main Street. He'd first seen her from the window of his school bus as she emerged from her house to walk to school. At recess that day, he'd approached her and pulled out a miniature Matchbox truck and car from his pocket and handed them to her. "Want to play?"

She smiled and followed Gabe to a large oak tree, where they sat and pushed the cars in the dirt. In the days to follow, the two spent every recess together climbing the playground equipment, chasing each other in a game of tag, or just talking about their families or what had happened in their class the hours before.

At lunch, Gabe carefully placed his tray of cafeteria food on the table and saved a seat for Cat. His mom was the busy county sheriff and bought his school lunch each day. Cat had a stay-at-home mom who made her lunch, which often included delicious sandwiches, soup, and home-baked goodies. Gabe looked forward to the days when Cat agreed to trade lunches, especially on days near holidays when Cat's lunch included an assortment of gourmet treats.

It was on April 7th of his second grade year that everything changed. Gabe's teacher, Mrs. Harrison, held his class back from recess for five minutes because Billy Eden was talking, which was not unusual for him. Billy talked incessantly to anyone who would listen. Once they were released for recess, Gabe looked everywhere for Cat. He couldn't find her at first, but then spied her talking adamantly to Ralphie Smith, who had a reputation as being the class bully. The thought of Ralphie hurting Cat tore at his insides and Gabe raced toward them. He had to protect her. But before he could reach Cat, Ralphie had pushed her to the ground where she hit her head.

Gabe pulled at her arms to help her up but Cat did not respond. She lay there lifeless on the ground. Soon Mrs. Harrison arrived, and a circle of kids surrounded them.

"Gabe, two County EMTs are giving a talk in Mrs. Olympia's class, please run as fast as you can and bring them here!"

One EMT returned with Gabe while the other drove the ambulance near the playground, opened the back, and pulled out a gurney, then rushed back to Cat, who was not responding to Mrs. Harrison's efforts at CPR. The EMTs lifted Cat's small body and placed her gently on the gurney, then covered her face with an oxygen mask before positioning her in the ambulance. Gabe threw himself against the closed ambulance door, begging the EMTs to let him go with Cat. Mrs. Harrison wrapped her arms around him and held him close to her as he cried hysterically.

He never saw Cat again. For weeks, he asked Mrs. Harrison and his mom about her. They each answered that she'd been transferred to a hospital in Indianapolis. Finally, Mrs. Harrison shared that Cat's mother had withdrawn her from school and the house where she once lived was empty. Gabe became convinced that Cat was in heaven where his mom said people go after they die. He'd spent the rest of the school year mourning for his best friend, worrying his mom so much that she took him to a doctor.

He fell into a light sleep. The beep of his laptop announcing a new email woke him. Glancing at his clock, he noted it was 6:30. Pulling his laptop off his bedside table onto his lap, he logged in and read the message.

Hello, Little Sheriff Bro.

It's time to introduce you to our game. Here's how it works: We contact you, and you contact your big brother, Sheriff Brody Chase. Once you receive our email, you need to act fast, because the message goes to the media at the same time.

We're leaving a little surprise in the alley behind the Morel Bar and Grill. And Gabe, this one's for you.

If the Jim Ryder case is any indication of his team's detective skills, Sheriff Chase and his blithering band of idiots will never stop us, no matter how many clues we leave.

This is going to be the best game ever.

— Gamers

Gabe's insides turned to ice. The email had been sent by Abby, at least it had been sent from her email address.

A dark cloud blanketed the morning sky, and heavy rain pelted the windshield of Gabe's truck, blurring the glass, as he raced to town. He'd trace the email back to its true origin.

It had been sent from Abby's IP address, and if this was her idea of a joke, he wasn't laughing. What the hell? She'd been missing for days.

Was the email sent from Abby's laptop in her apartment? Did she send it? Did someone hack her account? Please let this be a bad joke. A wave of apprehension swept through him, and he prayed he'd find Abby alive and well.

He dug his cell phone out of his pocket and called Cameron. No answer. When he heard the voice mail message, he hung up. What message could he leave that wouldn't sound completely insane?

The Morel Bar and Grill was one of the less-desirable establishments in town, and was just off Main Street where the city hadn't started its rejuvenation project. Gabe was unsure the Morel Bar and Grill owners had ever heard or used the word "rejuvenation." Their building was in disrepair with peeling gray paint, cracked and chipped red brick, a roof that needed replaced, and a couple of bullet holes in its windows. At night, its parking lot was packed with Harleys, pickup trucks, and Shawnee County deputy cars. The deputies were inside breaking up fights. This early in the morning, the lot was deserted.

Gabe turned left on Covington Avenue, and then made another left into the alley that ran behind the bar.

There was something or someone leaning against the building that Gabe couldn't make out, thanks to the blinding, driving rain against his truck window. Dressed in a black golf shirt and jeans, Gabe searched the truck for a rain poncho or jacket, until he remembered he'd left them at the house. Leaping out of the truck, he slammed the door shut, and turned up his collar as he hunched down, running and slipping in the rain until he could see what was against the brick-lined building. His hair hung in wet slicks against his neck, and water dripped into his eyes and mouth as he drew closer. Wiping his eyes, he could see clearly.

Propped up near a dumpster overflowing with trash was a young woman. Her skin a purplish hue and her head bent, she was completely nude, her body peppered with droplets of rain. A plastic bag, beaded with moisture, covered her head and was secured tightly at her neck, while her arms and legs were bound with duct tape.

Gabe yanked his cell phone out of his pocket and punched in his oldest brother's number. As soon as he heard his voice, he said, "Brody, I just found a body in the alley behind Morel Bar and Grill. Get here fast."

"Gabe?"

"Just get here, Brody. It's bad."

Gabe disconnected the call and jammed his cell back in his jeans pocket. Careful not to disturb the crime scene, he bent to try to get a closer look at the victim's face. His gut clenched as he fought the nausea rushing up his throat. He had to be wrong. This body couldn't be Abby's. He remembered the end of the email — "this one's for you". What did that mean?

Pushing back to his feet, he swayed and scrambled back until he smacked against the building with his shoulder. By then Gabe heard a siren. The sheriff's SUV skidded around the corner and raced up the alley toward him, trailing a boil of muddy water behind it. Brody braked to a stop, jumped out of the vehicle, and ran toward him.

"Gabe!" As soon as the words flew out of his mouth, Brody saw the body and froze. "Sweet Jesus. What sick bastard did this?"

Running back to his vehicle for a plastic tarp, he returned to the body, carefully covering it to prevent the loss of even more trace evidence being rinsed away by the rain.

Slowly, he walked around the body. Like Gabe, he was careful not to disturb the scene. Pulling his cell phone out of his pocket, Brody tapped a name in his speed dial list. "Cam, we've got a body in the alley behind Morel Bar and Grill off Covington Street. You know the drill. Get the coroner and crime scene techs down here ASAP. Send some deputies to block the alleyway and seal off the crime scene. Come right away and bring Carly with you."

Turning to his brother, Brody said, "Tell me what's going on? How did you find the body?"

"I think it's Abby," Gabe whispered.

"Who?"

"Abby Reece."

"You mean the girl you brought to Carly's party?"

"Yes." Gabe swallowed hard, still fighting the urge to vomit.

"Okay, let's start over. How did you find her body?"

Wordlessly, Gabe pulled a folded printout of the email out of his back pocket and handed it to Brody, who opened and read it.

"When did you get this?"

"It came this morning at six-thirty, before I left the house."

Movement drew their attention to the far end of the alley where a local news truck was maneuvering into a parking space.

"No!" Brody shouted, waving his arms. "This is a crime scene. Move your truck and back off!"

Three patrol vehicles, followed by Cameron's unmarked car, came to a screeching stop in the middle of the street. A brawny deputy climbed out of his vehicle and directed the driver to park the news truck across the street from the alley, while another deputy stretched yellow crime scene tape across the alley entrance from one building to the other. Once that was finished, he raced to the other end of the alley to do the same.

Reporters from radio, television, and newspaper arrived and were clamoring for answers to their questions. But the officers ignored them. A couple had cameras that they aimed down the alley toward the victim.

Running toward the group, Cameron directed his attention toward a deputy who was standing near the alley entry-way. "Well, if it isn't Deputy Gail Sawyer. I didn't recognize you without the giant black medical boot on your foot."

"It made quite a fashion statement. Didn't it?" Gail returned sarcastically.

"Good to see you off desk duty and back in the field," Cameron said. "I need you to move the media all the way across the street."

"They're not going to like that much."

"Do I look like I give a shit what the media likes? Get them away from this crime scene. The first photo any of them get of the victim is on your head. Move it."

Carly Stone pulled her rain coat's hood up to cover her head, and got out of her car to join Cam. She'd left the house right after Brody got the call from Gabe. The two made their way down the alley toward Brody and Gabe, who looked like they were having a heated discussion.

"Sweet Jesus, Gabe. Do you know how bad this looks? You're dating the victim and you're the one who finds her body?" The lines of Brody's face were etched with concern. "Go back to my office. Wait for me so we can talk. Don't talk to anyone until I get there."

"Bullshit, Brody. I am not waiting at your office. You're not going to treat me like a suspect. I had nothing to do with this, and you have to know that. I've been searching for Abby since I learned she was missing. I'll be at Mollie's Cafe. And if you decide to meet me there, come as my *brother*, not the county sheriff."

Sadly, Gabe glanced at the body one more time, then got into his truck and left.

Brody approached Cameron and Carly. "The body was found in that position about twenty-five minutes ago. There's no purse or wallet, so no identification. I covered her with the plastic sheeting so we wouldn't lose any more trace evidence than we already have from the rain."

"The crime scene techs are on their way, as is the coroner," Cameron told Brody as he inched toward Carly, who was already bent over the body.

"Unusual," Carly remarked softly as she lifted the tarp

to scrutinize the body.

Brody eased close to her, and got under her umbrella. "What's unusual?"

"Her body has been posed. That doesn't happen often. A very small percentage of murder victims are left staged in an unusual position like this."

Brody eyed the body curiously. "Why do you think she was posed?"

"The killer or killers want to thwart our investigation. In addition, they posed the body to shock the finder, as well as the investigators. It's the killer's perverted, cheap thrill."

"Sick," Brody said with disgust.

Carly bent down to look closer at the victim's face beneath the plastic bag covering her head. "Brody, she looks familiar."

"Yeah, I think so, too," said Cameron, who bent down next to her.

Brody whispered, "Gabe thinks it's Abby Reece, the woman he brought to Carly's party."

"Oh, no. It can't be," Carly said sadly.

"What do you think? Crime victims are only people we don't know?"

"C'mon Brody. You know what I meant," said Carly.

"I was thinking about Gabe. I saw him here earlier, and even from a distance, I could tell he was upset. Is he the one who found the body?"

"Later. Can't talk here."

Carly quickly replaced the plastic tarp and backed away, as Coroner Bryan Pittman arrived with two of his assistants. "How many of you are trampling all over my crime scene?"

"Not even one. Wouldn't think of it, buddy," said Brody. "You know you've been saying that for years, and not once has a member of my staff compromised a crime scene."

"Just keeping people on their toes. That's all." Bryan hid a wicked grin. He and Brody had been best friends for years, and there was nothing better Bryan liked to do than give the sheriff a hard time. It distracted him from the unpleasantness of crime scenes.

Slipping on a pair of latex gloves, Bryan moved close to the body, pulled up the plastic sheeting, and examined the plastic bag on the victim's head. "I don't think suffocation is a stretch here." He paused when no one laughed. "A little coroner humor." Grinning as the others grimaced and shook their heads, he slowly inched his way around the body.

Bryan then looked back at Brody. "This is a secondary crime scene. This isn't where the murder occurred. I won't know until the autopsy if she was raped and/or tortured prior to death. Our killer is fearless, stupid, or unfamiliar with this area, considering the time it took to pose the body. There are drunks ambling through this alley from the bar all hours of the night."

"Interesting." Carly focused her attention on the only thing the victim was wearing. "Check out her shoe. It looks like a vintage brocade-covered high heel, the kind girls wore to the prom back in the day. It's at least two sizes too big for her."

"You're right," Bryan responded. "It doesn't look like it belongs to her. I'll send it to the State Police Crime Lab in Indy for trace evidence and DNA testing."

Thoughtfully, Brody rubbed his chin. "If the shoe doesn't belong to the victim, who does it belong to?"

Next to him, Cameron stopped writing in his notepad. "If this isn't the first kill, the shoe could lead us to another victim."

"Please don't let this be another serial killer in this county. Please," Brody groaned.

Cameron pulled Brody aside. "I saw Gabe here earlier. Where did he go?"

"I told him to wait for me in my office, but he insisted on Mollie's."

"Is he waiting for you as a brother, or a suspect?"

Brody shot Cameron a glare. "What are you getting at?"

"Conflict of interest. You can't, and no one from your team can interview Gabe about this. He's the sheriff's brother." Cameron paused for a second, and then added, "Right now, Gabe needs his family. We need to get an outside investigator who doesn't know our family to talk to interview Gabe."

"I overheard Blake Stone telling Carly that he just hired a new detective. I'll call Sheriff Brennan to see if we can borrow him."

"Seriously? People know how close you are to Tim Brennan and Blake Stone, which leaves us wide open for accusations of conflict of interest. In fact, there isn't another sheriff in this state that you don't know. We need to go to another agency entirely."

"I'll call Dan Walters with the Indiana State Police. But I hate to turn over a crime that happened in our county to another agency." Brody ran his fingers through his hair, wet from the rain.

"I don't think we have to. The state police could send one of their detectives to interview Gabe, and maybe they could even expedite the DNA processing of the shoe placed on the victim. We could share the case, work alongside them. We can avoid the potential allegation of a conflict, and still maintain our involvement."

Brody nodded and fished his cell phone out of his pocket to call Dan Walters.

On Covington Avenue, a white utility van crawled past the alleyway next to the Morel Bar and Grill so its occupants could rubber-neck the activities in the alley. Inside the van, dressed in white painter's coveralls and caps, Evan and Devan watched as the body they'd left hours before was loaded into the coroner's van.

"And so the game begins," Devan's mouth pressed into a smirk as he rolled down his window. "There's no one behind us, so stop the van."

Braking, Evan peered down the alley. "I don't see Gabe Chase."

"Neither do I, but there's the sheriff. He doesn't look very pleased, does he?"

Evan laughed and took his foot off the brake. "I predict he'll become less and less pleased as the game progresses."

As soon as Gabe sat down in a booth at Mollie's Cafe, he realized what a mistake it was to choose her restaurant to wait for his brothers. Across the room, Mollie Adams honed in on him like a heat-seeking missile. She shot across the restaurant and slid into the seat across from him.

"Not a good time, Mollie," said Gabe, as his waitress poured a cup of coffee. "Just leave the pot," he told her, then glanced at Mollie, wishing she would leave him alone.

"After what I did, I doubt a good time will ever come for one of the Chase brothers to want to talk to me," Mollie said, swallowing the tears forming at the back of her throat. "I need your help, Gabe."

"What do you need *my* help with?"

"I need for you to talk to Cameron for me."

"Mollie, there is no way in hell I am going to talk to Cameron for you. You chose to smother Brody with kisses in his hospital bed after his surgery. What in the hell were you thinking? You knew Brody was in a relationship with Carly. Most importantly, you knew how Cameron felt about you."

"I'm guilty. I know. I don't know what came over me. When I heard Brody had been shot, I rushed to the hospital. My original intent was to find Cameron and wait for word about Brody's condition. But when I asked at the nurses' station, they said Brody was in recovery and I could visit with him for a minute."

"And the rest is history. I already lived this experience; I don't need to relive it, Mollie."

"Please ask Cameron to talk to me and give me another chance."

"Not going to happen."

"Why not?"

"*You* chose to tell Cam for months that he was the one you were in love with — not Brody. You chose to molest Brody in the hospital. I mean, the guy was still under anesthesia. What were you thinking?"

"I can't explain what I did. I have no clue what came over me. I've been over Brody for years."

"You couldn't have hurt Cam more if you'd stabbed him in the chest. He's been in love with you for years. He thought you loved him, too," Gabe said. "If he ever forgives you, that's his decision. I'm not intervening on your behalf."

Wiping tears from her cheek, Mollie went back to the kitchen.

Gabe's cell vibrated on the table. The call was from Kaitlyn, the very last person on earth he wanted to talk to right now. What would he tell her? He'd just found a body in an alley that looked an awful lot like her sister. Bryan hadn't made an official identification of the body yet. Gabe ignored her call and prayed she was nowhere near the crime scene.

Brody was right. If the body was Abby's, he'd be

considered a person of interest — the last thing a private investigator building a business wants to be. A sickening sense of guilt washed over him. How could he be concerned about his business when a young woman just lost her life in such a violent way?

Gabe ran his fingers through his thick hair and thought about the email and how it had come from Abby's laptop. Brody needed to get possession of her laptop and have the crime scene technician team examine it for prints and DNA. The email was signed "Gamers," which meant there was more than one of them. They'd written they'd left a "surprise" behind the bar specifically for him. Were the Gamers people he knew, or people who knew him? If the body was Abby's, did they target her to get back at him for some reason? Or was it his brother, Brody, they had the beef with? If the killers thought of this as a game to test the sheriff's detectives, this would not be the only victim unless they caught them quickly.

Gabe was so engrossed in his thoughts, he didn't notice that Brody had entered the restaurant until he sat down at his booth. Within seconds, Mollie was hovering over them with a pot of hot coffee. Once she warmed up Gabe's brew, she poured coffee into a mug for Brody.

"Are you having breakfast, Brody? We've got fresh cinnamon buns this morning."

"No thanks, Mollie. Just the coffee."

Brody waited until Mollie headed back to the kitchen, then leaned across the table. "Talk to me. Start from the beginning."

Gabe explained how he'd learned Abby was missing and that he was looking for her.

"Why didn't you or Cam discuss this with me?" Brody interrupted, obviously annoyed his brothers left him out.

"There was nothing you could do. She was missing from Tippecanoe County, out of your jurisdiction."

"Besides being the sheriff, I'm your brother. A woman you dated goes missing. You don't think I'd be interested in that?"

"I'm sorry, Brody. Everything was moving so fast. All I knew was that I had to find her." He paused, remembering the email the killers had sent him. "You have to get Abby's laptop from her apartment. I traced it back to its IP address, and the email I showed you from the killers is from her laptop."

"How do you know where Abby's laptop is? I thought you two broke up?"

"It was there when I searched her apartment."

"When was this?"

"The day I found out she was missing, and talked to the West Lafayette police."

"They gave you permission to search Abby Reece's apartment?"

"She'd given me a key, and I wanted to see if there was anything in her apartment that would tell me where she was."

"In other words, you compromised what could have been the crime scene and illegally searched a missing person's apartment. What were you thinking, Gabe?"

A tone sounded and Gabe looked down to read a text from Kaitlyn. She was waiting for him at his office. That's all he needed. What in the hell was he supposed to say to her?

Slapping a twenty dollar bill on the table, Gabe said, "I have to go."

"We're not through talking, Gabe," Brody insisted.

"Kaitlyn is waiting for me at my office."

"Who's Kaitlyn?"

"Abby's sister. She hired me to find Abby."

Brody shook his head. "You've got to be kidding."

"No." Gabe slid out of the booth.

"Gabe, you have to be interviewed. If the body is identified as Abby Reece, you not only dated her, you found the body. A detective from the Indiana State Police will be here this week. Stick around so I can find you."

"State Police?"

"Yes, since you're my brother, it's an obvious conflict of interest for anyone from my staff to do it."

"Right," Gabe muttered.

"Another thing. I have to suspend you as our computer forensic consultant."

"Really? Then who is going to examine the contents of Abby's laptop?"

"I'll have to find another consultant."

"Wait a minute. I know who you can hire. Call Anne Mason-Brandt."

"Anne? I know she used to own a computer-related company, but she's not qualified to do computer forensics."

"Yes, she is. She got certified about six months ago. Anne does a lot of work for Frankie Hansen's P.I. business. She'd do a good job, Brody."

"I'll call her, but in the meantime, stay close."

Later that day, Brody was in a dark rage when he barged into Michael's office, hitting the door back against the wall with the flat of his hand.

"I just heard something that can't be fucking true!"

From behind his desk, Michael leapt to his feet and held up a hand in restraint.

"Calm down, Brody."

"Seriously? Calm down?" Brody was incredulous. "I just heard that Ryder's been moved out of maximum security to an undisclosed location. Is this true?"

"Yes, the FBI moved him yesterday."

"What the hell is going on?" Brody couldn't stop the raw fury that slammed into him every time he thought about it. "Is it also true you're working on a plea bargain with that animal?"

"Quiet down, Brody. The entire floor can hear you."

"How can I calm down when I just heard you're talking about a plea bargain with Jim Ryder?"

"Sit down so we can discuss this," Michael motioned to a guest chair on the other side of his desk. "You may not know that I started my career as a cop. I've been on your side of law enforcement. I understand what you're feeling."

Brody sat down, but on the edge of his seat and leaned toward the prosecutor. "We risk our lives to get the bad guy, and then once he's in the legal system, everything works to his favor. He gets out and commits the same crimes and the cycle starts again."

"It's not like that," Michael explained. "We have him on

seven counts of murder. I'm one hundred percent certain he's going to get the death penalty."

"Then why the plea bargain?"

"We have him for killing seven girls, seven counts of murder, and if we give him death, that's all we'll ever have a chance of solving. We think there are more victims." Michael paused, elbows on his desk, searching Brody's face for signs of understanding. "We have DVDs of Ryder beating, torturing and raping ten additional victims, and we have no clue who they are or where he put their remains. Ryder is the only one who can tell us. He says if he gets the plea agreement, he'll tell us who they are and show us where their remains are."

"How do you know he's telling you the truth? Ryder's a prolific liar."

"We have an interrogation analyst from the FBI listening to every conversation we have with him. So far, the analyst says he's telling the truth. There are more victims we haven't identified and remains we haven't found. Jim Ryder is the only way we'll find those victims and give closure to their families."

"After what's he's done, that freak doesn't deserve to live. He should get as much mercy as he gave his victims."

Michael leaned back in his chair. "Does he deserve to live? Hell, no. He's a monster. Do the families of the unidentified victims deserve to know what happened to their missing daughters so they can give them a decent burial? Yes, they do. If we can give it to them, we owe them some sense of closure. In the end, they are the only people who matter in this. They've suffered enough."

CHAPTER FIVE

A clap of thunder vibrated through Gabe's office, shaking the windows, vibrating the floors, and startling Kaitlyn. The wind had picked up and rain pinged against the windows, blurring the glass and collecting on the sidewalk and street below. She turned on Gabe's desk lamp to illuminate the darkened room. It was morning, yet the stormy skies made it seem like evening had come.

Another siren, the third one within thirty minutes, pierced the momentary stillness. Kaitlyn returned to the window in time to see another county deputy cruiser racing toward the other side of town. The car created a wave of water that drenched a woman huddled under an umbrella, entering the building's lobby below.

Lifting her mug to her lips, Kaitlyn discovered the coffee was cold and bitter, which made her wonder just how long she'd been standing at the window. She heard more sirens, and wondered what had happened so early in the morning. For that many officers to race to a crime scene in this small town, it must be serious.

Anxiously, Kaitlyn paced in front of Gabe's office window and looked for him in the street below. She checked her watch. Where was he? Why wasn't he responding to her texts? She told him she'd return this morning. Why wasn't he here?

Remembering the night before, the thought of his kiss sent shivers of desire racing through her body. It shouldn't have happened. What was she thinking? After all, she'd hired the man to find her sister. Starting something with him would only complicate things. Besides, was she ready to trust another man after what Mitch did to her?

Footsteps sounded from the stairwell, and soon a shadow appeared on the frosted glass of Gabe's office door. Kaitlyn raced to open it.

To her surprise, a woman stood before her, squeezing rain water from her long, dark hair. Every piece of clothing the woman wore was soaked and dripping water onto the floor.

Carly did a back-step to make sure she was indeed at Gabe's office. Yes, his name was printed in black letters on the frosted glass of the door. She was as surprised to see the young fair-haired woman at the door as the she seemed to be to see her.

She smiled and extended her hand. "Hi, I'm Carly Stone. I'm looking for Gabe."

"Gabe's not here."

"Are you one of Gabe's clients?"

"Yes, I'm Kaitlyn Reece. I hired Gabe to find my sister."

Carly's heart thudded when she heard the last name "Reece." Was this woman Abby's sister? "Your last name sounds familiar."

"My sister, Abby, is missing. You may have seen one of the missing flyers, or maybe heard her name on the news."

"That must be it." Shedding her soaked raincoat, Carly folded it over her arm.

"Please come in. I'll find some towels for you. You must be freezing in those wet clothes."

Carly watched as Kaitlyn opened a set of pocket doors and entered Gabe's private living area. Clearly it wasn't the young woman's first visit to Gabe's office. She knew her way around. Why hadn't Gabe told her that he was hired as a P.I. to find Abby Reece? Soon Kaitlyn returned with a couple of thick white towels. Carly wrapped one around her shoulders and began dabbing at her wet blouse and pants with the other.

"I think they call this kind of storm a toad strangler," said Kaitlyn with a giggle.

"I don't know about the toads, but it looks like it made a good try at strangling me,"

Kaitlyn eyed Carly with renewed interest. "I think I've seen you in the paper. Aren't you the profiler the sheriff hired last year?"

"Yes, I am."

"Has the sheriff made any progress finding my sister?"

"I believe the West Lafayette police have your sister's case in Tippecanoe County. It's outside the sheriff's jurisdiction. But I'm sure they're doing all they can to find her," Carly said. Although if the woman's body they'd found earlier in the alley turned out to be Abby Reece, the case would be turned over to Shawnee County and Brody's team. She prayed Kaitlyn didn't ask more questions about her missing sister. Glancing down at her watch, she realized Abby Reece's autopsy would begin in a couple of hours. She couldn't stay much longer, but she really wanted to see Gabe and make sure he was okay.

Loud footfalls on the stairs caught their attention, and soon Gabe burst into the room, out of breath, as soaked from the storm as Carly was. He glanced at the two women, muttered something under his breath, and stripped off his jacket to hang it on the coat rack.

Grasping Carly's arm, he glanced at Kaitlyn. "Sorry I'm late. I need to talk to Carly about a private matter in the hallway. I'll be right back."

Closing the door behind him, he turned to Carly. "You didn't tell her about the body in the alley, did you?"

"Of course not, and here's a question for you. Why didn't you tell me that Kaitlyn hired you to find her sister?"

"It just happened a couple of days ago."

"I'm not judging, Gabe, but don't you think it makes things even more complicated? I mean, you dated Abby, and now she's missing. Then you are hired by her sister as a private investigator."

"At this point, everything I do makes my life more complicated," Gabe responded, clearly frustrated. "I was already looking for Abby when Kaitlyn asked me to help. I couldn't say no to her."

"Brody told me you found the body in the alley, and that you think it might be Abby. How did you happen to find the body?"

"It's a long story, Carly. Ask Brody about it. I just talked to him." He tiredly ran his fingers through his hair and sighed.

"I'm sorry, Gabe. I came here to see if you needed to talk. Is there anything I can do to help you?"

"Yes, you can tell me if the body is identified as Abby Reece as soon as you know."

Gabe found Kaitlyn sitting on the sofa in his living area. She looked worried and anxious. He wanted to fold her in his arms and make the burden on her slender shoulders slip away.

"Where have you been? I told you that I would be here at nine o'clock."

"I'm sorry. Something came up." It wasn't a lie, but was close. He refused to tell Kaitlyn that her sister might be lying in the morgue without a definite identification. What if the woman's body wasn't Abby after all?

"I heard police sirens. Do you know what is going on?"

"No. Maybe it was another fire. Brody told me they think we may have a serial arsonist." The lie came out smoothly, and he prayed she believed him. Skillfully, he changed the subject before she had a chance to ask a question.

Kaitlyn eyed Gabe and wondered why he'd just lied to her. There were men who tell award-worthy lies, but Gabe wasn't one of them.

Just as she was about to confront him, he pulled off his

wet T-shirt, revealing broad shoulders, a rock-hard chest that tapered nicely down to a rippling six-pack, tight waist, and slim hips. The man was exquisite. There was no other word for it. The room temperature seemed to raise a couple of degrees. Kaitlyn's heart jack-hammered against her ribs as she tried to throttle the dizzying current of excitement racing through her body. Forcing her eyes to his face, she found Gabe watching her with a smile that slowly tipped up one corner of his mouth.

Embarrassed she'd been caught ogling him, Kaitlyn's face burned a dark scarlet. Rising to her feet, she struggled to compose herself. She glanced at her watch. "I need to go. My new teacher orientation starts in fifteen minutes."

"New teacher?"

"Yes, I got hired as a third grade teacher at Morel Elementary. I'm filling in for a Mrs. Grey, who went on maternity leave."

"That's great, Kaitlyn. Congratulations." Gabe walked her to the door.

"I think so, too. I love kids, and teaching them has been my dream since childhood. I'm pretty excited." Good Lord, she was chattering, filling in the empty space that lay between her embarrassment and attraction. The faster she could put some distance between herself and Gabe, the better.

"I can tell. It's good to see you smiling." He handed Kaitlyn her umbrella.

With a deep sigh of relief, Gabe watched Kaitlyn from the window as she strode down the rain-dampened street toward her car. Thankfully, he was able to avoid telling her that they may have found her sister's body.

Why did he feel so protective toward Kaitlyn? Okay, the feelings he had for her were more than just protective. Even knowing it was a mistake to get involved with her, he couldn't seem to stop himself. He wanted her, and the heat in her eyes a few minutes ago told him she felt the same way.

At eight o'clock that night, Brody, Cameron, and Carly waited for Bryan Pittman in the sheriff's conference room. The coroner was scheduled to present his autopsy report about the young woman whose body they found in the alley that morning.

Carly and Cameron had attended the autopsy earlier in the afternoon, and had painstakingly slipped items into evidence bags. Cameron had photographed the vintage brocade-covered high-heel shoe found on the victim. Carly had been correct. The shoe was two sizes too large for the victim. It was a size eight, and the victim wore a size six. If it wasn't Abby's shoe, whose was it? Cameron planned to email the shoe photo to a sizable state law enforcement email list to find out if the shoe was linked to any of their cases. Since a small percentage of bodies are left posed, he would attach the photograph of the posed body he'd taken at the crime scene, along with the shoe photo.

Realizing Brody would want him to head the homicide case, especially if the victim was Abby Reece, Cameron had spent the day re-assigning some of his cases to Ron Bergman and Sal Murray on his detective team.

Carly had researched the life of Abby Reece on the Internet, first comparing her photo on Facebook to that of the body in the alley. Though they still lacked an official identification, she was certain the body was that of Abby Reece. Next, she used her findings to start a preliminary victim profile. Abby Reece was not in a high-risk occupation, like a prostitute, which involved casual sexual encounters with strangers. She was a college student who may have had casual sexual encounters, but they probably took place in the relative safety of the college campus in a dorm room or apartment.

Of course, once Bryan officially identified the body, Carly would talk to friends and family members to generate more detail about the victim's lifestyle, and how it may have contributed to her death. Hopefully she'd be able to have enough information to start a profile of the killer. Questions whirled in Carly's brain like a tornado. Was the killer organized with a plan, or a specific preference of killing? Did he have a fantasy that only particular victims would fulfill? Did he know his victims, or did he target strangers?

Carly glanced at Brody, who seemed anxious and concerned. Why wouldn't he be? His younger brother could be named as a person of interest in a murder case. She wished there were something she could do to ease the worry lines on his face. If they were alone, she would have straddled him on his chair and kissed him until his worries disappeared — at least momentarily.

Bryan, in a lab coat, entered the room, laid a file folder on the table, then wordlessly walked to the coffee pot to pour himself a cup, and sat next to Cameron.

"Is it Abby Reece?" Brody was tense and impatient.

"When she went missing, her mother gave the West Lafayette Police Abby's dental records." Bryan began. "Yes, our body is Abigail Lynne Reece."

"Cause of death?" Brody's mouth dipped into a deeper frown.

"Asphyxiation. She was smothered inside the plastic bag we found covering her head," Fatigue settled in pockets under Bryan's eyes, and he threaded his fingers tiredly through his hair. "There was bruising on her upper arms that could indicate one person held her down while she was struggling to breathe, while the other tightly wound the duct tape around her neck, ensuring no air would enter the plastic bag on her head. By the way, there was a partial print on a section of the duct tape."

"Excellent," said Brody.

"Bryan, do you think there are two killers, working together?" asked Carly.

"That would be my guess. It would make the abduction and murder that much easier."

"That explains the signature on the email Gabe received. It was signed 'Gamers' plural, indicating more than one person," Brody said.

"Was she sexually assaulted?" Carly asked Bryan.

"No."

"That's odd." Cameron pulled out a photo of the body at the crime scene. "We found her nude. Why would the killers leave her posed like that in the alley?"

"One thought that comes to mind is that the killers are not motivated by sexual gratification," said Carly. "Maybe their goal is to dehumanize their female victims by stripping them of their clothing, and posing them in a sexual manner in a public place."

"After reading the email they sent to Gabe, I think their motive is to play games with law enforcement. They posed the body as if to say the county sheriff and his detectives are too stupid to catch them," said Cameron. "Which is one fucking wrong assumption!" Anger narrowed his eyes and stiffened his jaw.

"Did you just say 'victims' plural?" Brody asked of Carly. "Why do you think there are more victims?"

"I think this crime is too organized to be a first killing. The killers took time to painstakingly plan the abducting, killing and posing of Abby Reece," she replied. "Not only that. They crafted the email that they sent to Gabe and the media."

Cameron added, "There is also the line in the email, 'This may be the best game ever,' which I think indicates this is not the first time they've killed, or taunted law enforcement."

"I'm sorry," Carly said to Brody. "I know that's the last thing you want to hear, especially after the Jim Ryder case. Their killings may not have occurred in Shawnee County, and the bodies may or may not be found here. But believe me, there are other victims."

"Damn it!" Brody slammed his fist on the table, causing Bryan's coffee to slosh out of his mug. Brody's expression was clouded in anger. He handed Bryan a napkin. "The media is going to have a field day with this. County residents are still pissed off we didn't catch Jim Ryder sooner, not to mention the maniac was one of our own deputies. Now this."

"We'll get them," promised Cameron. "That's why I'm putting out an email with information about the note and photos of the crime scene, as well as the shoe, to all state and federal law enforcement agencies. We might get lucky and get a lead."

Brody looked at Bryan. "Did you give the shoe she was wearing to the Crime Lab in Indy to process any trace evidence or DNA?"

"Of course. I'll let you know if I hear anything from them."

Cameron added, "I'll find out the brand of shoe. I want to know if the shoe is one that is hard to find. Is it expensive? If we can track it down to where it was purchased, we might be able to get a buyer's name."

"Try the vintage shops." Carly handed him a short list of shops in the area.

"Bryan, when was time of death?" asked Brody.

"Judging by her body temperature and state of rigor mortis, I think she died between midnight and two in the morning."

"That fits, Gabe got the email from the killers at 6:30 this morning. That gave them plenty of time to send the email from Abby's apartment, drive here, and pose the body."

Bryan pushed his chair back, gathered his paperwork in a file folder, and prepared to leave. "Call me if you have any more questions. I'm heading home for a couple hours of shut-eye." He left the conference room, closing the door behind him.

Brody turned to Cameron. "Let me know when you've notified the next of kin."

Cameron rose and moved to the door, then turned and asked, "Isn't it just the sister and the mother?"

"Yes."

"What about the West Lafayette Police? Do you want me to contact them?"

"No, I'm heading to my office right now to tell the chief their missing person has been found dead in Shawnee County, and it's now our case. I'll request they send her file to you," said Brody.

"Thanks. It's getting late, so I'll contact Abby's family tomorrow morning."

"No problem."

Once Cameron left the room, Brody pulled Carly to him and kissed her quickly on the lips. "There's no reason for you to stay late, too. Why don't you head home? I'll see you later."

Carly nodded in agreement and watched as he left the room. Once she heard him on the phone in his office, she pulled out her cell and dialed Gabe's number to honor her promise to tell him if the body in the alley belonged to Abby.

Within seconds she felt a large, warm hand clenched around her own, removing her cell phone from it. Snapping to attention, she looked up to find Brody leaning over her as he read the display on her cell phone. Her heart stopped as she met his gaze. Carly was speechless. She had never lied to Brody and wasn't going to start now.

"I know why you're calling Gabe, and we need to talk," Brody said coldly. "But not here. I'll see you at home." He pocketed her cell phone and left the room.

Great. Just great. There was nothing she disliked more than fighting with Brody, especially when it was so obvious she'd crossed the line. She should have told Brody of her promise to Gabe. The call made it look like she was going behind his back — which she was. Worst of all, she knew how he felt. She would have felt the same way if he'd gone to her brother, Blake, with one of her issues, and not told her about it.

Parking in front of Gabe's office building, Cameron got out of his car and glanced up. It was not surprising that lights were on in Gabe's office. Working hard had always been his own remedy when he had a problem. Though, he'd never had a problem like being a suspect for a murder. Gabe was the ex-boyfriend, which meant he went to the top of the suspect list.

He wasn't looking forward to telling his younger brother that Abby Reece had been murdered, but he didn't want anyone else to do it, either. He and Gabe were close, and nothing was going to change that. It was bullshit that anyone might think that Gabe would hurt anyone, especially someone he'd dated.

Reaching Gabe's office, Cameron knocked, and then opened the door to find Gabe at his desk, working on his computer.

"Cam, what are you doing here?"

"Do I need an excuse to come see my brother?"

"Sit down. Want some coffee?"

"No. I've had so much caffeine today, I'll never get to sleep. Not that I'll have time for that tonight."

"What's going on? I know you're not here at this time of night just to visit," Gabe's voice was rough with anxiety.

"Bryan was able to make identification of the body through dental records. It's Abby Reece." Cameron watched the shock of discovery flash over his brother's face. "I'm sorry, Gabe." This was the part of his job he hated, notifying people of the death of a friend or loved one. He felt even worse delivering the news to his brother.

Gabe rose from his seat and walked to his window, wordlessly peering out at the darkness of night, the street alit with the street lamps below. Cameron wondered what he was thinking but said nothing, letting his brother soak in the news. It wasn't like the Chase brothers were strangers to pain. Years ago when their mother was the county sheriff, she'd been shot by a drug dealer who thought she was going to search his trunk full of meth. He wished she were here. She'd know what to do to make Gabe feel better.

Finally Gabe turned toward him. "Do Kaitlyn and Abby's mom know?"

"No. I'll tell them tomorrow."

"I'd like to go with you when you tell Kaitlyn."

"Why?"

"Because I care about her."

"Gabe, I heard you'd taken her on as a client, but are you in a relationship with her?"

"No. Can't I care about her without being involved with her?"

"But you want to, don't you?"

"Shit, Cam. Are you going to make a federal case out of it?"

"I can't believe you're getting involved with the sister of your ex-girlfriend, who is now a murder victim. A little messy, don't you think?"

Gabe swiftly changed the subject. "Is it your case now?"

"Yes, but not officially. When I left the office, Brody was calling the West Lafayette police."

"I can help you, Cam."

"Not sure that's such a good idea. You're too close to the case."

"Bull. Private investigators work with the police all the time."

"Not when the P.I. is the ex-boyfriend of the victim, and on a short suspect list."

"Well, then let's get me off the list. Has Brody scheduled a State Police interview? He told me that's what was going to happen. Let's get it over with."

Cameron slipped his cell out of his pocket and sent a text to Brody, asking him when Gabe's interview would take place. There was a brief knock on the door before Brody entered the room and sat next to Cameron, holding his cell phone.

"Got your text," Brody said to Cameron. To Gabe, he said, "The interview is tomorrow at ten in one of our interview rooms. Indiana State Police is sending a detective named Robynn Burton. I hear she's one of their rising stars."

"I'll be there."

"Be cooperative, Gabe. Tell her all you know."

"Why the hell wouldn't I cooperate?" Gabe's lips thinned with irritation. "I've done nothing wrong."

"She'll ask what you were doing last night during the time of the murder. Do you have an alibi?"

"I was with Kaitlyn."

"The victim's sister?"

"Yes, I caught her at a bar doing some amateur investigative work. She'd had one drink too many, and I brought her back here. We talked until around two this morning, and then I drove her home."

Brody seemed satisfied with his answer. "I'm sorry, Gabe."

"Which part are you sorry about? The mini-inquisition or the fact Abby is dead?"

"I had to ask about your alibi, and of course I'm sorry Abby is dead."

"Then reinstate me." The determination in his bottomless brown eyes was unmistakable.

"You haven't been officially cleared yet," Brody pointed out.

"But I will be."

Carly heard the familiar hum of Brody's SUV as he parked outside the house. She'd tried for hours to concentrate on the work she should be doing in her office, but had not been too successful. Listening to his footfalls on the stairs, she swiveled her chair away from her computer and toward the door.

Brody appeared in the doorway, loosening his tie and unbuttoning his shirt sleeves, and shot a fierce look in her direction.

"You didn't trust me to tell my own brother about Abby? What the hell, Carly? Do you think my abilities to be a good brother are that bad?"

"Oh, Brody, I'm so sorry. I promised Gabe I'd call when there was an identification of the body."

"But you didn't trust me to make that call?" He leaned on the door frame, as if he had all the time in the world to hear her response.

"Sometimes you're too hard on Gabe. You act like nothing he does meets your approval."

"You obviously have problems with the way I treat

Gabe, yet you haven't said a word. What's that all about?"

"I don't know."

"Bull. It's trust, Carly. You still don't completely trust me."

She folded her arms across her chest. "That's not it."

"Yes, it is. You *can* trust me, Carly. I would never hurt you like your ex. I know he's part of this. That you'd compare me to him pisses me off. Don't you know that every time I think about what he did to you, I want to rip Sam Isley's head off?"

"Brody, put yourself in my place. I thought I loved him and that we'd someday get married. Finding him on his office desk having sex with an agent I was training is a visual I have a hard time getting rid of."

"I understand, baby. But cheating on you is something I'd never do. I'm in this for the long haul. I want to marry you, Carly." She got to her feet and moved to the doorway, where he pulled her close. Fingers entwined in her soft hair, his other hand caressed the line of her back, down to the first hint of her round behind. Pressed against his rock-hard body, Carly felt every nerve come to life as he nibbled on her ear and planted light kisses down her neck.

"Brody, I'm crazy about you. I'm just not ready to get married. You promised you'd be patient."

"It's hard to be patient when I know how right we are for each other. I want to make it official. I want to celebrate with our friends and family. I want babies someday, and I see how you interact with your brother's kids, Shawn and Mylee. I know you want kids, too. So what's the hold up?

Moving back to her desk, Carly sat down and said, "Your parents didn't divorce, Brody. You have no idea what it's like for kids. You don't know what Blake and I went through. I can't do that to a child we might have. I just can't."

"You wouldn't have to, because we're *not* getting divorced."

"You can't predict that."

"And you can't predict that we will."

"Please, Brody, give me a little more time."

Carly rose from her chair and walked slowly toward him until they were inches apart, her eyes never leaving his. Brody remained motionless as she began unbuttoning his shirt. In a low, sexy voice, she said, "Do you remember what you promised we'd do to break in my new desk?

Nodding, he replied, "Okay, now you've found a soft spot."

"What's that?" Carly asked seductively.

Brody backed her toward her desk, and then with one swipe swept away the papers on it. Once she was perched on the desk, he parted her legs and pulled her toward him until she was aligned with the impressive, hard ridge beneath his zipper.

"Make-up sex."

It was entirely too early in the morning for Gabe to be knocking on Kaitlyn's door. He'd had a sleepless night, grew tired of tossing and turning, and finally rolled out of bed, making his way to the kitchen. After scrambling some eggs and making coffee, he watched the morning news. The media already had the Abby Reece murder story, and it was only a matter of time before Kaitlyn saw the story. Gabe showered, dressed, and raced out to his car, violating speed limits until he got to her house. He'd gotten Cameron to agree that he could tell Kaitlyn, but now that the moment was close at hand, and he was standing on her porch, dread washed over him.

Wearing only a pink satin nightshirt, Kaitlyn met him at the door, gave him a once over, and said, "You have bad news about Abby, don't you?"

"She's gone, Kaitlyn."

Her blue eyes widened in disbelief. "What do you mean? She's gone because she ran away, or she's gone forever because she's dead?"

"I'm sorry, but she's dead," Gabe said softly. "Her body was found yesterday."

The breath whooshed out of her as if she'd been sucker-punched. Her sister was dead, and she'd never get the chance to tell her she was sorry. The time would never come for Kaitlyn to make amends, or to tell her sister that she loved her.

She flew into Gabe's arms, making him stumble back a couple of steps before he regained his balance. He backed her inside and closed the door behind them. Gabe held her close as the hard, wrenching sobs she couldn't hold back filled the room. She clung to him, inhaling his woodsy, very male scent, while soaking the shoulder of his shirt with her tears.

Gabe picked her up, taking her to an easy chair in her living room, where he cradled her in his arms, kissing the salty tears from her cheek. Kaitlyn felt the pain in her chest ease as she soaked up the warmth of his body, the gentleness of his kisses, and the strength of his arms that held her. It was as if the world melted away, and she wished she could stay like this forever. Her hand on his powerful chest, she could feel his heart beat through her fingers. Impulsively, she hooked her arms around his neck and kissed him. A hot blush crept over her body as she tightened her grip on him and deepened the kiss.

More than anything, Kaitlyn needed someone to hold her, kiss away her sorrow, and make her forget for a while. She needed Gabe. She needed and wanted the man who haunted her dreams, the man who aroused her like no other man ever had.

A low moan slipped past her lips, a husky helpless sound of want.

"I want you, Gabe," she whispered.

"Honey, I'm not sure this is the time —" He didn't want to cross any lines she'd later regret.

"Yes, it's the right time," she interrupted, placing two fingers on his lips. "Make love to me. Please, Gabe. I need you."

Suddenly she was up in the air as he swept her, weightless, into his arms. In her bedroom, she pulled at his shirt until he lifted it over his head and tossed it on the floor.

Kaitlyn tugged her nightshirt over her head, and then wrapped her arms around his waist to press against him, feeling the heat of his hard abs against her breasts, hearing the hammering of his heart. Every hormone in her body sizzled. She fumbled with the metal button of his jeans, until he gently pushed her hand away. Pulling his wallet from his pocket, he placed it on her bed stand. Jeans and boxers fell to his ankles with a whoosh. God, he was sexy, from his broad shoulders, down to his muscled legs, and everything in between.

Tenderly, he eased her down onto the bed, stretched out alongside her, and kissed her as if he'd been waiting for a long, long time to do just that. Her senses reeled, and she wished the kiss would never end.

Raising his mouth from hers, he gazed into her eyes. "I want something more from you, Kaitlyn. If you want a quickie or a one-time thing, I'm not the right guy."

"I want more, too," she whispered.

His lips recaptured hers, more demanding this time. His tongue explored the recesses of her mouth, sending delicious shivers of desire racing through her. Kissing the sensitive spot behind her ear, he then trailed kisses down her neck, and in the hollow of her throat. God, she wanted him. He tasted and felt better than she'd imagined. Like a thousand times better.

Burying his face in her breasts, he drew one nipple at a time into his mouth, with tantalizing possessiveness. Her body throbbed in areas she'd never known a body could throb, while her nerves danced as he leaned toward her. In one fluid motion, he covered her body with his own, bracing his weight on his arms. Feeling his erection pressing between her legs, she rocked beneath him, slowly and erotically. Absorbing the heat of him, she wanted all he could give. She wanted him deep inside her, and now, before she burst into flames.

"Now, Gabe, please," she moaned impatiently, as her body arched, her thighs opening almost of their own volition.

Leaning on one arm, he retrieved a foil packet from his wallet, opened it with his teeth, and quickly covered himself. Kaitlyn arched her hips again as he drove inside her, making her gasp at the force of it. He was thick, hard as steel, and she relished every inch. Thrill after erotic thrill shot through her as he possessed her body, until she was hurtled beyond the point of return.

She clung to him desperately as he thrust in and out, rocking her hips, until the hot tide of passion raged through them both. She whispered his name again and again, quivering inside, unable to wait another second as each thrust brought them closer and closer to the fiery flames that engulfed them, leaving them shattered with his last, powerful thrust.

Rolling over, he took her with him, holding her close against him. Settling her head on his shoulder, she listened to the steady beat of his heart and each breath he took. Before long, sleep overcame her and she contentedly closed her eyes.

Carly watched as Brody ate his breakfast. She'd put off telling him as long as she could. It was now or never.

"Brody, I'm going to interview Jim Ryder next week."

Choking on his coffee, he knocked over his mug, the hot liquid spilling on the table before him.

"Carly, would you please repeat that? Because I thought I heard you say you were going to interview Jim Ryder," asked Brody incredulously, his voice low and angry. "That couldn't have been what you said."

Handing him a dish towel, Carly said firmly, "You heard correctly. I'm seeing him next week."

Dabbing the spilled coffee with the towel, he asked, "Why on earth would you want to visit that sadistic son of a bitch?"

Carly retrieved the coffee pot and refilled his mug. "I received a call from Dr. Richard Anderson this week."

"Who's he?"

"Dr. Anderson is a renowned BAU profiler and researcher. I completed many of his courses while with the FBI," Carly explained. "He said the agents assigned to get information from Ryder about additional victims and dump sites were getting nowhere. Ryder won't talk to them."

"Why you? Why can't the famous profiler and researcher interview Ryder himself?"

"He thinks Ryder may be more apt to talk to me." Carly focused on her plate, toying with her food, moving it back and forth, but not eating it.

"There's something else. What aren't you telling me?" Brody asked, leaning across the table.

"Ryder asked for me. He'll talk if I am the one who interviews him."

"As the guy who loves you and doesn't know what he'd do without you in his life, I can't tell you how much I oppose this idea," Brody began. "You were at the trial and heard his rants. Sweet Jesus, Carly, the man shot you. Ryder hates you because he blames you for his getting caught."

Gabe pulled the sheet over Kaitlyn's body to ward off the morning chill. He loved how her body felt pressed against him, her arm across his waist, and one long leg thrown across his thighs. Reveling in the feel of her, he listened to her quiet breathing, knowing she'd fallen asleep. He'd never felt so content, so connected. It scared him to put his heart out there, but he decided she was worth the risk. There was no escaping the fact he was falling hard for Kaitlyn Reece.

Kissing her on the top of her head, he managed to slip out from underneath her without waking her. Finding his boxers on the floor, he slipped them on and went to the kitchen to make a pot of coffee.

Before long, Kaitlyn appeared in the kitchen, wearing a

silky robe. Gabe pulled her into his arms, kissing her hair and neck. "Next time, we go slowly. I want to explore every delicious inch of you."

Her arms wrapped her arms around his waist. "Looking forward to it."

"Would you like me to make you breakfast? I checked your fridge and you have eggs, bread, and maple syrup. Would you like some French toast?"

"Did you hear my stomach growling? I'm famished, but I need to know more about what happened to my sister."

Gabe nodded and opened the refrigerator door to pull out eggs, milk, and bread, along with the maple syrup.

Finding her remote, Kaitlyn flicked on the small flat screen television anchored on her kitchen wall, and the morning news appeared. A local news anchor stood in an alley next to what looked like a local bar. "This is the site where the body of Purdue University co-ed Abby Reece was found yesterday—"

Gabe grabbed the remote from her hand, quickly turning off the TV and the newscast.

"Oh, God, no," Kaitlyn moaned, her voice trembling, tears flooding down her face. "Her body was found in an alley? How did Abby die? Tell me everything. I mean it. Don't leave anything out."

Leading her to the living room, Gabe sat on the couch and pulled her down next to him. "I'll tell you anything you want to know."

"How did she die?"

"Abby was murdered." It pained him to see the misery etched in her face.

"Who would want to kill my sister? I mean, she had her faults. But no one deserves to be killed and dumped in an alley like garbage. Who found her body?"

Gabe paused for just a moment, and then said, "*I* did, Kaitlyn. I found her body."

"You found her body yesterday and didn't tell me?" A mixture of anger and fear filled her blue eyes.

Gabe reached for her hand, but she pulled it away. "I couldn't tell you until she was officially identified by our coroner. I wasn't absolutely sure it was Abby. I didn't want you to suffer needless pain if the body wasn't hers."

"How did *you* happen to find her?"

"I got an email from her killers."

"What the hell is going on?" Kaitlyn jumped to her feet, and began rattling off questions. "Did you say 'killers,' as in more than one? How do you know more than one person killed Abby? Why would they send you an email about killing my sister? How did they know that you even knew her?"

"Starting with your first question, I know more than one person killed her because they signed the email as "Gamers," plural, indicating there is more than one of them. We think there are two of them, and they're playing a sick game with law enforcement."

"Why would they send *you* an email about killing my sister? How did they know that you even knew her?"

"I think they were stalking Abby. Maybe they saw me with her at some point," Gabe began. "The email was more about their contempt for my brother and his detectives, than it was about Abby."

"Why does that not make me feel better? All I know is that the bastards killed my sister and I'll never get the chance to tell her I love her." A single tear slid down her cheek.

Gabe pulled her into his arms, holding her close and stroking her hair. "I'm so sorry this happened, Kaitlyn."

Kaitlyn pushed him away. "Oh my God. My mom! My mom can't hear this on TV. I have to go to her house. She needs me."

"My brother, Cameron, is the detective assigned to the case. He should have told your mom about Abby's death by now."

"I don't want her alone at a time like this. We'll have to

plan a funeral." Kaitlyn led Gabe to the door, and then added in a low voice, "This conversation isn't over."

Gabe's cell vibrated and he pulled it from his pocket to read a text from Cameron. "I have to get dressed for an interview. I need to leave for the sheriff's office. I'll call you later."

"Interview?" Kaitlyn asked, as she followed him back to the bedroom and watched him get dressed.

"An Indiana State Police Detective is going to interview me about Abby's murder." As soon as the words left his mouth, he wished he could yank them right back. If Kaitlyn wasn't suspicious of him before, she would be now.

"Why does a detective want to talk to you about it?"

Gabe paused for a second, and then said, "I'm on a list of suspects."

"Why?"

"I dated Abby. I found her body. Hell, if I was a cop, I'd suspect me, too."

A flicker of doubt crossed her face for a fraction of a second, but Gabe noticed it and said, "Are you wondering if you just made love with a killer?"

"No, of course not," Kaitlyn said, not sounding too convincing, even as she shook her head.

"She was murdered between midnight and two in the

morning on Thursday," he explained, watching her intently. "Do you remember what was going on during that time frame?"

"Oh, God. Wednesday was the night you caught me in the Hoosier Bar and Grill. You took me to your office, and then drove me home around two in the morning on Thursday, and we talked in your truck when we got here."

"Since I was with you, it's literally impossible that I could have murdered your sister."

"Oh, Gabe. I am so sorry."

"You were right about what you said before. This conversation isn't over. I'll call you later."

CHAPTER SIX

The small room was lined with plastic storage bins, each labeled with a name. Devan and Evan worked carefully around each one as they scrubbed the floor with bleach.

"After we get the floor done, we'll strip the bed and take the sheets to the Star's Laundromat. With enough bleach and hot water, we should get any trace of Abby Reece's DNA out of them," said Evan.

"Did you learn that from *C.S.I.* or *Forensics Files*?" asked Devan. "Man, you watch too much television."

"You should thank me. What I learn about forensics could keep us safe from Indiana's death penalty. Lethal injection has no appeal for me," Evan replied with a smirk.

"Get a grip. Our ages alone will do that. No chance of the needle until we hit eighteen. Sometimes you can be so dense."

"Who was being dense when he chose to attend the Ryder trial? Who was the dim-wit who knocked Gabriel

Chase's laptop out of his arms? Do you think he won't remember the description of who did that?"

"That's enough!" Devan snapped. "It was worth the risk to get extra credit from my English teacher. The bitch was going to fail me. And Chase's laptop was in the wrong place at the wrong time. I couldn't resist."

"Both were needless risks. You were probably the youngest person in the court gallery. Did you really think no one would remember you later?"

"Shut up, you fucking idiot."

"Who was being an idiot when he passed a note to Ryder through his attorney, who can now identify him?"

"I used a hair color spray and wore colored contacts. He will identify a kid with brown hair and brown eyes."

"Why take the risk?"

"I wanted Ryder to know that we admire him, and we're taking up where he left off," said Devan. "Don't worry. He won't know who we are. I signed the note 'Gamers.'"

"Whatever." Evan pushed the mop to clean the last inch of cement flooring. He bumped against one of the clear plastic bins and it tumbled to the floor, spilling its contents.

"Damn it!" He began picking up clothing, shoes and

jewelry, stuffing them back into the container.

"Whose container is that?" asked Devan, making no effort to help his brother.

Evan checked the bin's label. "Sharon Maud. Remember her? For a skinny, drug-addicted whore, she sure was a fighter. She almost kicked your ass," Evan said, making a considerable effort not to laugh. His twin was not one to make the object of a joke. His rage was instant, his temper something to be feared.

"Hell, yes, I remember her. She's the one who blackened my eye, and I had to wear Mom's makeup for a week so no one would notice it at school. The bitch got what she deserved."

Evan remembered the beating of Sharon Maud. He'd had to pull his brother off of her dead body, which Devan had beaten beyond recognition. It was an ugly memory he'd like to forget. He preferred his killings to be less-messy, no blood at all, if possible.

To avoid one of his brother's tantrums, Evan changed the subject. "Let's get on your laptop and look for our next girlfriend."

"Girlfriend? Is that what you're calling them? What the fuck have I told you about targets? They're off-limits. If I catch you making puppy eyes at another target, like you did Abby Reece, I'll beat you until you can't stand up."

"Sorry, Devan. Poor choice of words," Evan responded. Eager to redirect his brother's focus, he asked, "Where's your laptop?"

Heading for a couple of folding chairs near the door, Devan sat down on one of them, pulled the portable computer onto his lap, and turned it on.

Evan joined him and watched as the system found a wireless network. Soon they were on Facebook.

"We need a victim who will cause such a county uproar that it will be hard for Sheriff Chase to contain." Devan said.

"I have an idea. Go to Abby Reece's page and pull up her friends."

"What for? We're done with her."

"Humor me. Pull up her friends."

Soon the laptop screen filled with names and photos of Abby's friends. Evan pointed to a photo at the center of the page. "Click on this one."

"I'm looking. So what?" Devan became increasingly frustrated and angry.

"Calm down and really look at her."

"Kaitlyn Reece? Are you fucking kidding me? Who said this game was a family affair? She's Abby's sister, you idiot."

"C'mon. Doesn't she look familiar?"

"Yeah, she resembles her sister but not much. She looks like that actress on *Friends*. What are you getting at?"

"She's the stacked blonde we saw going in and out of Gabriel Chase's office building."

"So what? She may have hired him to look for her sister."

"Yeah, that's possible. But what if they're involved? You know, dating, having sex, and so on. Can you imagine how freaked out he'd be if we snatched another one of his girlfriends? And if he's freaked out, his sheriff and detective brothers would be, too."

Devan leaned back in his chair and gave the idea consideration.

"C'mon. This could be a blast," Evan urged.

"No. The answer is no. Making her a target now doesn't work. We need to kick the game up a notch by targeting someone who's important from Morel. We need to snatch a local woman whose disappearance and murder will set this county on fire, upping the pressure on the sheriff. Let's add some excitement to this game, so we can watch the media go nuts. We can sit back and enjoy every second."

"So why wouldn't Kaitlyn Reece inspire this kind of

county hysteria?"

"Because she just wouldn't. Drop it, Evan! Drop it." Devan's scowling face reddened as he searched Facebook. After a couple of minutes, he paused. "What's the name of that beauty queen who's from Morel? Remember how Mother was raving about her?"

"What's so special about a beauty queen?"

"She's the first African-American beauty queen from Shawnee County. I can't believe you don't remember Mother gushing about how pretty and smart she is. According to Mother, she's like the Shawnee County sweetheart of all time."

"If she's so popular, why have I never heard of her? Why can't you even remember her name?" Evan knew better than to push his brother, but couldn't resist.

"Stop being such an ass-hat. I'll remember. Give me a second. I know her name starts with a 'D.'" He sat quietly for a moment, and then nearly jumped out of his chair. "It's Destiny. I know it is. Destiny Cooke." In no time, Devan pulled up Destiny Cooke's Facebook page. "Look at her in this picture wearing her pageant crown. She's perfect."

"Oh, yeah? Read this posting. She's about to get married to an Indiana State Police Trooper. Still think she's perfect?"

"Just adds to the challenge. I love a good challenge,

especially when it comes to one of our games."

With Dr. Richard Anderson at the wheel, Carly sat quietly, thinking of how she'd approach Jim Ryder to get the most relevant information from him. Anderson turned off U.S. Route 136 and onto a country road that ran through farmland on either side of the road. She had no idea where they were as they headed to the secret location where the FBI was holding Jim Ryder.

Anderson broke the silence. "The Bureau's interest in Jim Ryder is two-fold. First, we want to find out if there are additional victims. If so, where are they buried or discarded? We also want to study him, learn all we can about his personality, his background, and development. When and why did he start killing?"

"What have you discovered so far, Dr. Anderson?"

"Please, call me 'Richard,'" he said, pausing as he passed a slow-moving car. "Ryder's crimes exhibit the stages many serial killers display," he continued. "Fantasy, stalking, abduction, killing, and disposal."

"I agree," said Carly. "The only difference between Ryder and the more infamous serial killers like Bundy and Ridgway is that he did his stalking online."

"Don't forget John Robinson in Kansas, who in the early nineties roamed social networking sites, offering jobs, and a BDSM experience to his victims if they'd join him in Kansas —"

"Victims who were later found in chemical drums at his farm and in a storage facility," Carly interrupted.

"You know the case?"

"Yes, and there *are* similarities between Robinson's and Ryder's killings," Carly admitted, and then changed the subject. "Have you received any valuable information from Ryder about his background?"

"Not directly. He refuses to talk to any of the agents or to me. Once we had a sample of his DNA, we ran it through CODIS and got a hit from a cold case in Francis, Utah, population 919."

"Ryder is connected to a cold case in Utah?" Carly asked with disbelief. She'd tried getting more information about Ryder's background from the deputies who worked with him. But none of them talked to Ryder about anything but day-to-day activities, gossip, etc. "Tell me more about the cold case."

"It seems Ryder's real name is Jim Dawson. He and his sister, Erin, grew up in Francis. It's such a small town, the agent we sent there had no problem getting information from residents who knew them."

"What did he have to do with the cold case?"

"His parents were found dead in their bedrooms from multiple knife wounds. I've seen the crime scene photos, and it was a horrific act. The early responders looked everywhere for Jim and Erin, but they were gone. The detective assigned to the case didn't know if the killer had abducted the two, or if they were the killers."

"What did the agent find out about their childhood?"

"The father was the town drunk, and the mother, a shy, timid woman, didn't work outside the home. Neighbors reported that they heard screaming from the house when the father was drunk and beat the wife and both kids. According to Child Protective Services, nothing is in their records that suggest anyone reported the abuse."

"Neighbors don't want to get involved, so the abuse continues," Carly commented.

"After the parents' murder, the Dawson teens disappeared off the face of the earth. Later, the car Jim Dawson drove was found abandoned in Indiana. With new identities, Jim and Erin Ryder started their new lives in Shawnee County, working odd jobs to support themselves. They both earned GEDs, and Jim eventually graduated from the Police Academy to become a deputy for Shawnee County."

Thirty minutes later, Anderson turned onto a long gravel driveway leading to a farmhouse, a weathered barn, and several huge, arched steel buildings. Doors were open on two of the steel structures. One housed a single engine airplane; another was filled with bales of hay from top-to-bottom. Anderson pulled up and parked in front of the third building, where several agents guarded a door. Carly immediately recognized Brody's SUV parked nearby, and wondered why he hadn't mentioned he'd be here today.

"Sheriff Chase is here?"

"Yes, he's questioning Ryder after you finish your interview with him. Sheriff Chase is going to show Ryder a map of Shawnee County to see if Ryder will tell him where additional victims are buried."

"Has Ryder admitted there *are* additional victims?" asked Carly.

"Yes, but he refuses to give any specifics. We hope you can help in that area."

Two armed agents approached either side of the car. Recognizing Dr. Anderson, they focused their attention on Carly.

"Good morning, sir. I see you have a guest," said one of the agents, peering into their vehicle, his hand resting on the gun holstered at his side.

"This is Special Agent Stone. She's here to interview Mr. Ryder."

"May I see your identification?"

Carly and Dr. Anderson handed their Bureau identification to the agents, who reviewed each card, then opened the car doors and led them inside the building. Though it looked like a pole barn from the outside, there were offices and several cubicles inside.

Leading them down a long hallway, one of the agents said to Carly, "Special Agent in Charge Isley is waiting for you."

Hearing the name, Carly tensed. Surely there was another agent in the Bureau with last name 'Isley.' He couldn't be the same man with whom she'd had an affair when they both worked in the Tampa field office. Saying nothing, she kept moving.

They hadn't walked far when she spotted Brody standing before an office and talking to whoever was inside. She was several feet away when Sam Isley entered the hallway from the office, and her stomach dropped to the floor. Both men stared at her as she approached.

"Dr. Anderson," said Isley. "We've brewed a fresh pot of coffee for you, sir."

Anderson smiled, heartily shook Isley's extended hand, and then darted into what looked like a break room across the hall.

Isley turned to Carly and warmly greeted her, "It's good

to see you, Carly."

Coldly shaking his hand, she turned to Brody. "Good morning, Sheriff."

Brody told her good morning as if it were the first time he'd seen her that day. He gave no indication she had awakened in bed next to him that morning, or that they'd made love the night before.

To Isley, she said, "I was surprised to hear that you're heading this project. Isn't it a bit unusual for the Bureau to assign a special agent in charge of an Indiana project from their Tampa field office?"

"I'm assigned to the Indianapolis field office now. I moved from Tampa a couple of months ago," Isley said, inching intimately close to her, prompting her to step back.

Carly couldn't look at him without remembering how much she used to care about him. That was before she caught him screwing her trainee in his office, on his desk. The anger and pain were still very real, and she detested him for it. Had he succeeded in destroying her trust of any other men, as Brody suspected? She couldn't allow Isley to have that kind of control over her life. Not if she wanted a future with Brody.

Brody's eyebrows shot up in surprise. "I wasn't aware that Brad Roth was no longer heading the Indy office." A muscle flicked angrily at Brody's jaw as he glared at the special agent in charge.

"I took over last month. Brad accepted a position with the Bureau's field office in Denver to be closer to his ex-wife and kids."

If there was one thing Carly didn't need as she prepared to interview Ryder, it was the thoughts and emotions now spinning in her brain. Why would Sam Isley make a lateral career move to a position in Indiana, and leave his cushy assignment in Florida? If he made the decision to be closer to her, he was in for an epic disappointment. Sam Isley was her past. Brody Chase is her future.

Frowning at Isley, she asked, "Where is Jim Ryder? Is he ready for my interview?"

"Follow me."

Isley took Carly and Brody to an observation room where Dr. Anderson sat at a conference table, next to a woman she didn't recognize, watching Jim Ryder on a huge, flat screen monitor mounted on the wall.

SAC Isley quickly made introductions. "Sitting next to Dr. Anderson is Special Agent Susan Black from our field office in D.C. Susan is an interrogation analyst, who will advise us on Ryder's truthfulness in answering any given question." Special Agent Black, who appeared to be a very serious woman, simply nodded. "This is Special Agent Carly Stone, who will be interviewing Mr. Ryder first this morning.

Standing next to her is Sheriff Brody Chase, whose jurisdiction is Shawnee County, where Mr. Ryder committed his murders and was captured. The victims we know about were all found in the sheriff's county. He will question Mr. Ryder immediately after Special Agent Stone."

"Mr. Ryder appears to be annoyed and a little agitated this morning," Dr. Anderson observed, referring to the closed-circuit television. "I'm told he's been sitting in the interview room for close to twenty minutes."

"Ryder perceives himself as an important person, and doesn't like to be kept waiting."

"I agree," said Dr. Anderson. "Like most sociopaths, our Mr. Ryder is quite the narcissist, pumped up with self-importance."

Isley said to Carly, "The room is outfitted with state of the art camera and audio equipment. There are also armed guards just outside the room, who are ready if you should need help. Ryder is handcuffed to his chair by his wrist and ankle. The chair is bolted to the floor."

"I'm not afraid of Ryder," Carly stated calmly to Isley, while offering a smile to Brody, whose expression was a combination of tension, anger, and protectiveness. Clearly he still did not agree with the decision Carly had made to interview Jim Ryder.

"Perhaps that is why he will talk to only you," Dr.

Anderson stated. "I doubt there have been many people Mr. Ryder has encountered, especially women, who didn't fear him."

Brody spoke up, "None of my deputies feared the bastard. They thought he was a good ol' boy, one of their buddies."

Dr. Anderson adjusted his glasses. "I don't doubt that, Sheriff. Sociopaths are consummate actors and prolific liars. Outwardly, they appear very normal and know how to blend in. They're very good at charming others when they want to."

"You keep referring to Ryder as a sociopath. I'm convinced he is a psychopath."

"If I were a psychiatrist, I would agree with you. But to a criminologist like me, Jim Ryder is a sociopath. As a criminal, a psychopath is erratic and disorganized, with a tendency to leave clues, because he or she acts on impulse. Psychopaths are fearless and take excessive risks. They are unable to maintain normal relationships or keep a job for very long." Anderson paused, then nodded to Carly for her to take over the explanation.

"As a sociopath, Ryder's crimes were very organized and he was careful about not leaving clues like forensics on his victims or at his crime scenes, which made it difficult for Sheriff Chase's team to catch him. He appeared to have maintained a relatively normal relationship with his sister, Erin, and provided for her, thanks to his position as a deputy. That is, until the day Alison Brown escaped. I'm sure he blamed Erin for that, and killed her."

Anderson turned to Carly. "It's time to interview Mr. Ryder. We don't want him too worked up about waiting when you question him. Remember what we talked about in the car. Before you ask him about additional victims and dump sites, get him into a dialog about his personality, background, and development. It's useful for us in the Behavioral Analysis Unit to understand when and why he started killing."

"Yes, sir." To Brody, she shot a smile to reassure him that she was going to be okay.

Rising from his seat, Brody said, "Special Agent Stone, may I talk to you before you interview Mr. Ryder?"

"Of course." Carly quirked her eyebrow questioningly.

She followed Brody into the hallway. After he closed the observation room door, he pulled her close and whispered in her ear, "I love you, Carly, and I know if anyone can get information from Ryder, you can."

"Thank you, Sheriff." Her voice was laced with tenderness. "If you have no plans for later, I'd like to show you how much I love you in return."

His mouth eased into a seductive smile, and her

hormones did an excited little dance. "It sounds like I'd better call the office after this and tell them I'm heading home early."

"Sounds like a plan."

After making sure no one was in the hallway to see them, Carly lightly kissed him on the lips, then returned to the observation area in order to enter the interview room.

"Good morning, Mr. Ryder. I apologize if I kept you waiting."

His eyes undressed her as she moved from the door to the table where he sat, making her skin crawl with revulsion.

Sitting across from him, she waited for him to respond, which he did in seconds. "You can call me Jim, and I'll just call you Carly."

"Sorry, but that's not going to work for me. You'll refer to me as Special Agent Stone," Carly began. "In addition, let me set up some ground rules. You will at all times treat me with respect and answer my questions honestly, per the plea bargain agreement."

His eyes blazed with sudden anger. "You're such a cold, uppity bitch."

"Fine," she said as she leapt to her feet. "I won't mind telling the prosecutor that you're not cooperating. I'm sure he'll want to rethink the plea agreement."

As she headed for the door, Ryder called her back. "Wait. I can be cooperative."

She turned to glare at him, and then returned to her seat. "Are you ready to get started?"

"Yes."

"Let's start by talking a bit about your childhood. What was it like? Where did you grow up?"

"Seriously? Are you trying to shrink me?"

"Not at all," Carly insisted, meeting him eye-to-eye.

"Fine. I grew up in a small town in Ohio. My dad was a high school principal, and Mom was a nurse. Is that what you wanted to know?"

"No kidding," Carly said. "I heard you and your sister, Erin, grew up in Francis, Utah, as a member of the Dawson family. Your father was the town drunk, and your mother was a weak-willed woman who did nothing to protect her children from his beatings."

Ryder looked as if she'd slapped him across the face. He stared fiercely at her from across the table.

"So let's start over. Tell me about your childhood."

Ryder exploded. "What the fuck does my childhood have to do with the additional victims I agreed to talk about?"

In her calmest, most soothing voice, Carly said, "It would really help me to understand your side of things if you'd give me some information about your background. I just want to get to know you better before we move on to the subject of additional victims."

A suggestion of annoyance mixed with distrust hovered in his eyes as he spoke. "I grew up in Francis, Utah. Yeah, my father was the town drunk. He was a mean, merciless man who took pleasure in beating up his family, among other things."

"What other things?"

"Never mind."

"What other things did your father do?"

Ryder hesitated for a moment. "When he got drunk, he came home and raped my sister repeatedly while she screamed her lungs out. There. Are you satisfied? Is that the kind of dirt you wanted to hear?"

"I'm sorry that happened," Carly said with sincerity. "I'm sorry for Erin. What did your mother do to help your sister?"

"Not a goddamned thing."

"That must have been tough for you, to listen to her cries for help when you were too young to do anything to help her. That must have made you feel very weak."

"Weak? You don't know what you're talking about."

"I only meant you were too young at the time to stop your father."

"Oh, I was young, but that didn't hold me back from putting a permanent stop to his abuse. One of the best things I ever did was to plunge that butcher knife into the old man's chest." Ryder flashed a cold smile, as if remembering how the violence gave him pleasure.

Disgusted, Carly swallowed back the bile rising to her throat. "And your mother?"

"She could have stopped the old man from beating us, from raping Erin again and again, but the bitch did nothing. The mother-of-the-year asked for it. She had it coming to her. She made me kill her."

"So you're admitting you killed your parents?"

"Do you think you tricked me into admitting I killed my own parents with your superb questioning techniques, Special Agent Stone?" Ryder ripped out the words impatiently. "What do I have to lose by telling you I murdered those two losers? I'm not stupid. I'm in prison for the rest of my life. Am I sorry about killing my parents? Hell, no. They're my favorite kills."

"The girls you caged in your basement. Were they weak like your mother? Did they ask for it? Did they make you kill them?"

"Hell, yes, they did. Weak little bitches. All they did was blubber and beg me to stop. They made me kill them."

Carly gritted her teeth to prevent lashing out at him. He was such a sick, evil bastard. Just sitting in the same room with him made her want to vomit.

She heard a knock at the door, which was a signal to stop the interview for the day. A guard opened the door and waited.

Forcing herself to be polite, to play to his narcissistic personality, she said to Ryder, "Thank you for talking with me today."

"Always a pleasure, Special Agent Stone," he answered sarcastically.

"I'll be back to talk to you again."

"Check with my staff for appointment availability."

Cameron stood before the window of his office. He'd received a call from Detective Burton, who said she'd be in Morel within fifteen minutes to interview their suspect. *She* didn't mention that their "suspect" was the youngest of the Chase brothers. *He* didn't mention that she was about to interview for a murder a man he would give his life to protect. That was the part that gave him the most angst. He couldn't protect Gabe in this thing. It wasn't like the time the school bully bloodied Gabe's nose as he stole one of his Matchbox cars in the playground. Cameron had chased the kid seven blocks after school before he finally reached him and tackled him to the ground. Nobody messed with his brothers. Not back then. Not now.

He wondered what this female detective would look like. She was probably tough as nails and had the body of a quarterback. Law enforcement was hard on women. The ones who succeeded had to be as tough and as smart as their male counterparts. If this detective was a shining star, rising in the ranks, then she had to be very effective at what she did. He just hoped she was fair-minded, and that her questions were objective. Gabe did *not* murder Abby Reece. It wasn't in him to kill anyone, especially not a woman.

A white Indiana State Police car pulled into the parking lot and took a space in the third row. A couple of seconds passed, and then a dark-haired woman in a navy pantsuit emerged from the car and headed toward the building. Wearing her dark hair in a serious bun at the back of her head, she carried a black leather pad-folio, and slipped her keys into her jacket pocket.

Cameron looked her up and down. He couldn't help himself. His weakness was curvy women, and this one had luscious curves in all the right places. The kind of soft-as-sin curves she couldn't hide under her business suit. And he was a bastard for mentally undressing this woman when his brother could be in so much trouble.

Cameron raced to the lobby and met her at the door.

"You must be Detective Chase," she said.

Cameron forced his attention away from her full, sexy mouth." And you must be Detective Burton."

"Call me Robynn," she replied, as she glanced around the lobby.

"I'm Cameron." He shook her hand, inhaling a wisp of her perfume and noting the deep hunter-green color of her eyes. A man could get lost in those eyes. He knew he could.

"Has your suspect arrived?" Robynn sounded all-business.

"Yes, he's in the interview room."

"You put him in an interview room?"

Cameron paused for a moment, thinking this was a strange question. Of course, Gabe was in an interview room. Wasn't she here to interview him? Where else would he be?

"Come this way." He led her through the lobby, and then down a long hallway to the observation room where they could see his brother through the one-way glass window.

Gabe had his hands behind his head and his feet on the metal table. He looked angry and impatient, making Cameron wish he'd spent more time calming him down. Emotions were not going to help him. Robynn would be looking for emotional responses, and could view Gabe's anxiety as a sign of guilt.

Holding her folder to her chest, Robynn gazed at Gabe for several minutes before Cameron asked, "Are you ready to interview him?"

"I like to take things slow."

"Good to know," Cameron offered with a suggestive grin. What was it about this woman that had him wondering what she'd look like without her clothes, under him in his bed?

"I meant I don't like to hurry interviews." Robynn's face colored to a rosy blush.

"Duly noted."

"Do you have a conference room here?"

"Yes, we have two of them. One is large with a long, oval conference table; the other is a lot smaller, with a round conference table."

"Is the smaller one available?" Robynn asked, as she turned her attention back to her suspect.

"Let me check." On his cell, Cameron checked the

conference room's availability, and then reported back. "Yes, it's available. Why did you want to know?"

"Please reserve it. That's where I will interview Mr. Chase."

"But our interviews are usually held—"

"I imagine your interviews *are* usually held in that room. But mine aren't done in interview rooms ever," she began heatedly. "I'm not one of those *Law and Order* interviewers where there is a lot of yelling, and I threaten to kick my suspect's ass. I don't think that kind of aggressive interview style works well. It's probably the best way to get a suspect to clam up and give you absolutely *no* information you need or want."

Cameron simply nodded. There was no way he was getting into a debate with this detective over interview styles. He could care less how she interviewed his brother, as long as she cleared him and got him off the suspect list. "One small conference room it is."

"Would you please show me where it's located?"

"Sure. Follow me." Cameron led her back down the long hall until they reached the conference room. Opening the door, he followed her in. "Will this suit your needs?"

Scanning the room, she replied, "Yes, quite nicely." She took a seat, pulled out her folders along with a small tape recorder.

"I'll get Gabe."

"Not so fast. Sit down, I want to talk to you first."

"Not a problem." Cameron sat down across from her. "Fire away."

"Tell me about your victim, Abby Reece."

"It's early in the case, but here's what I know," Cameron began. "Judging from her Facebook page, she was a bit of an exhibitionist. She's got about sixty photos of herself in various stages of undress."

"So you think she asked for it?"

"Hell, no. There is no victim, ever, who deserves to be murdered." Cameron shot her a glare and continued, "I'm saying that by posting all those photos of herself, she was making every sexual predator on the Web aware of her. Not the kind of attention any woman would want."

"What evidence do you have?"

"She was wearing a shoe that did not belong to her. I sent it to your state police crime lab. Maybe you could push that along, so we get the results sooner rather than later."

"I'll see what I can do."

"Other than that, we have a partial print and an email from the killers."

"I read the email you provided. How do you know Mr.

Chase didn't send that email to himself?"

"Because the email's IP address was traced back to Abby Reece's laptop at her apartment."

"Any witnesses?"

"None that have come forward. Like I said, it's early. We haven't had much time to conduct our investigation."

"I see. What evidence do you have that indicates Mr. Chase may have committed this murder?"

"His name is Gabe, and you can drop the 'Mr. Chase' bit. You know he is my younger brother."

"I meant no offense. Let's try this again. What evidence do you have that indicates your brother, Gabe, may have committed this murder?"

"We have no evidence whatsoever that Gabe is involved."

"Then why am I interviewing him?"

"He dated the victim and they'd broken up weeks before she was murdered," said Cameron. "He wants his name cleared."

"Understood. Just so *you* understand, when I question him, he gets no breaks because he's the brother of the lead detective in the case, as well as the county sheriff."

"We don't want special treatment. Any more

questions?"

"Not now, but you need to know my boss wants me to investigate the case with you. He's calling the sheriff about it."

"I don't need you or anyone else looking over my shoulder to make sure I do the right thing."

"Not suggesting that. My boss thinks the Indiana State Police and I can be of help to you."

"Brody is creating a task force. I'll ask him to add you to it."

"Excellent. Thank you. Now if you'd please ask Gabe to join me, I'd appreciate it."

Cameron gazed at her, trying to penetrate the deliberate blankness of her green eyes. Was that a dismissal? Did she really just dismiss him?

Finally, he left the room to fetch his brother. This woman was getting on his last nerve, yet he couldn't get past how attracted he was to her. When was the last time he was this drawn to a woman? Oh, yeah, that would be Mollie, and what an incredibly stupid mistake that was.

Cameron opened the interview room door, and then stood in the door frame for a moment watching Gabe tapping his fingers on the table.

"What's up, Cam? Where's the detective who's supposed to question me?"

Instead of answering, Cameron crossed the room and punched Gabe in the arm.

"Ouch! What was that?" Gabe jumped to his feet.

"Remember that game we used to play in the car every time one of us saw a VW?"

"Slug Bug?" He answered as he slugged Cameron in the arm. "Yeah, I remember."

Throwing his hard, muscled arm around Gabe's neck, he said, "Well, do you remember my famous choke hold?"

"From high school? Seriously?" Gabe struggled for release as Cameron laughed between grunts, while his brother demonstrated a few moves of his own. Finally Gabe broke the hold, grabbed his brother's thumb, twisted his arm behind his back, and threw him face-first to the floor. Then he braced his knee on Cameron's back to hold him down.

"Where did you learn that move?"

"Duh. The police academy?"

"What the hell is going on in here?" Brody bellowed as he entered the room, closing the door behind him. "Let him up, Gabe."

"*He* started it."

Brody looked at him incredulously, his hands on his hips. "What are you? Twelve?"

Cam, still lying on the floor, couldn't control his burst of laughter. Gabe's sense of humor took over and he began laughing in return.

"You two are crazy." In spite of himself, Brody chuckled. "Do I want to know what started this?"

"No!" Cameron and Gabe said in unison.

"Is the Indiana State Police detective here yet?"

"Yes," said Cameron. "She's waiting in the small conference room for Gabe."

"Thanks for letting me know," Gabe called over his shoulder as he rushed from the room.

As soon as his footfalls could be heard down the hall, Brody asked, "What was that all about?"

"Just doing my part to distract and calm my brother down before his interview. Think it worked?"

Brushing himself off and straightening his clothes, Gabe entered the conference room, took one look at Detective Robynn Burton, and knew that beyond her sweet smile, he was facing an opponent capable of kicking his butt and keeping him on the suspect list. So he shook the hand she extended, and shot her his most devastating grin. The one that usually had women swooning. When he saw it had no effect on her, he quietly sat down.

"Hello." Her voice friendly and calm.

"Nice to meet you, Detective Burton."

She leaned back and relaxed in her chair like they had all the time in the world, like this was a social call she'd been looking forward to. "May I call you Gabriel?"

"Most people call me 'Gabe.' "

"Gabe, tell me about yourself."

Gabe noted how Detective Burton appeared as if she were looking forward to learning all about her new friend. Not a chance.

"I grew up in Shawnee County. After high school, I trained to be a cop, graduated from the police academy, and then decided to go to college. I graduated from I.S.U. in Criminology and Criminal Justice. I'm a licensed private investigator."

"Indiana State University?"

"Yes, in Terre Haute."

"Good school. I graduated from I.S.U., too," Robynn looked at her notes. "Don't you do something with computer forensics?"

Just as he'd known, she'd already read his background.

She was just chatting him up to get him relaxed and running his mouth, saying things that might implicate him in Abby's death. He'd used the same technique in the past.

"I'm certified in computer forensics, and I'm sure you already know I consult with the sheriff's office when needed."

Ignoring this information, Robynn asked, "How long did you date Abby Reece?"

"About a month or so."

"Why did she break up with you?"

"She didn't really break up with me. It was a mutual decision."

"How angry were you when Abby broke up with you? Angry enough to kill her?"

"Like I already told you, it was a mutual decision. Was I angry? Not even close. I was relieved. I didn't kill Abby Reece."

"When was the last time you saw her?"

"After a friend's birthday party. I drove her back to her apartment."

"From what I hear, Abby had a lot of boyfriends and lovers. You had to be hurt or jealous. Is that why you killed her?"

"I didn't kill her." Gabe shook his head.

"If you didn't murder her, who did?"

"I don't know, but there are a lot of guys who might have."

"Why do you say that?"

"Abby used men. Notches on her headboard and so on. She was very open about how she liked sex and having many partners," Gabe began. "There was also her Facebook page, which was like a beacon beaming a signal to every sexual predator in the universe."

"I've heard about her page, but haven't had time to visit it yet," Robynn said, before glancing at her notes. "Do you have an alibi for the night Abby Reece was murdered?"

"Yes, I do," said Gabe, wishing there was a way he could avoid involving Kaitlyn. "I'd asked a client not to do investigating on her own. I found her at a bar doing just that, so I drove her to my office. We talked for hours and I took her home around two in the morning."

Pulling out a pen, she asked, "Who is this client? I will need to contact her."

"Kaitlyn Reece." He paused for her reaction.

"Any relation to the victim?"

"Kaitlyn is Abby's sister. I mean *was*. She hired me to find Abby when she learned her sister was missing."

"Did she realize you and her sister had dated when she hired you to find her?"

"Yes," Gabe replied. There was no way he was telling this detective how Kaitlyn had seen him in Abby's apartment, copying her laptop's hard drive. She'd slam the cuffs on him faster than one could say "tampering with evidence."

"She was hiring a private investigator, not an ex-boyfriend of her sister. Besides, I was already looking for Abby."

"When you were looking for Abby, did you discover any information that could help with this investigation?"

"Yes," Gabe responded.

"Have you shared this information with your brother, Cameron?"

"I didn't have a chance. I tried to, but Cam got a call and had to leave."

Robynn glanced at her watch. "I'm hungry. Let's go to lunch. Why don't you ask Cameron if he wants to join us?"

"Hey, Detective Slug-bug," Gabe said, his voice laced with sarcasm, as he picked up his laptop next to his desk.

"Is your interview over?"

"Not sure. Detective Burton wants you to go to lunch with us."

"Lunch? She's taking a suspect out to lunch?"

"So it seems. Do you want to go or not?"

Cameron smiled as he put on his suit jacket. "Wouldn't miss it."

Robynn Burton was waiting for them in the lobby. "Glad you can join us, Detective Chase."

"Thanks for the invitation."

As they stepped outside, she turned to Gabe. "Where is a good place to eat?"

With a mischievous grin, he pointed to Mollie's Cafe. "Mollie's has the best food in town."

"Then Mollie's it is," Robynn responded, as she began walking in the restaurant's direction.

Gabe glanced at his brother, whose pained expression almost made him laugh out loud. Cameron's avoidance of Mollie Adams was probably about to end.

It was only eleven o'clock, so the lunchtime rush hadn't begun and good tables were plentiful. When one of Mollie's waitresses arrived to seat them, Robynn quickly said, "We'd like a table in the back. And if you could avoid seating people around us until you absolutely have to, I'd appreciate it."

Once they were seated, the waitress took their drink orders and headed back to the kitchen. Returning a short time later, the waitress distributed their drinks and whispered to Cameron, "Mollie would like to talk to you before you leave."

"Please tell her that this is a really busy day, and I don't have time. Thank you."

Robynn studied her menu. "What's good here?"

"I'm getting the breaded tenderloin sandwich with fries," said Cameron. "Best tenderloin in the county. It overlaps the bun by at least an inch."

"Talked me into it," Gabe placed his folded menu on top of Cameron's.

Robynn said, "It seems we are all ordering the same thing. Thank you."

Once the waitress left, the detective was all business. "Detective Chase—"

"Cameron."

"Cameron, your brother here tells me that he made some discoveries during his search for Abby Reece that could help the investigation. I'm sure you'd like to hear what he's found. I know I would."

She pulled her tape recorder out of her pocket, turned it on to record, and set it in the middle of the table.

To Cameron, Gabe said, "This was what I was trying to tell you when you raced off for that call." The last thing Gabe wanted was for his brother to think he was holding out on him, and was only prompted to give him this information because a State Police detective asked.

Cameron nodded and said, "Go on."

"You've seen Abby's photos on her Facebook page?"

"Who hasn't?"

"She made herself a target for every sex predator in the country, so it might be a good idea to do a house-to-house sweep of registered sex predators in Shawnee County. We also might suggest the same be done in Tippecanoe County where she went to Purdue. Who has an alibi for the night Abby was murdered? Who doesn't?"

"I agree," Cameron replied.

"The email sent by the killers was sent through Abby's laptop at her apartment."

Her left eyebrow rising suspiciously, Robynn asked, "How do you know her laptop was at her apartment? How do you know that the killers didn't take it?"

"For one thing, her sister, Kaitlyn, told me." This was a creative twist of the truth, but Kaitlyn *had* seen Abby's laptop in her sister's apartment the day she was watching him download its hard drive from the closet. Not that

Detective Burton was going to get this information from him. That would put him on the fast track to a tampering with evidence charge, among others. Not to mention he'd lose his computer forensic certification.

"In addition, when I received the email, I tracked the IP address to Abby's apartment."

"Explain how you did this."

"When tracking computers, we look at the IP address, which identifies the network card in your computer. That's how I knew the email came from Abby's laptop."

Glancing at Cameron, he said, "You have to get possession of Abby's laptop right away. The killers may have left prints on it. In addition, we need a warrant for her Internet Service Provider to get transcripts of her emails."

"I sent an officer with a warrant to Abby's place in West Lafayette this morning." Cameron checked his watch. "He may be on his way back to Morel with it at this very moment."

Robynn said to Gabe, "I know about your certification and that you consult for the sheriff's office, but you *cannot* touch this laptop. A good defense attorney could get anything of evidentiary value tossed out by revealing you were once a suspect in the case. You could severely impact the prosecution's case."

"I realize that," said Gabe. "That's why another

computer forensics expert will be handling the laptop."

"Who?" asked Cameron.

"Anne Mason Brandt. She got her certification last year and is excellent at what she does. Anne has done a lot of work for her husband, Michael, who is a prosecuting attorney. Her examination of a suspect's computer helped crack the serial arson case he had last month."

"I think I've heard of her," said Robynn. "Didn't she once co-own a computer company in Indianapolis?"

"Yes."

"Wasn't she stalked by a former employee, who murdered customers that complained about him?"

"Yes. He killed the co-owner, too. Thank God, that's behind her. She's happily married with twins, and consults out of her home."

"Back to Abby's murder case," prompted Cameron. "What else do you have?"

"I talked to Emily Smith, one of Abby's friends, and she was supposed to meet Abby at Hoosier Sports Bar and Grill the night she disappeared. Emily bumped into her boyfriend on the way to the bar and spent the night with him instead of meeting Abby. She said she tried to call Abby to tell her she couldn't make it, but just got her voicemail."

"So you're assuming Abby went to the bar alone," said Robynn.

"I'm not assuming. I *know* she did." Gabe pulled out his laptop. "I have the surveillance tape from the bar." He set his laptop on the table, and turned it around so they could see the display. "Here is Abby leaving the bar at closing and walking to her car."

"Okay, we believe she was at the bar," Robynn remarked.

"There's more. Let me rewind a bit. See these two men in hoodies who leave before Abby? Watch as they get into a white van and wait there for thirty minutes. It's a long shot, but what were they waiting for? Were they waiting for Abby to leave the bar?"

"Did they follow her when she left?" asked Cameron.

"No, they took off before she came out," Gabe replied.

"Then I don't see how they're related to the case. Two men outside a bar having a conversation before they leave means nothing. They left before the victim did."

"Cam, Kaitlyn talked to the bartender on duty the night Abby disappeared. He told her that two men were focused on Abby that night, and that they left before she did. Show him the surveillance tape and see if the two men on the tape are the same ones who danced with Abby."

Cameron paused thoughtfully for a moment, and then said, "I intend to talk to the bartender anyway. I'll show him the surveillance tape and ask him about these guys. Depending on what he shares, I'll get a sketch artist out there."

CHAPTER SEVEN

Cameron leaned against the door frame behind Carly and Gabe, who sat in visitor chairs in front of the sheriff's desk. Cameron was pleased that once Gabe was cleared of any involvement in Abby's murder, Brody hired him back as the computer forensics consultant. Although Gabe couldn't deal with any of the computer forensics found on Abby's computer, he could advise Anne Brandt, who was handling that work.

"So tell me why we're meeting with an Indianapolis Metropolitan Police Detective," asked Brody. "You realize this might be valuable time wasted that we could use to catch our killer."

"Any piece of information, no matter how small, could help us solve Abby's homicide." Carly drummed her fingers on the arms of the chair.

"And stop the killers from adding more victims to their list," added Gabe.

"Let's hear him out." Cameron didn't believe in

overlooking even the slightest possibility. "I wouldn't have let him drive down here from Indianapolis if I didn't think his theory had merit. If he's right, and our cases are connected, his findings might help us crack our case."

"Sounds like I'm outnumbered," said Brody dryly. "Cam, while you get our guest from the lobby, the rest of us can head toward the conference room."

Indianapolis Detective Wayne Griffin was a short, stocky man, whose lined face wore the stress of chasing criminals. He entered the conference room with a thick file folder under his arm, and an evidence bag in his hand, which he slid to the center of the oval table. It contained a shoe that matched the one worn by Abby Reece.

Cameron introduced the detective to the sheriff.

"I heard you have a profiler working your case," Wayne said to Brody.

"That would be me. I'm Carly Stone. Good to meet you," Carly interrupted with an outstretched hand that the detective clasped briefly.

"Glad to meet you, too. You're one of the reasons I'm here. I could use your expertise," said the detective. "We've been chasing our tails for a year. Every time we think we might be close, another body is found."

"Know the feeling. Got the T-shirt. We had a serial last year." Brody's jaw tightened.

"Jim Ryder, right?"

Brody nodded. "So you can imagine how happy we were to find the body of a Purdue coed posed naked in an alley near a local bar." Brody paused for a moment and added, "I'll be honest, Detective. I don't see how our cases are connected." Indicating a seat at the conference table for the detective, Brody sat down. The others followed suit.

"Cameron filled me in on your homicide," Wayne began. "I won't argue with you. The M.O. is different from the prostitute murders we're working. But the fact is — the shoe found on your body was identified by our fifth victim's mother as belonging to her daughter, Sara Cassity."

"Go on," prompted Brody.

"We've had five prostitutes murdered in a year. It seems nobody cares if a working girl gets knocked off, except their families. We hear from most of them every day. Not much empathy from the public, though. Most think the girls deserved what they got."

"Unfortunately," Carly began. "Blaming women working in high-risk occupations for the violence done to them is too common. What most people don't realize is that many girls enter the sex trade because they're on the street after running away from physical and sexual abuse in their own homes. A lot of them are homeless. They put themselves in so much danger selling sex to strangers."

The detective nodded in agreement, and then continued. "When Cameron agreed to let me discuss our murders with all of you, I jumped at the chance." Wayne took out five photographs. "Let me introduce you to each of our five victims, and then I'll go through a list of similarities between their murders and Abby Reece's slaying. You can tell me if you see a stronger connection between our cases than just the shoe."

He tapped on the first photograph, slid it to the center of the table, and said, "This is Darla Green. She was a meth head who was seventeen-years- old when she died. A known prostitute, Darla had no police record — at least not yet."

"She looks older than seventeen." Brody studied the photo before he passed it to Gabe.

"Working the streets will do that to a person," Wayne replied dryly.

Pointing to the second photo, which was a mug shot, the detective said, "Meet Sharon Maud. Sharon's mother reported her missing two days before we found her body. She was nineteen-years-old, and had been arrested for solicitation and drugs."

"Was Sharon close to her mother?" asked Carly.

"Yes, they saw each other or talked by phone every day. Her three kids live with her mother."

"What about the others? Did they have a mother or friends close to them, who they might have shared their activities and whereabouts?"

"No, not really. The majority of these girls were loners."

"The next picture is of Val Staley. She was a runaway from Chicago who lived in the Indianapolis area for six months prior to her murder. No arrest records. She was only fifteen."

Wayne referred to the fourth photo. "Marie Engle was an eighteen-year-old stripper who trolled the area truck stops, offering sex for extra money to support her two kids."

"Our last victim is Sara Cassity, also age eighteen. She used to work around Tenth Street, but friends say she moved to the truck stops because she thought it would be more lucrative. Like Darla and Sharon, Sara had a drug problem she was feeding."

Brody spoke up. "So far I'm not seeing much in the way of similarities by comparing your murders to ours. Our victim was in her twenties, and an attractive university student. She wasn't involved in drugs, or a high-risk trade like prostitution."

"Let me continue. I think you'll find my team's analysis

of the murders interesting," Wayne said. "Our victims were all prostitutes who worked the area truck stops selling sex from cab-to-cab as the trucks lined up for rest or fuel breaks."

Gabe turned his open laptop around to show the others an online news headline. "Are these killings referred to by the media as the 'Truck Stop Murders'?'"

"Yeah. All of the victims were hitting the area truck stops to sell sex to the truckers."

"What time frame are we talking about?" asked Cameron.

"We started finding bodies last January. The latest victim, Sara Cassity, was found in June," said Wayne.

"And then Abby Reece was found this month," Brody noted.

"Do you think you have *one* killer?" Gabe asked.

"There's a possibility there are two. We tried to track down a white bakery van seen on a couple of the truck stops' surveillance tapes. It turned out to be a dead end because the bakery listed on the sign had one of their magnetic van signs stolen, and we couldn't make out the license plate in the tape. We did talk to a clerk who remembers two men got out of the van wearing baker's uniforms underneath black hoodies. They came inside and bought Cokes. He didn't offer much of an I.D. He only got a quick look at one of the men. He said the one who paid for their items looked young, maybe even a teenager."

"Gabe spotted a white van on one of our surveillance tapes." Cameron said.

"Was it a white 2012 Chevrolet 1500 utility van?" Wayne asked Gabe.

"Yes." Gabe nodded.

"That's the problem," Wayne remarked, scratching his head. "Do you realize how many white utility vans there are in the Indianapolis area alone? It will take forever to track them all down."

"Where were your bodies found?" asked Brody.

"The bodies were found dumped in rural areas. We found one on a creek bed, another in a ravine, and the rest in wooded areas not far from a road. Every one of them was naked. No personal belongings to be found."

"Since you found them near a road, it sounds like your killer wanted the bodies to be found sooner rather than later," said Carly. "This may go back to the killers' need for recognition." She paused for a moment, then went on. "However, your killers didn't want you to identify the victims right away. That's why they stripped each of their belongings."

Cameron spoke up. "No rural dump site for our

victim. Her body was found in an alley near a local bar. Her body was posed, not just dumped."

Carly shrugged her shoulders. "Cam, there is still our killers' craving for recognition that may be escalating, since now they are notifying the press."

"That's true, Carly." He turned to the Indy detective. "What was the cause of death? Were the five women killed in the same way?"

"One of our victims was severely beaten, but like the rest, the cause of death was suffocation. Each was found with a plastic bag secured around her neck. No fingerprints. No DNA from the doer."

Brody leaned forward, his elbows on the table. "Interesting. Abby Reece had a plastic bag over her head that her killers used to smother her. However, she was not beaten."

"Don't forget the shoe Abby Reece was wearing," the detective said. "Except for Darla Green, our victims were nude, and wearing a piece of jewelry, shoe or another personal item that belonged to one of the other victims."

"Seriously? Now we're getting into similarities!" Gabe said.

Carly paused a moment before speaking. Glancing at Brody, then at Wayne, she said, "I think the murders *are* connected, and our killers have purposely changed their mode of operation. They've even changed their victim preference by moving from prostitutes to a coed. That's unusual for serial killers, but I think that is exactly what they are doing. They placed Sara Cassity's shoe on Abby Reece's foot to make sure they got credit for killing the five prostitutes in Indianapolis. They want us to know they've killed before. They're proud of the fact the Indy police haven't caught them, but on the other hand, they crave recognition."

Destiny Cooke parked her new crimson pearl Honda Civic outside the First Baptist Church on U.S. Route 136, south of Morel city limits. Scanning the parking lot, she spotted her parents' Lincoln and Justin's Indiana State Police car. This was the second best day of her life. The first best day was when Justin asked her to marry him; the second was tonight's rehearsal and dinner, and the third would be their wedding day on Saturday. She was the luckiest girl in the entire universe, and she'd gladly debate anyone who thought differently.

Pulling down the visor to check her look in the mirror, she applied some lip gloss and powdered her nose. After all, she had to look her best for her fiancé, who was the hottest and most handsome man she'd ever laid eyes on. Destiny made that decision the first time she saw him sitting on her school bus her freshman year. By her sophomore year, they only had eyes for each other, and despite her parents' objections, they were going steady. It wasn't just that he was white and she was African-American. They said she was too young to be focused on just one boy. But they didn't know Justin like she did. He was her soul mate in every way.

The two became engaged their junior year at college. By then, her parents had come around and rejoiced as much as she did. In three short days, she and Justin would be married, just like she'd dreamed every day since she met him. He'd just finished his probationary period for the State Police, and she'd accepted a job at Purdue University where she would graduate. Everything was working out so perfectly.

Destiny had gotten out of her car, locked it, and was walking toward the church when a white van pulled into the parking lot. A young man in a baker's uniform called out his window, "Hey, are you Destiny Cooke?"

She eyed him warily until she spotted the "Grand Events Catering" magnetic sign on the side of the van. "Yes, I'm Destiny."

"Well, congratulations, Ms. Cooke," he said as he hopped out of the van. "We're the caterers for your rehearsal dinner tonight. And may I say we've cooked and baked up quite a feast. I think you will agree."

"I'm sure everything will be wonderful." Destiny turned

to head to the church.

"Ms. Cooke, if I could have just a minute of your time, there's something very special I need to show you before you go inside."

"Couldn't it wait? I don't want to be late for the rehearsal."

"It's really important or I wouldn't ask. My boss says he'll fire me if I don't get your signed approval on this special cake we baked for tonight." When she hesitated, he added, "Please, Ms. Cooke. I need my job."

"Well, okay. As long as it doesn't take much time."

He crossed his heart with his index finger. "Cross my heart. I promise. Just a second. That's all."

Leading Destiny around the van to the back, he grasped her arm as he opened the double door. Another man, wearing a baker's uniform, jumped out. A hypodermic needle was in his hand.

Jerking her arm away from the first man, she made a break for the church, but only got as far as the front of the van when she was grabbed from behind. Stomping on his instep as hard as she could, she broke away from him as he bent, howling with pain. Destiny had gotten close to the church and to help when the second man reached her, slamming his stun gun against her neck until she collapsed.

Devan picked up Destiny's limp body, shoved her into the back of the van, and then raced to the driver's seat, while Evan, retrieved the syringe of Rohypnol.

At her second interview with him, Carly pushed the map of Shawnee, along with surrounding counties, across the table to Ryder, who glanced at it and said, "This looks just like the map Sheriff Shitface tried to show me the other day."

"You will refer to him with respect and call him Sheriff Chase. And yes, this is the same map."

"I am not surprised Sheriff *Chase* shared his map with you. He's sharing a lot of things with you these days, isn't he? Like his bedroom, his bed."

"Stop it."

"What's the matter? Don't your fellow agents who are watching and listening to this interview via closed-circuit television know that Special Agent Stone is living with Sheriff Chase, and shares his bed on a nightly basis?"

Furious, Carly pushed her chair back and headed for the door. She had her hand on the door knob when she heard Ryder whisper something.

Stopping at the door, she looked back and asked, "What did you say?"

"Gamers. Is that name familiar to you?"

Returning to the table, she sat down. "Let's get back to the map. Let's talk about additional victims and where you buried them."

"I'm bored with those questions. Let's talk about the Gamers," he said with a smirk. "You need me more than I need you, so I'm changing the subject to the case you're working."

"What case?"

"You know I'm talking about that Purdue coed murder. What was her name? Abby something. Perhaps I can help with that."

"Let's make something very clear. This is not *Silence of the Lambs*. You are *not* Hannibal Lecter, and I am *not* Clarice Starling. We definitely don't need your help to solve a murder case."

"What would you say if I told you I received a note from the Gamers?"

"I'd say that you were lying. Agents turned your cell upside down and there was no note."

"But there *was* a note. I used to be a cop. Do you really think I didn't know my cell would be searched?"

"If the note exists, where is it?"

"I ate it, and it wasn't all that tasty."

"No more games, Ryder," Carly seethed. "Additional victims? Where are they buried?"

"They attended my trial."

"Who?"

"The Gamers. Well, at least one of them did. According to the note, I'm one of their heroes, and they intend to take up where I left off. What better way to impress me than a murder the good sheriff and team are chasing their tails trying to solve?"

"You're a sick, vile excuse of a human being, Ryder."

The now-familiar knock at the door signaled the end of the interview.

Ryder's grin was decidedly nasty. "And that is why I am so interesting to you."

Carly entered the observation room where Special Agent in Charge Sam Isley, Dr. Anderson, Susan Black, and Brody sat around the conference table.

"Before you ask, yes, he is telling the truth about whoever he is referring to as the Gamers," Susan Black said to Carly.

"I'm confused," said Sam Isley. "Who are the Gamers, and what the hell is Ryder talking about?"

Brody spoke up. "Recently a Purdue University coed was murdered. Her body was found naked and posed in an alley beside a seedy bar in Morel. The Gamers — whoever they are — took credit for the killing and promised more."

"Do you think they really contacted Ryder?"

"Yes, I'm sure of it," said Susan Brown.

"If I have profiled them correctly, they are the type of men who crave recognition, possibly even from someone like Ryder. Heaven help us if Ryder is their role model," Carly stated, her expression troubled.

"There's another thing of which I'm sure," Susan Brown began. "You should go back in there and show Ryder the victims' photos. Get him to tell us where they're buried."

Sam and Dr. Anderson nodded in agreement, so Carly returned to the interview room.

"You're back again, and so soon." Ryder sneered at her.

Laying a folder on the table, Carly eased herself down and met Ryder's eyes head-on. "I'm going to show you some photos of girls who have disappeared. Each of them communicated with you online. I want you to tell me their names, and where you buried them."

Ryder smirked. "I'd be more interested in some photos

of you, preferably without clothes."

Ignoring his remark, Carly pulled a stack of 5" by 7" photos from the folder. She held up the first one. "What is her name?"

"I don't know."

"I think you *do* know her. You and she communicated on Teen Chat for six months before she agreed to join you in Morel."

"Like that's a good clue. Are you kidding me?"

"She's from Battle Lake, Minnesota. We have a copy of her bus ticket to Morel. She arrived in December, three years ago. Ring a bell?"

"Oh, yeah, that's Leeann something? Can't remember her last name."

"Leeann Stetler was her name." Unfolding the Shawnee County map, she pushed it across the table to him. "Where did you bury her?"

"I might have buried her in my back yard."

"Hear that sound, Ryder? That's my bullshit alarm going off. Don't make the mistake of lying to me. I was there the day the Shawnee County deputies excavated your yard, front and back. No bodies were found."

Shifting in his seat, he stared at the map. "We'll have to come back to that one. I recall having a damn good time with her, but I can't remember where I put her. Doesn't mean I won't remember. I just don't right now. Give me time to think about it."

Carly pushed Leeann's photo into the folder, then picked up another from the stack. "Who's this girl?"

Squinting as he considered the girl in the photo, Ryder said, "That one really looks familiar. Let me think."

"Here's a couple of hints. She was only fourteen when this school photo was taken —"

"Wait!" Ryder held up his hand. "That's Delores Fulton. She called herself 'Dee.' I remember her because Erin got sick and couldn't meet her at the bus station. I had to go instead. I was scared shitless that someone would recognize me and ask me what I was doing there. Luckily, it was before any surveillance cameras were installed. Her bus was ninety minutes late, and then she made a fuss about not getting in my truck because she didn't know me. I finally persuaded her that I was Anthony's father and that he was meeting us at the house."

"Where is she?"

"I don't think I buried her in Shawnee County. In fact, I didn't bury her at all. I dumped her in Tippecanoe County in a corn field near Shadeland. I kept waiting for the farmer to find her and report it. But no one did."

"We'll check it out." Carly withdrew another photo,

which she gave to Ryder.

Scrutinizing the photo of the girl, a slow, evil smile spread over his face. "Joy Marshall," Ryder said. "That little bitch would be hard to forget. She bit me and left scratches so deep on my arms, I had to wear long sleeves in the heat of summer that year."

Carly pointed to the map. "Show me where you dumped or buried her."

After several minutes of moving his index finger across different areas of the map, Ryder stopped. "It's here. I think I buried her in this area. "

Carly looked at the area he was pinpointing. "Can't you narrow it down?"

"No, I can't. At least not with a map. I'd have to take you there."

A knock on the door notified Carly to stop the interview. "That's enough for now. I'll get one of the guards to come in so you can take a break."

"Always good to see you, Special Agent Stone."

In the observation room, Carly spread out the map so that Brody could identify the area Ryder indicated. "I know where this is," he began. "It's located off State Road 341, just east of Hillsboro. The area is miles and miles of flat land, with equal parts of farmland and forest. There aren't many houses in this part of the county. It might be a good place to dump or bury a body, but it's a terrible place to find one."

"Then we'll have to take Ryder with us to find the exact location of the body," Isley said.

"You're joking, right? You can't be suggesting taking Ryder anywhere outside this secured location," said Brody incredulously.

"You seem to be forgetting who's in charge of this project, Sheriff," Isley's face heated with anger. "We go early next week."

Destiny regained consciousness, blinking to focus her eyes. The room was a drugged haze and she struggled to clear her mind. Why did she feel so dazed? Where was she? After she attempted to sit up but couldn't, she looked at her wrists and legs. They were secured to the bed with silver duct tape. She tried to scream, but the sound that came from her was muffled by the duct tape over her mouth, until there was little sound at all. How had this happened to her? It was then she remembered the young caterer and how he'd lured her to the back of the van. She'd seen the stun gun just a second before he forced it to her neck. Destiny recalled another man, who bound her with duct tape before he placed a needle in her vein.

Destiny took in her surroundings. Her wrists were taped to a wrought iron headboard, her ankles to the footboard of the bed. A couple of folding chairs were at the end of the bed, and rows of plastic bins, stacked high, were to her right. On the other side of the bed were smaller bins.

Turning back to her right to get a better look, Destiny saw that each of the stacked bins was labeled. On each white label appeared a name. Darla Green was listed on one bin, another had the name Sharon Maud. She read the labels from left to right until she came to the name Abby Reece. Why did that name sound so familiar? Searching her mind, she remembered. Abby Reece was the Purdue student who disappeared and was found murdered. She visualized Abby's photo from a poster she'd seen on campus.

Oh, God. Had she been abducted by Abby Reece's killers? Did the names on the plastic bins' labels represent others who had died at their hands? No, that couldn't happen to her. Not now. Not when she and Justin were so close to realizing their dreams. Justin would find her. She knew he would. He was with the State Police, and he'd have the entire department out looking for her.

Tension tightening the rugged features of his face, Brody disconnected the call and slipped his cell phone in his pocket. Racing into the house from his SUV, he saw Carly and Cameron waiting for him at the dining room table.

"We have to go. Just got a call from Justin Andrews."

"The state trooper?" asked Cameron.

Brody blew out a breath and nodded. "He reported his fiancée, Destiny Cooke, missing!"

The siren blared as Brody sped through Morel to the opposite side of town. Cameron alerted Bryan Pittman to send a couple of his crime scene technicians to the First Baptist Church. Deputy Danny Wilson was on patrol and was closest to the church, so Cameron tasked him with securing the scene and keeping the rehearsal dinner guests inside the church.

"If she is, indeed, missing, this may be the work of the Gamers." Carly commented from the passenger seat.

"Or it may be a soon-to-be bride with cold feet," returned Brody.

"I know Destiny and Justin. They've been together since high school. I don't think this is a case of cold feet," said Cameron from the back seat. "They're one of the closest couples I've ever met. I planned on attending their wedding Saturday. "

"Justin said he'd gotten to the church before Destiny arrived, going straight there from work. Who the hell in his right mind abducts a woman from a parking lot where a state trooper's vehicle is parked?" Brody shook his head with frustration.

"That's the thing about thrill killers," said Carly. "The more danger and risk, the better the high. Could abducting the fiancée of a state trooper be any riskier?"

Reaching the church, they parked alongside the road and walked to the parking lot in back of the church. Three county sheriff patrol cars secured the perimeter. A patrolman was waving on bystanders, as well as the media. Deputy Wilson had already strung crime scene tape to secure the scene, and Justin Andrews stood talking animatedly on his cell phone. Disconnecting his call as soon as he saw the sheriff, Carly and Cameron walking toward him, he said, "I need your help to find Destiny before the worst case scenario in my mind comes true."

"Why do you think she's been abducted?" asked Brody.

"Follow me over here." They'd moved closer to a row of vehicles. "This new Honda Civic is Destiny's car. Notice the disturbance in gravel several feet away to the left?"

"They look like drag marks to me," offered Cameron. "That's a decent tire print in the bare dirt over there, too. If the crime scene techs can get a good mold, we have a chance of identifying the tire, and possibly even the vehicle."

"When was the last time you talked to Destiny?" Brody asked Justin.

"She called me around three this afternoon. I have a habit of running late from work, and she wanted to make sure I got to the rehearsal on time. I got here early to please her." His face clouded, unshed tears glistening in his eyes. "Destiny is my world. This cannot be happening. We have to find her."

"Justin, I have to ask you the standard questions." Brody said, as Cameron spoke with Deputy Wilson, and Carly went inside to talk to the guests.

"Hurry up and do it. We're wasting time."

"Was Destiny having problems with anyone? Any conflicts?"

"No. Everyone loves Destiny. She has a way with people. Always did."

"Where was she prior to driving to the church?"

"She was at the community center. Destiny meets with a group of troubled teenage girls every Thursday after school."

"Would any of them want to harm her?"

Justin paused to consider the question. "I doubt it. Most of the girls have no role model or parent who is interested in what happens to them. They know Destiny cares. She may be the one person in their lives who does."

Hating his next question, Brody ran his fingers through

his hair. "Justin, have you and Destiny been getting along?"

"Yes. Ask anyone. We're very happy and I can't wait to marry her on Saturday. We have to find her."

"Where were you during the time she disappeared?"

"I was with Reverend Powell in his office. He wants me to lead a youth basketball team for the church."

"Did anyone see anything during that time?"

"I don't think so. When I realized her car was parked in the lot, I looked everywhere for her, inside the church and out. Everyone was looking. Surely if someone had seen something, he or she would have spoken up."

Inside the church, Carly sat with the bride's parents, Anthony and Bobbie Cooke. She engaged them in preliminary conversation in an effort to calm them down, and then asked, "How were Destiny and Justin getting along?"

Anthony answered, "Those two kids grew up together. They've been in love for a long time. Sure, they had their spats, but nothing serious."

"Do you think if Destiny decided she didn't want to get married that Justin would hurt her?"

"For one thing, Destiny has wanted to marry Justin since high school. She's never wavered in that," her father claimed, nervously clutching his wife's hand.

"Even if she had backed out, I don't think Justin would hurt her. He might do some heavy-duty begging to get her to change her mind. But he wouldn't hurt her." Bobbie Cooke dabbed her eyes with a tissue.

"Has anything odd happened today or this evening? Think carefully. Has anything out of the ordinary happened besides Destiny's disappearance?" Carly asked.

"Nothing I can think of—" said Anthony.

"Now wait a minute," Bobbie interrupted. "The caterers never arrived. They were supposed to be here at five o'clock to set up the rehearsal dinner, but they're still not here."

"What is the name of the caterer?"

"Just a second." Bobbie searched her purse. She pulled out a small slip of paper and handed it to Carly. "Grand Events Catering is their name. They called me and said they were a new business, and that Reverend Powell recommended them. Well, that was enough for me. I hired them."

"And this is the phone number they gave you?"

"Yes, right there on the bottom of my notes."

"Thank you, Mr. and Mrs. Cooke. You've been very helpful."

Carly left through the front entrance of the church and dialed the caterer's phone number as soon as she was outside. She let it ring and ring, hoping to get a voice mail. After too many rings to count, she called the operator and asked for the business number of Grand Events Catering. After a few moments, the operator said, "I'm sorry, but I am not finding that name in our business *or* residential section."

Carly disconnected the call. She'd bet anything the 'business' number was linked to a burner cell, which was probably tossed out a vehicle window or thrown in a dumpster after the catering details were settled. She hurried to tell Brody the news and her theory.

"What kind of uniforms do caterers wear?" asked Brody, once he'd heard her out.

"I guess it varies. They could wear just a simple bib kitchen apron, or some type of traditional chef or baker coat. Why are you asking? No one saw them because they never arrived."

"Remember the white van in Wayne Griffin's truck stop surveillance tape? The clerk said the passengers were wearing black hoodies over baker's uniforms. Then Wayne later discovered the magnetic baker sign on the van was stolen."

"Exactly. I still think the killers of the Indy prostitutes are the Gamers, who then killed Abby Reece, and have now abducted Destiny Cooke."

In the weeks to follow, the search for Destiny Cooke pulled an entire county together as missing flyers were posted around town, and searches were organized by residents. Brody's deputies combed the area with search dogs and helicopters. Pleas were made by her tearful parents on local news television stations, and social media was aflame with news of her disappearance.

CHAPTER EIGHT

Deputy Gail Sawyer couldn't sleep, so she decided to treat herself to the breakfast smorgasbord at the historic Morel Hotel. Besides having great food, like her favorite blueberry pancakes, bacon, scrambled eggs with cheese, and pumpkin muffins, the hotel's restaurant was the only one in town that opened before six in the morning.

New owners were renovating the hotel, and a van filled with house painters pulled in next to her, prompting her to leap out of her squad car and race around the building to the front door. If there was one thing Gail couldn't tolerate, it was a long line.

As she approached the hotel's veranda, Gail had that funny feeling in her stomach that something was off, not as it should be. Taking a closer look, she noticed someone seated in the last of six rocking chairs. The rocking chair at the end was turned at a 90-degree angle compared to the rest. The back of the chair was facing her, and whoever sat in the chair was not rocking, and in fact, was not moving at all.

Letting the painters pass her, she waited until they were inside the hotel before climbing the steps and advancing toward the last rocking chair. Gail's intuition kicked in and there was no other choice but to check on that person in the chair.

"Good morning," Gail called out. She got no response.

Reaching the chair, Gail slid into position against the porch railing to stand directly in front of the person to take a closer look. *Oh, God, no.* Feeling light-headed as the blood drained from her face, she fought the nausea that crept up her throat and braced herself. Seated in the rocking chair was a young African-American woman in her twenties, completely nude except for an old-fashioned locket on a gold chain around her neck. On her head was a plastic bag, secured with duct tape that wrapped tightly around her neck, just above the necklace. Someone had intertwined the tape through the slats in the rocking chair to keep her body upright.

Gail's hand trembled as she pulled out her cell phone to call Detective Cameron Chase, who arrived at the scene twenty minutes later.

The shrill ring of the kitchen landline phone jerked Gabe to attention as he helped himself to another serving of sausage and biscuits. He picked up the receiver.

"Gabe, another body has been found!" Cameron shouted. "Open your email. Did you get another one from the Gamers?"

Shocked, Gabe dropped the coffee mug he was holding and it shattered into a million pieces, spraying coffee on his pants and floor.

"Tell me this is a bad joke."

"Gabe, I wouldn't play with you about something like this. She's naked and posed, just like Abby Reece. Check your email."

He raced upstairs. Once Gabe reached his room, he opened his laptop to look at his incoming email. There it was — an email from 'Destiny Cooke, and he didn't know anyone by that name. Opening the message, he soon realized it was the one Cameron was asking about.

"Found it."

"Read it to me, Gabe."

Hello, Little Sheriff Bro.

We've got another surprise for you. Making 'history' this time. You'll find her at the historic Morel Hotel.

Like last time, this email goes to you and the media.

Act fast to catch us — if you can. But of course, you can't.

—Gamers

P.S. Have to hand it to you. Give credit where credit's due and all that shit. You've got extremely good taste in women, Little Sheriff Bro. The sister is smoking hot. Could she be next?

"Those sick, perverted bastards!" Cameron swore. "Trace the email. Where did it come from? Call me right back."

Gabe traced the email back to its origin, which was the address of a home owned by a Justin Andrews. Plugging his name into one of the law enforcement databases to which he had access, he discovered that Justin Andrews worked as an Indiana State Trooper. Using Destiny's name as a search term, he quickly discovered her Facebook page, which was bursting with photos and news about her upcoming wedding when she would marry Justin Andrews.

He called Cameron and told him the email had come from Destiny Cooke's email account.

"Goddamn it all to hell," Cameron said sadly. "I thought this was Destiny's body. I just didn't want to believe it."

"Sorry, Cam."

"No, I'm the one who's sorry — for her parents and fiancé, Justin Andrews. I hate having to tell them that we found Destiny, and she's never coming home. It will rip their worlds apart."

Cameron said he was sending a couple of deputies to

Justin's home to see if the Gamers were still there, and Gabe ended the call.

His heart froze as he re-read the note's postscript. "The sister is smoking hot. Could she be next?"

The Gamers were referring to Abby's sister, Kaitlyn! She was the next woman on their list to kill.

Throwing on his clothes, he raced to his truck. Glancing at the Honeymoon Cottage, he saw that both Brody and Carly had already left for work. He had to get to Kaitlyn. He thrust the gear to drive and catapulted out of the main house's long lane to the road. Once he reached town, he had to slow down to get through Morel traffic on route to the rural road that led to the house Kaitlyn was leasing. It was Morel's version of a traffic jam, and it seemed every vehicle in the entire county was on the road, residents going to work, kids on busses heading to school, farmers on tractors heading toward their fields, and semi-trucks loaded with grain. Gritting his teeth and clenching the steering wheel, frustration danced in his stomach as he maneuvered through town.

What if he was too late? What if the killers had already abducted Kaitlyn? Leaving city limits, he floored the accelerator and passed slower moving vehicles until he reached the road that led to Kaitlyn's house. Skidding to a stop in her gravel driveway, he slammed the gear to park, and jumped out of the car. Pounding frantically on her front door, he got no response, so he raced to the garage and saw that her car was gone. Taking a deep breath, he tried to calm himself. Did the Gamers already have Kaitlyn? Was he too late?

Calling her on her cell phone, he got no answer. Then it hit him. Kaitlyn was a teacher. It was after eight o'clock by that point, so maybe she was in class. She had to be. He got back into his truck and headed back to town. Once he reached Morel Elementary, he drove to the teacher's parking area and spotted her VW in the third row. Thank God.

A wave of gratitude washed over him as he pulled out his cell phone. Sending a text to Kaitlyn, he told her he needed to talk to her. Seconds later, she returned his text with: "In class now. Meet me at my house this evening with a large veggie pizza with extra cheese, and we can talk all you want."

When was the last time he felt so close to a female in such a short time, and so terrified he might lose her? Never.

Gabe's truck was immediately stopped by a young deputy as he pulled up to the Morel Hotel.

"I'm sorry, sir. I'm going to have to ask you to turn your vehicle around and leave. This is a crime scene," said the deputy in as stern a voice as he could muster.

"I'm Gabe Chase—"

"I don't care who you are," he interrupted. "Turn your truck around."

Gabe reached into his back pocket and pulled out a badge that he flashed before the deputy's eyes. It was a replica of his mother's badge. Years before at her funeral, the new county sheriff gave one to each of her sons. Brody and Cameron wore theirs on their belt buckles. Gabe always had his mom's badge in his back pocket. Luckily, the deputy hadn't taken a closer look.

"Sorry, sir. Park your truck over there. The crime scene is on the veranda."

As Gabe approached the building, he spotted Brody and Cameron at the far end of the veranda with Deputy Gail Sawyer. Joining them, he bent down to examine the body under a small blanket and wondered how a human being could get a thrill out of destroying another. Beneath a plastic bag, Destiny Cooke's eyes bulged, her mouth formed a silent scream, and her facial features were frozen in terror. A dark rage bubbled through his veins. Like Abby, Destiny's life was just beginning when monsters smothered her, leaving nothing behind but pain for her loved ones. He felt a hand pull at his arm and looked up to see Brody.

"C'mon, Gabe. You shouldn't be here."

Taking a cleansing breath to calm himself, Gabe said, "Did Cam tell you about the email? Kaitlyn is next on their list, and I have to move her to a safe place."

"All of the safe houses are full. Why don't you move her into our main house? In addition to the ones you and Cam have, there are four more suites."

"You're right. I just hope I can convince her to leave her house."

Brody frowned thoughtfully and said, "You do realize, if she is their next target, they're stalking her."

"I know. That's what I'm afraid of."

"She's a teacher at Morel Elementary, right?"

"Yes, and if she insists on working, I'll take her to and from school."

"The killers can probably recognize both your cars. Take one of the drug-seized vehicles parked in the helicopter hangar. There are a couple with tinted windows."

"Thanks, Brody."

"Talk to Carly. She's worked undercover and may have some ideas on how to disguise Kaitlyn. Carly can make it as difficult as possible for the Gamers to identify her."

Their attention was diverted to the coroner's van, which had just driven through the yard and parked close to where they were standing.

Bryan Pittman and a couple of crime scene techs

bounded from the vehicle and joined Cameron and Deputy Sawyer on the veranda. They'd moved closer to the victim near Brody and Gabe.

"Who the fuck covered the body with a blanket?" Bryan bellowed the second he saw the victim. Instantly angry, a small vein near his left eye bulged as his face grew red.

"I did, sir." Deputy Sawyer admitted, a little stunned by his rage.

"No, shit?" Bryan said, and then added, "I could have sworn you were at the training session I gave for deputies and firemen a couple of months ago."

"Yes, sir. I was there."

"Then you must have forgotten my first rule of what *not* to do at a crime scene!"

Glancing at Brody and Cameron, Gail said, "I was just preserving the dignity of this young lady. No one deserves to be staged naked in a public place."

"She's dead, Deputy. Dignity is not her most important issue now," Bryan said. "Do you remember the part of the training when I discussed how covering bodies transfers material, contaminants, and other forensic evidence from one part of the crime scene to another?"

"I do now, sir," Gail responded, as embarrassment

flooded through her.

Brody broke in. "Deputy Sawyer, why don't you assist Deputy Wilson? Make sure no one who shouldn't be here gets inside the grounds."

Once she reached the road, Brody turned to the coroner. "Hey, Bryan. Could you have said all that a little louder? I don't think the folks on Main Street heard you."

"I can't count how many times I've told your deputies not to cover the victim with a blanket," said Bryan, still frustrated. "Move over. I can't see the victim."

Brody moved aside and Bryan crept closer to the body. "She's posed like Abby Reece's body, and has the plastic bag over her head, too. Looks like Abby's killers have struck again."

To the crime scene technician taking photographs of the crime scene, he said, "Get a close-up of that gold necklace she's wearing."

Cameron said, "I noticed that necklace, too. It's an old-fashioned locket like Mom used to have. Those things open, and usually there's a photo of a loved one inside. I knew Destiny Cooke, and I don't see her wearing something like that."

Bryan examined her arms. "There are no defensive injuries, which suggest she was restrained, probably by the same type of duct tape we see on her now. If we get lucky and the killers didn't wear gloves, we might lift a print from the duct tape. I've got a tech who's a genius at lifting prints with super-glue."

"How fast can you make an official identification?" Cameron asked.

"I'll call you. I've got her dental records, so it won't take long."

Just before dark, Gabe pulled into Kaitlyn's driveway, turned off the ignition, and sat in his truck assessing the house and surrounding area for places where intruders could hide.

Kaitlyn's house was a one-level renovated farmhouse, painted a pale yellow with white shutters and trim. A porch ran the front of the house, and two white rocking chairs with fluffy, floral cushions sat on the porch. There was a bright floral wreath on the front door. The home looked like something out of one of his mom's old *Country Living* magazines, with all the feminine touches that suited Kaitlyn.

Next to the house was a relatively new two-car garage. A dense wooded area lay to the right of the property and behind it. To the left was a corn field that went on for as far as he could see. The closest neighbor was at least a mile or two away. The place failed miserably for security. Intruders had multiple options to enter and hide on the property.

Gabe needed to quickly move Kaitlyn into a suite at their main house before it was too late. How hard would Kaitlyn, who could be stubborn as hell, fight him to stay in her own home? Any place would be safer than this one.

Getting out of his truck, he balanced the large pizza on the palm of one hand, and carried a bottle of wine in the other. Kaitlyn met him at the door with a radiant smile, making him wish he was not here to tell her there had been another murder and she was next on the killer's list.

Inside, he noticed lit candles on her dining table, along with china, silverware, and wine glasses. It was set up for romance, and his conversation would be anything but.

Kaitlyn wore a snug, silk tee that accentuated her round breasts, in the exact shade of ocean blue to match her eyes, along with a worn pair of jeans that clung to her like a second skin. Kaitlyn had a body that pushed all his buttons in a very big way. He wanted to pull her hard against him and kiss her all the way to her bedroom, then make love to her for hours.

Instead, Gabe handed the pizza to Kaitlyn, who placed it on the table. At the kitchen counter, he popped the wine bottle and she wound her arms around his waist as she kissed him. A spike of heat caught him low in the gut, and if he didn't get some control, he'd take her right in her kitchen.

Gabe led her to the dining room. "Are you hungry?

I'm starving." He poured their wine and pulled out a chair near him for Kaitlyn.

Suddenly a small dot of red light appeared on the wall next to them.

"What is that?" asked Kaitlyn.

Recognizing it as the laser light from a gun, Gabe grabbed Kaitlyn out of her chair and hit the floor, landing on top of her.

"Ouch!" She squealed. "Okay, I get it. You're into rough sex. But you're killing my back. Besides that, I'm famished. Can't we have pizza first?"

Gabe shifted, balancing his weight on his elbows, placed his hand over her mouth, and whispered, "Kaitlyn, that red light is from a laser mounted onto a gun. Someone is outside."

"Oh, c'mon. You can think of a better reason to jump me than that."

Shots rang out, shattering the window, as well as the china and wine glasses on the table, shooting splintered glass projectiles throughout the room and cutting Gabe's back.

Now terrified, Kaitlyn tightened her arms around Gabe, clamping down like a vise grip, as her heart hammered against her chest.

"Damn it!" Gabe cursed. "I left my gun in the glove

box in my truck."

"Gun? I've got guns!" Kaitlyn pushed at him. "Get off me. They're in my bedroom closet."

Looking down at her, Gabe shook his head. "Why am I not surprised?"

"As much as I'm turned on by your buff, sexy body pressing against mine, if you could please roll off of me, I'll get my guns."

"Oh, hell no. You're not going anywhere. I'm a private investigator. I think I can find your closet. Wait here and don't move until I get back."

The shots continued as Gabe army-crawled on his belly to her bedroom. Inside her closet, he found a loaded shotgun propped upright in a corner, and a loaded handgun on a shelf.

He returned to Kaitlyn and gave her the handgun. "I assume you know how to use this. Stay here while I circle the house to find out where the shooter is."

Climbing out a back window, Gabe pressed himself against a tree as he eyeballed the woods in back for any signs of activity. Finding none, he moved to the side of the house that faced a thicket of trees. Headlights flashed on just beyond the trees, and a motor roared as the vehicle headed toward the road. Gabe raced to the road and reached it just in time to see the tail-lights of a van speeding toward town.

Pulling out his cell phone, he called Cameron to send backup, and for crime scene technicians to search for spent casings from what he guessed to be a semi-automatic rifle used by the assailants.

Back inside the house, a terrified Kaitlyn flew into his arms. "You're safe now, Kaitlyn. They're gone. But we have to talk."

Leading her to the sofa, he made her sit down, then he sat beside her, holding her hand. "Something's happened that you need to know about. Abby's killers have claimed another victim — Destiny Cooke."

"Oh, no. I saw the media coverage of her disappearance and prayed she'd be found safe. Her poor family."

Gabe took a folded piece of paper from his pocket. "Just like before, the killers emailed me." He handed it to Kaitlyn to read.

Once she reached the end of the note, she looked up at him. "I'm next, aren't I?"

"Not if I have anything to do with it," Gabe began. "I want to move you to a safer place. I think it was the killers who shot up your house."

"But where can I go?"

"Move into our main house. The house is divided into

suites because my parents thought they'd turn it into a bed and breakfast or lodge someday. Cam and I live in two of the suites. There are four left for you to choose from. Brody's made sure the house and property security is top notch. You'll be safe there."

Kaitlyn headed for her bedroom.

"What are you doing?"

"I'm packing. You don't think I'm going to fight you to stay here by myself, do you?"

Gabe was vigilant about watching the wooded area, where he saw the vehicle headlights from her front porch. After a while, he stepped back inside. Listening to Kaitlyn packing her things in her bedroom, he walked around her living room.

"Hey, Kaitlyn. Are you almost ready?"

"Not yet, and quit bugging me, Gabe."

Chuckling to himself, he examined the contents of her three bookcases, which were floor-to-ceiling and crammed with education textbooks and romantic suspense novels. His attention was drawn to the second shelf of the first bookcase where a Matchbox car sat in the midst of tiny shards of glass that had blown in from the dining room. He picked it up.

The Matchbox car was a 1976 Pontiac Firebird in metallic blue with orange tinted windows and chrome interior. The tiny toy Firebird was identical to the car his mother drove in high school. He turned it over to see the underside, and right where Brody had scratched it with a nail, was the letter "C" for Chase. There was no mistaking this was the Matchbox car Gabe had given to Cat in the second grade.

He'd had this feeling since the first time he met her that there was something very familiar about Kaitlyn. Could Kaitlyn be the girl he nicknamed Cat in the second grade? There was no other explanation for her having his toy car in her possession.

All this time, he'd thought Cat had died. He'd mourned for her, but he'd never forgotten her, thanks to the constant replay in his dreams of the day she left in the ambulance.

A siren in the near distance broke into his thoughts. Soon Cameron and Seth Ziegler, a crime scene technician who specialized in ballistics, arrived.

Meeting his brother on the porch, Gabe led Cameron and Seth to the side of the house where the windows were shattered.

"Not to mention your truck. You're lucky you weren't hit!" Cameron said to Gabe.

"I think he used an assault rifle, possibly a semi-automatic. His van was parked over there in that thicket of trees."

"I'll head over there and see if the shooter left any spent bullet casings," said Seth.

"White van?" Cameron asked.

"I saw the vehicle, but couldn't see a plate or anything by the time I ran to the road."

"I've got my detectives looking for a white van. They tell me in Shawnee County alone, there are over two hundred. Who knows how many white vans are in the surrounding counties? My gut tells me the killers live in this county, so I've got them running down each one, taking a special look at the 2012 Chevrolet 1500 utility vans on the list."

"Good idea. These sick freaks need to be caught, and soon." Gabe's voice was low and trembling with anger. He couldn't get the ugly visual of Abby's and Destiny's posed bodies out of his head. And now they wanted Kaitlyn.

"No argument there, bro," said Cameron.

Soon Seth returned, holding several spent casings. "I've got an AK-47, and I'll bet you my next pay check that is what these were shot from. I'll give you a final verdict in a couple of days." He headed for his vehicle, then drove back to his lab in town.

"Have you told Justin Andrews about Destiny's death?" Gabe asked his brother.

"I didn't have to," said Cameron. "After you left, he rammed his car through the barricade by the road and pushed down two of my deputies who were trying to stop him from getting to the veranda. Bryan and I tried to keep him from her body, but he was so pumped with adrenaline, he cannon-balled us to get to her."

"Oh, shit."

"It was the worst thing I've ever seen. Justin threw his arms around the rocking chair where Destiny's body was propped and wouldn't let go of her. The man was hysterical," said Cameron. "It took two deputies, Bryan, and me, to get him to let go of Destiny and the chair. Bryan gave him something to calm him down, and I walked him to his truck. We sat inside talking for a good thirty minutes. Then he went with me to tell Destiny's parents."

Just then, Kaitlyn appeared on the front porch, dragging behind her two large pieces of luggage.

"Looks like you talked her into moving into the main house."

"After her house was shot up, it didn't take much persuading."

"Don't blame her."

Running to the porch, Gabe secured the luggage. "Cam, this is Kaitlyn Reece. Kaitlyn, this is my brother, Cam."

"Hi, Cam. Welcome to our shooting." Kaitlyn made an attempt at a smile. "You two look a lot alike. One could certainly tell you are brothers."

"So I'm told. It's good to meet you, Kaitlyn. Wish it were under better circumstances."

Gabe led her to the garage, where he opened the door and packed the luggage into her car. He helped her into the passenger side, and then got behind the steering wheel after he pushed the seat back as far as it would go. VWs like Kaitlyn's weren't designed for big men like himself. He felt the metal Matchbox car in his pocket rest against his thigh. Turning the key in the ignition, he glanced at Kaitlyn and thought of how he longed to see his Cat again. He pulled her to him and kissed her soundly and quickly on the lips. "I'll keep you safe, Kaitlyn." Losing her again was not going to happen. Not on his watch.

Evan crept across the dining room and into the family room where his father's gun collection was kept in a gleaming mahogany gun cabinet. Unlocking the cabinet door with the key he'd found in the top drawer of his father's dresser, he quickly but carefully placed the AK-47 in its place among the nine other guns his father had collected. A creaking sound in the floor startled him, and he spun around until he was face-to-face with Devan.

"What the fuck is going on? Where have you been with Dad's AK-47? Are you suicidal or just stupid?" Devan demanded.

"Be quiet before you wake up everyone in the house."

Evan locked the cabinet, slipped the key in his pocket, and climbed the stairs to his bedroom, with Devan close on his heels.

"You didn't answer me. What were you doing with the old man's assault rifle?"

"I was shooting rats at the old junkyard," Evan lied. Who knew what Devan would do to him if he found out he'd been to Kaitlyn Reece's house and used the rifle to give her a good scare. It was a bonus that Gabe Chase had been there. Not that Devan would get that. Not that he'd ever tell Devan about it.

"Since when do you shoot rats at the junkyard without me?" asked Devan suspiciously.

"You were at football practice, and I didn't want to wait until you got home."

"Next time, wait for me."

"Is that an order? Since when do I need a chaperone?"

"Since I say you do," barked Devan, as he drilled his index finger into Evan's chest.

"Sure, whatever you say, Devan." The last thing he needed was for his anger-ball brother to go ballistic and wake up his parents. The punishment for being out this late would be grounding for a month with no access to his cell phone, laptop or any other electronic device. Who knows what his militaristic father would do to him if he found out he took his prized AK-47 from the gun cabinet without permission.

Gabe sat on the bed in the suite Kaitlyn chose and watched her unpack. One-by-one she pulled out each article of clothing and hung it neatly in the closet.

"Am I safe in here unpacking?" Kaitlyn asked.

"Yes, why?"

"I was just wondering why you were guarding me."

Gabe pulled out the Matchbox car, holding it in the palm of his hand.

Kaitlyn snatched it from him. "What are you doing with this? Did you take it from my bookcase?"

"It's a great replica of a Pontiac Firebird. Where did you get it?"

"I can't remember. I just know I've had it since the

second grade. I asked my mom about it. But she doesn't know where I got it. She said I refused to let go of it, even in the hospital as they wheeled me to the operating room."

Kaitlyn turned to place the toy car on the top of her dresser.

"Cat?"

Hearing her old nickname, she whirled around. "Why did you call me that?"

"I started calling you 'Cat' in the second grade. When my school bus passed your house, there was always a cat in every window. So Cat became my pet name for you."

"You knew me in the second grade?" Kaitlyn asked, bewildered.

Gabe nodded and then asked, "May I see your toy car? I want to show you something."

Handing him the car, she sat next to him on the bed and watched as he turned the car to show her its underside. "My brother, Brody, used a nail to scratch the letter 'C' for Chase on all of our metal Matchbox cars and trucks. This isn't just any Matchbox car. It's a 1976 Pontiac Firebird in metallic blue, exactly like the one my mom drove in high school. *I* gave this to you, Cat. You were my best friend in the second grade, and I've been missing you since the day you were taken away from the schoolyard in an ambulance."

Sadness entered Kaitlyn's eyes as she gazed at him, along with a vulnerability he hadn't seen before. "I wish I could remember you. There were all sorts of things I couldn't remember after the surgery. But you shouldn't have been one of them. I think, subconsciously, I remember our friendship. Mom said I was fierce about the toy car. A nurse tried to take it from me before they wheeled me into the operating room and I bit her."

Gabe liked the thought that something he'd given to her, even in the second grade, meant that much to her. He could feel the warmth of her body as she pressed against him, placing her small hand in his.

"Mom said everyone thought Ralphie Smith had seriously injured me when he pushed me down."

"I did, too. That's why I picked a fight with him and he kicked my seven-year-old ass."

"Oh, Gabe, it wasn't his fault," Kaitlyn began. "His mother brought Ralphie to the hospital to make him apologize. I had a mild concussion, but that isn't why I passed out. It was far more serious than that. I had what is called an atrial septal defect."

"What's that?"

"Basically, it's a hole in the heart. Many children have them, but mine was large and was negatively impacting my health. My doctors felt it was best if they performed open heart surgery to stitch it closed."

Kaitlyn paused for a second, and then stood before him, pulling her shirt up over her head to reveal a long white scar that ran from just under the hollow in her throat, to in-between, and below her breasts. "That's how I got this."

"Cat, I'm sorry." Gabe took a deep, cleansing breath to soothe the apprehension that filled him as he thought of how close he'd come to losing her forever.

"Why didn't you say anything about it when we made love?"

Lightly running his finger down the scar, he said, "I didn't notice it. If I had, I would have told you how beautiful I think it is. Without the surgery, you might not be with me now. Your scar tells the story that you survived. And for that I will be forever grateful."

With his large hands, Gabe encircled her waist, pulling her closer until she stood between his legs as he sat on the bed. Removing her bra, he dropped it to the floor, and then removed her panties. He trailed light kisses from the beginning of the scar to the ending, his hot breath softly fanning her skin. Burying her hands in his thick hair, she sighed with pleasure. There was no fighting her overwhelming need to touch him, to be close to his warmth. Her body ached for his touch.

Standing, Gabe reclaimed her lips, one hand on her

back and the other on her bottom, crushing her soft body against him, building a fiery heat that rushed through her like a forest fire. His tongue traced the soft fullness of her lips and explored the recesses of her mouth until her every cell erupted with a need. Gabe effortlessly picked her up and laid her gently on the bed.

He began a slow and sexy strip tease as he lifted his shirt above his head and tossed it aside, revealing a broad chest, muscled arms, and impressive biceps without an ounce of fat. His body radiated strength, determination and heat. She lay there on her back watching him, wanting him. He pulled a foil packet from his pocket and laid it on the table. As if in slow motion, he unzipped his jeans, kicked off his shoes, and pushed his pants to the floor until he was completely naked. Stretching out alongside her, he kissed her until she was drunk with desire.

Balancing himself on his elbows, he hovered above her, kissing her with his entire body, igniting a bone-melting fire that spread through her blood. He took the foil packet from the table, opened it with his teeth, and covered himself. His fingers found the nub of her passion as his steel drove into her. Then he pumped and thrust, rocking her hips, sending her into a heated frenzy from which she thought she may not recover. Shaking with desire, he groaned as she clung to him desperately, as they tumbled over the last edge of pleasure, unable to wait another second.

He whispered something in his low, sexy voice as he planted gentle kisses on her face and neck, before he rolled off her. He lay next to her, pulling the sheet to their waists, when she asked, "What was it you whispered to me?"

He grasped her face and held it gently, kissing her slowly and thoughtfully. "I love you, Cat. I don't think it's too soon to tell you. I think I've loved you since I was seven-years-old."

"I hear we have another victim," said Bradley Lucas, as he entered Brody's office without knocking. Bradley plopped down in one of the visitor's chairs in front of Brody's desk and waited for an answer, as if he had asked a question.

"Hello to you, too, Mr. Lucas," Brody offered sarcastically.

Bradley Lucas was the county commission president, making him the sheriff's direct supervisor. He could be a horse's ass when he wanted to, throwing his weight around like an Army general.

"I thought our agreement was that you brief me immediately after the event. Why did I find out we have another murder on our hands from the morning news?"

"I spent most of the night at the crime scene and then the autopsy," Brody replied.

"You should have called me to the crime scene when it was first discovered."

"We had too many people at that crime scene as it was, putting the forensic evidence in jeopardy," said Brody, annoyed that Lucas felt it was his right to be at a crime scene, even though he was a civilian.

"Next time anything like this happens, you call me first," Bradley commanded, his face red and blotchy with anger.

"The victim is Destiny Cooke."

"The beauty queen?" Bradley interrupted. "Shit. Nothing like taking out the county darling. What kind of animals did this?"

Shrugging, Brody continued, "Where we found her on the veranda of the Morel Hotel is the secondary crime scene. She was murdered somewhere else, then the killers brought her to the hotel and duct-taped her body to a rocking chair."

"Well, the surveillance tape should tell us who did it."

"Sure would, if any surveillance cameras existed at the hotel. But none do. The owners are spending their money on renovating the building, not security."

Lucas shook his head with obvious frustration. "Well, shit. What else do you know?"

"Just like Abby Reece, Destiny died of asphyxiation

when she was smothered inside the plastic bag we found covering her head."

Grimacing, Bradley said, "What a way to die."

"We think there are two killers. One secures the plastic bag with duct tape around her neck, while the other one holds her down as she struggles to breathe."

"Any prints?"

"We got a partial print on the duct tape wound around Abby Reece's neck. No prints at all in Destiny's case."

"Any hits on the partial print?"

"Nope, which means at least one of our perps doesn't have a criminal record, making it that much harder to find the bastards."

"Speaking of Abby Reece, I heard a rumor that your brother, Gabe, was involved with her."

Glaring at him, Brody answered, "My brother was cleared of any involvement with her murder by a detective with the Indiana State Police. And you knew that before you asked me the question."

"You won't hear about either of my sons being involved with a murder investigation. The brother of the county sheriff shouldn't be either. It puts a suspicious cloud over the entire department."

"That so?"

"I have to tell you I am getting a lot of complaints about your performance with the Ryder case. I mean, the killer was a deputy in your own department. People are asking me why it took so long for you to catch him."

"What do you tell them?"

Ignoring his question, Bradley said, "I'm up for re-election next year. Don't expect me to fall on the sword for you, Brody. Not going to happen."

"I've never asked you to put your neck out for me."

"If these killings continue, it's a matter of time until the board asks for your badge."

"If the board thinks they can do a better job, they can have my fucking badge."

Both tempers at a flashpoint, Brody knew they'd accomplish nothing by continuing the conversation so he changed the subject. "How are your sons? I heard one of them got a touchdown at the game last Friday night."

"Dev almost won that game single-handedly," Bradley boasted. "He should have no problem getting an athletic scholarship for college."

"How's Evan doing?"

"He's still holding his own grade-wise. We're hoping he can snag an academic scholarship."

Kaitlyn followed Gabe inside the hangar on their property. The structure was giant and held the sheriff department helicopter, as well as several vehicles.

"Who flies the copter?" Kaitlyn asked.

"I do, when I'm needed. All three of us are licensed pilots."

"Is there anything you can't do, Mr. Chase?"

"I plan on showing you what I *can* do later tonight, Ms. Cat," A broad grin split Gabe's face.

Giggling, Kaitlyn pointed to three vehicles parked next to her VW, which they'd hidden here earlier. "Which of those did your brother say we could use?"

"They all have tinted glass, so you can pick. Which one do you want?"

"I like this one. It's a Mercedes, right?"

"Yes, this is the Mercedes SUV GL-550 in steel gray. Nice choice, Cat."

"I always wanted to test-drive a Mercedes SUV. Not that I'll be buying one anytime soon on a teacher's salary."

"Here's the deal," said Gabe. "I'll drive you to school each morning and pick you up in the afternoon."

"Then we'll go to your office, right?"

"No. There is a good chance the killers saw you

coming in or out of my office, so we're staying away from it. I have enough computer equipment to work from home, so that's what I'll do."

"Okay, but what if they are watching the school? They'll see me enter and exit."

"We're going to talk to Carly about disguising you. She's worked a lot of undercover assignments."

"Hey, did I hear my name?" Carly entered the hangar and joined them near the SUV. "Welcome, Kaitlyn. I'm so glad you'll be staying here. I need a little help breaking up all the testosterone on this property."

"Hi, Carly. It is good to see you again," Kaitlyn said, as the two women hugged.

"Gabe is right. I have some ideas on disguising you so the killers will have a hard time determining whether it is you. Come with me to the Honeymoon Cottage, and I'll show you some of my wigs and makeup tricks."

Kaitlyn followed Carly up the staircase to the loft, where one of the walls was a floor-to-ceiling window that offered a beautiful view of the trees and lake beyond. The large bed had an oak, vintage Eastlake headboard with geometrical elements and lightly incised carvings.

"That has to be the most beautiful bed I've ever seen,"

Kaitlyn exclaimed.

"It belonged to Dr. and Mrs. Chase," said Carly. "Did Gabe tell you the story behind the Honeymoon Cottage?"

"No." Kaitlyn shook her head.

"Dr. Chase built this house as a wedding present to his bride. They lived here until the main house was built."

"That is so romantic."

"I agree. The little touches he added to the house says a lot about how much he loved her."

Carly went to a closet and dragged a small trunk to the middle of the room. Pulling open the lid, she waved for Kaitlyn to join her on the floor as she withdrew some dresses.

"We look to be the same size, so these dresses should fit you. I was a school teacher in one of the roles I played, so there should be some appropriate clothing for you."

Kaitlyn withdrew a long halter dress with sparkling rhinestones on the silky black fabric. She held it against her. "Why do I have the feeling that this sexy number wasn't used in your school teacher role?"

The memory of the last time she wore the dress was not a good one. In fact, she thought she'd destroyed it. Carly took a deep breath and shook her head.

"Do you want to talk about it?"

"About what?"

"The bad thing that happened the last time you wore this gown," said Kaitlyn softly.

"I'm sorry. It's not something I talk about."

"But it still bothers you, right?" she asked. "We've only known each other for about a minute, but you can trust me. What's put in the vault, stays there. I promise."

"I was with the Bureau," Carly began. "We were chasing a very evil man who trafficked people and drugs. My supervisor found out he had a preference for women with dark hair and eyes like mine. So I was chosen to go undercover wearing a wire sewn inside this dress. At his favorite bar, I was to flirt with him, to get him to talk about something that could be used to indict him."

"But there's more to the story, isn't there?"

"Yes. My best friend, who was also an agent, went undercover and let the traffickers abduct her. Amy was wired and her cell had GPS on it, so we always knew where she was and what was going on."

"Go on," Kaitlyn gently urged.

"One day, she was in the back of a van driven by the traffickers, with three other women. I was following them at a safe distance, when the driver ran a red light during rush hour and I lost them."

"Is it normal for the FBI to have only one agent on surveillance?"

"This was during the time that budget cuts ran rampant."

"I see," said Kaitlyn. "Did you eventually find Amy?"

"Yes, I had her on GPS and could track where they were going. Once I reached the house, I hid the car and listened. They'd discovered Amy was wired. There was a lot of yelling. I called for backup and received direct orders not to move until additional agents arrived. I waited and waited and no one arrived." The thought made Carly's throat ache with regret. If only she hadn't followed orders and waited for backup. If only . . .

"Oh, no. What happened to Amy?"

"I heard a blood-curdling scream and her cries for help. I could hear the other women in the room crying hysterically."

"I had one handgun in my holster, and grabbed another from the glove box of my car that I shoved in my boot. I ran as fast as I could. When I reached the house, the women were being loaded into the van. I waited until the vehicle left, and then I stormed the house through the back door. But I was too late. Amy was dead. The traffickers made an example of her to keep the other women terrified and obedient. They'd beheaded her."

"Oh, God, Carly. I'm so sorry."

Carly wiped across her face with the back of her hand, surprised to feel the wet tears streaming down her cheeks. Revealing this to Kaitlyn had freed a lot of memories Carly had tried to lock away. She'd never forgotten what happened to Amy. Recurring nightmares made sure of that.

"I heard a sound at the back of the house and withdrew my gun from my holster. They'd sent a man back to clean up. He pulled a knife on me and I shot him, killing him instantly. After an internal investigation, I was ordered to see a battery of shrinks. I soon left the Bureau." She paused for a second, and then added, "I never had a chance to wear the gown because the leader of the traffickers disappeared, but every time I see it, I remember the day I lost my best friend."

Grasping Carly's hand, Kaitlyn squeezed it and said, "I'm glad you told me about it, Carly. Thanks for trusting me."

CHAPTER NINE

Carly stood with Dr. Anderson and Brody outside the arched steel building where the FBI was holding Jim Ryder. SAC Sam Isley and two agents were inside fetching Ryder, to guide them to the spot where he buried victim Joy Marshall.

Only thirteen-years-old when she died, Joy was the apple of her father's eye, the only girl with four brothers. Her parents, farmers from Anderson, spent their life savings searching for Joy, hiring a private investigator when her case became cold, and their area law enforcement officers moved on to other cases. Their faith never wavered, even after five years had passed. They still believed they'd find their only daughter alive and well.

"I think that taking Ryder along is the worst mistake we could make." Brody crossed his arms over his chest.

"I agree," said Carly. "Unfortunately, it wasn't our decision to make. If Sam wants him along, then he goes."

"Do you believe he's telling the truth about where Joy

Marshall is buried?"

Dr. Anderson interrupted, "If Agent Black believes Ryder is telling the truth, then he is. She's a gifted interrogation analyst and hasn't let the Bureau down yet." He returned to his small office inside the building. Dr. Anderson had no interest in digging for one of Ryder's victims.

"There's always a first," Brody mumbled softly as he leaned toward Carly.

Soon one of the agents guarding the facility opened the heavy door and Sam Isley walked out, holding one of Jim Ryder's arms, while Sean Mahoney held the other. Agent Jon Finnelly took up the rear. All three agents, along with Carly, wore the standard-issue navy all-weather jackets with white FBI letters on the back. Ryder wore a bright orange cotton jumpsuit with a gray hooded sweatshirt.

Carly liked Sean, who was a young agent from one of the Chicago field offices. Over coffee, he'd shared he was a newlywed whose wife had recently discovered she was pregnant. He missed her terribly and spent every available moment on his cell phone talking with her.

They led Ryder, who was shackled, to the huge white Suburban Brody was leaning against. "Isley, do you think you could get a vehicle more conspicuous than this battleship? Why didn't you just have FBI painted in big black letters on its side?"

Isley shot him a don't-screw-with-me glare. "Would you prefer a caravan of multiple law enforcement vehicles with lights and sirens? That wouldn't attract attention, would it?"

Ryder laughed out loud at the bickering. "Nothing like a good pissing contest between law enforcement officers."

"Shut the hell up, Ryder, and get in," Brody growled as he opened the side door. "You're sitting in the second row. I'll be sitting right behind you, so please, try something. Like Clint Eastwood said in the old *Dirty Harry* movie, 'Make my day.'"

Both of the young agents helped Jim Ryder into the vehicle, letting him sit by the window, while Agent Jon Finnelly from the Minneapolis office sat down beside him. Finnelly was a beefy, humorless man in his early thirties, and Carly thought he must have drawn the shorter straw to have to share a seat with Ryder, who was not slender himself. Carly and Brody settled down in the last seat, while Sam Isley got in the driver position and Sean Mahoney claimed the passenger seat.

Ryder twisted his neck to look back at Carly and said, "Hope you two lovebirds can control yourself in the back seat."

"Turn around and keep your perverse thoughts to yourself," Carly hissed.

SAC Isley turned the ignition to start the vehicle, then drove the Suburban down the long country lane to the road. As soon as he could, he caught U.S. 136, heading east toward Hillsboro. Twenty-five minutes later, he turned the vehicle onto State Road 341, just outside of Hillsboro. The two-lane highway led them through miles of flat farmland, with periodic thickets of trees and wooded areas. Isley slowed the Suburban as they passed an area dense with towering white pines, hickory, and oak trees.

"Is this where you buried her, Ryder?"

"No, sir," said Ryder. "Go a bit further. This area looks familiar, so we can't be far. Go slow."

Keeping the speed around twenty-five miles per hour, Isley rolled forward. They soon came to an ancient graveyard. Most of the tombstones were so faded, one couldn't read the letters, or were knocked over from the elements or vandals.

Ryder shouted, "Stop! This is it."

"You buried her in a graveyard?" Brody asked. "That's original."

"Back up and turn onto the dirt road that winds around the cemetery. See the wooded area in the back? We enter the woods where there are three black cherry trees standing together."

Isley backed the vehicle up until he could turn onto the

dirt road. He stopped and the two agents prepared to get Ryder out. Isley rounded the Suburban and threw the keys to Sean. "You can drive back."

Carly gazed out her window at the small graveyard. There was only half of a metal fence left to guard the place, and it was crooked and dotted with rust. There were simple faded markers, cracked urns, damaged older headstones along with ornate statues. Many of the ancient gravestones leaned together like old stones. Leaves, vines, overgrown grass, moss, and debris blanketed the cemetery. No one had visited or cared for this place in a very long time.

Like a small insect, a chill crawled up Carly's spine, and a shiver of panic raced through her veins. Something didn't feel right. In her line of work, she relied on her gut instinct or intuition to stay alive. Right now it was sending her a warning, loud and clear. Becoming increasingly uneasy, she grabbed Brody's arm. "Don't get out. Something's very wrong. I feel it."

"Carly, what could go wrong? The only one of us not armed to his teeth is Ryder. C'mon, let's get this over with."

Carly hesitated for a second, but then let Brody help her out of the vehicle.

Ryder was arguing with the agents. "Take these shackles off. How am I supposed to lead you through the woods and show you where I buried her with these on? I can barely walk."

Isley gave the okay to remove his prisoner's shackles. "But his handcuffs stay on."

Finding the three black cherry trees, the group entered the woods. Ryder was in front with Sean Mahoney. Sam Isley and Jon Finnelly were in back of them, with Brody and Carly taking up the rear. Agent Finnelly carried a shovel and wore a backpack filled with smaller digging tools and a digital camera.

The branches of the taller trees created a canopy that faded the light and created new shadows and dark patches. The path was not well-traveled, and they found themselves tripping over vines and weeds crossing the trail.

"How do you think Ryder found this place?" Carly asked Brody.

"We're still in Shawnee County, so no doubt he found it while he was a deputy on patrol," Brody replied. "Who knows? The sick bastard may have buried the girl while on duty. The thought makes me want to rip his head off." His words were sudden, raw, and very angry.

The wind picked up, making Carly wish she'd worn something warmer than her FBI windbreaker. Climbing over a dead tree that had fallen over the path, she picked up the sweet, rancid odor of death. It was a smell she'd never get used to, and it still made her want to retch. If Ryder was telling the truth, and she still had her doubts, he buried Joy out here around five years ago. The odor of death would have ridden the wind until it faded away long ago. Soon she spotted a dead raccoon surrounded by vultures, and quickly looked the other way.

"Are we almost there?" Carly asked Ryder impatiently.

"Just a bit further. There's an old sycamore tree, the tallest I've ever seen, near the spot."

Ryder had relaxed and seemed to be enjoying the outing, much like a high school kid on a field trip. He turned her stomach. She'd rather be anywhere than here with a sociopathic serial killer, proudly showing off where he buried the body of a thirteen-year-old girl.

"Is that it?" Brody called out, pointing at a huge tree with mottled bark standing near a creek.

"Yes, just over the creek a ways."

Using large rocks as a bridge, they crossed the creek and soon came upon a clearing, where Ryder stopped the group. "This is it," he said. "I'm sure of it."

He pointed to a spot and Agent Finnelly started digging. Once he'd dug about four feet across and down, he wiped the sweat from his brow and asked Ryder, "This isn't the spot, is it?"

Looking upset, Ryder asked for the shovel, which

Finnelly refused to give to him, so he used his hands to dig a bit more. Finally, he stopped and said, "No, this isn't the spot. Try over there by that bramble patch."

"Oh, do you mean that bramble patch covered with fucking poison ivy?" Finnelly barked.

"I said it was *by* the patch, not on it," Ryder said, as Finnelly jabbed the shovel into the hard ground near the bramble patch, breaking up the dirt so it would be easier to shovel.

When Finnelly stopped to rest, Sean Mahoney took the shovel from him and dug deeper. He, too, stopped digging when the hole was close to four feet deep.

Sean eyed Ryder. "There's nothing here. Is she even buried in these woods?"

"No, she's here. I know this is the spot." Ryder fell to his knees and dug frantically with his hands.

"Isley, make him stop," said Brody, his hand resting on his gun.

"No, let him dig. He knows this place better than we do. Let him find her body."

Ryder clawed the earth for several minutes as the bored officers scanned their surroundings. Carly heard a sound like the grinding of metal against metal. Ryder leapt to his feet holding a handgun, dropping a metal box to the ground.

"Slowly hand me your gun, and then unlock my handcuffs," he demanded, pointing his gun at Sean Mahoney's chest.

Once his handcuffs were removed, and the agent's gun was shoved in his pocket, Ryder wrapped his arm around Sean's neck in a choke-hold, pressing the gun to his temple. Breathing hard from the digging, Sean started to tremble as he realized his life was in the hands of a mad man.

"Freeze!" Ryder shouted to the others. "Slowly take out your weapons and put them on the ground. Kick them toward me." Pulling a dirty duffle bag from the hole, he shoved it at Sean. "Get their guns. If anyone makes a move, Sean here gets a bullet. Got it?"

A war of emotion raged inside Carly's mind as she watched the other agents drop their weapons to the ground. A mix of fear and anger did a wild tangle inside her as she fought off the panic that threatened to emerge. He'd kill them. Ryder would kill all of them. In his mind, he had no choice; they stood in the way of his freedom. Which meant *she* had no choice but to fight back.

Pulling her handgun from her holster at her waist, Carly noticed Ryder's attention was fixed on Sam, Jon and Brody, who stood beside her. Slowly and deliberately, she bent to one knee to lay her weapon on the ground, and then slipped her hand up her boot to reach the small Smith & Wesson handgun in her ankle holster. Before she could pull it out, shots rang out. Ryder, now holding Sean's gun, shot both

Sam and Jon and they collapsed to the ground. Their blood sprayed onto her like she had been standing next to an exploding red paint can. She wiped her eyes so she could see. Protectively pushing in front of her, Brody was shot and flew backward on top of her, knocking the air out of her lungs and her handgun out of reach. Even with the adrenaline surging through her, she couldn't move Brody's dead weight off her body. Please, God, she prayed. Let Brody be alive. Please. Closing her eyes, she pretended to be dead.

Ryder called out, "Hope you're alive, Special Agent Stone, you fucking bitch. I still have a score to settle with you. This ain't over. Not even close."

Pushing Sean Mahoney in front of him, Ryder headed down the path from which they'd come, toward the Suburban parked near the graveyard. Once they reached the vehicle, he forced Sean to unlock his handcuffs. Then he shot Sean in the chest and left him lying near an ancient tombstone. Fishing the keys out of Sean's pocket, he jumped in the large SUV, fired up the engine, and headed north on State Road 341 for ten miles. Fighting the panic ready to explode within him, he drove the speed limit and nearly had a cardiac when a sheriff's patrol car raced past him just before he'd gotten to Mellott.

Soon he turned onto Monroe Road, then turned left

onto a gravel road that led to the old stone quarry. Parking the Suburban at the quarry's edge, he reached in the back seat and grabbed the duffle bag filled with weapons, opened the door, and placed it on the ground. He then pushed the gear to neutral, leapt out of the vehicle and ran to its rear where he grunted as he pushed the heavy vehicle until it fell off the edge, a straight-down drop to the deep water below. Peering over the edge, he watched until the Suburban sank to the bottom of the quarry's basin.

Throwing the duffle bag over his shoulder, he crossed the two-lane highway and entered a forest on the other side, and pushed deep into the woods heading toward the Smith-Cedar house.

Ryder had first discovered the old house by accident while a deputy on patrol two years or so before he was arrested. A passerby had called dispatch to report they'd seen a light inside the Smith-Cedar house on Monroe Road, out past the quarry where the kids swam all summer.

It wasn't an easy house to find. He'd driven past it two times before he realized it was located about a fourth of a mile off a dirt road, shielded by giant red cedar trees that lined the front of the property. Illuminated only by a full moon, the two-story, early 1800s Federal/early Republic style house was graced by five columns in front, six windows with dark shutters on the lower level, and eight on the upper.

Though it was in various stages of disrepair, thanks to a series of renters, the old house must have been a beauty in its day.

There were no vehicles on the property, or any other obvious signs of trespassers, but he was paid to check it out, so he retrieved his flashlight from the glove box, got out of the squad car, and checked the front door. Finding the door locked, he moved to one of the windows, flashing a light beam inside, but saw nothing but an old fireplace and papers littering the wooden floors. He rounded the house to the back and found the door there unlocked, so he went inside.

"Anyone here?" he called out, his words echoing through the house. Searching from room-to-room, he found nothing that suggested squatters — no sleeping bags, oil lamps, cans of food, or anything else required for impromptu living.

Squatters were common in Shawnee County during the recession, where more homes were foreclosed and deserted than he'd ever seen before. People moved into abandoned houses and called them their own, with some success if neighbors were scarce. Homes like this vacant house were prime pickings.

Checking the house room-by-room, Ryder entered a lower-level bedroom and tripped over something, landing face-first on the floor with a thud, knocking the air out of his lungs, and stirring up a cloud of dust that choked him once he started breathing again. Cursing between coughs, he pulled himself up and dusted off his uniform. He found his flashlight that had rolled across the floor when he fell, and searched for whatever had tripped him. Aiming his flashlight, he found a groove in the wooden floor that blended in so well that one would have to be looking for it to notice it. Fingering the groove, he lifted until he heard the squeaking of a hinge, as a 5' by 3' trapdoor opened to reveal an ancient wooden ladder leaning against a rough rock wall, perched on a dirt floor about 6' below him. Ryder swung the flashlight beam until it lit up the room below. Hesitant about putting his two-hundred-and-fifty pound weight on the ladder rungs, he tried the first one and it held. The third rung cracked as he stepped on it, so he decided to jump the three feet to the dirt floor below.

The room was empty, filled only with stale, mildewed air, and over a hundred years of dust. He walked the perimeter of the room with his fingers running over the coarse, rough rocks embedded in the walls. Hearing only the echoes of his footsteps, he moved to the wall opposite the ladder. Besides the ceiling being lower in this part of the room, there was something else. Fresh air seeped from the wall near the floor. On hands and knees, he discovered the large rocks in the wall were loose. One by one, he pulled out rocks and set them aside. Before long, he realized he'd discovered a hidden cave, or possibly a tunnel. Gripping his flashlight tightly in one hand, he crawled about six feet or so, then entered a long corridor, just tall enough for him to stand up to walk. Lining the walls of the tunnel were rusting lanterns. Jutting off the passageway was a catacomb of rooms, some the size of a closet, others much larger.

It was true what Ryder had heard at the library long ago. Surfing the Internet on his laptop, using the library's free Wi-Fi, and searching for young girls to seduce online, Ryder overheard a conversation two of the librarians were having. In the 1800s, the Smith-Cedar house provided food and shelter for hundreds of runaway slaves. However, neither librarian mentioned that beneath the house was a tunnel with a maze of rooms that hid the fugitives from bounty hunters and plantation owners.

Wondering where the tunnel would lead, he moved forward until he reached another cave. Crawling, he'd reached the end of the cave when the beam of his flashlight hit upon another trapdoor, this one above him. On his back, Ryder strained as he pushed until he dislodged whatever was preventing the hatch from opening. Emerging from the cave, he discovered he was in a wooded area, thick with trees, which undoubtedly, was the escape route for slaves who found refuge in the tunnels he'd just left. Circling the trapdoor was about a half-dozen paper birch trees, which probably served as a marker for fugitives coming from the opposite direction, searching for the house and safety.

Re-entering the cave and closing the trapdoor, he crawled until he reached the main corridor, then plopped down on the floor. He couldn't believe his luck. No one had lived in this house for years, and although the county wanted to purchase the home for a historic landmark, the money wasn't in the budget. It would take years to raise enough. Too bad, so sad. The place was perfect for his purposes. Perfect.

Ryder could house his teenaged slaves here, instead of the basement of his house, which was much more apt to be discovered by the law. The Smith-Cedar place would also be a perfect hideout should he need it.

He spent the weeks and months to come preparing the place for his purposes. Hiding canned foods in one room, he placed them in a corner and covered them with rocks. In another room, he dug a hole in the dirt floor to hide a sleeping bag, a coat with hat and gloves, and clothing in sealed plastic bags. He dug another hole large enough to hold a covered plastic bin filled with candles, matches, lamp oil and lamps. Still another plastic bin held bags of charcoal and a small portable grill he could use outside to grill small animals he'd hunt, as well as heat his coffee. Finding an old shed on the property, he bought an old Toyota with cash, stole a license plate for it, and parked it inside.

Ryder raced through the woods, constantly looking

over his shoulder, listening for police sirens. He hoped he'd been successful in killing all of them. If he had, he'd be ahead of them for days, if not months or years. They'd never find him in the tunnels of the Smith-Cedar house. Did anyone even know about the tunnels? He doubted it. The Master was back.

In the distance, he located the circle of paper birch trees where the trapdoor to the tunnels and his safety awaited.

Carly wiggled out from under Brody's heavy body and reached for his wrist. Thank God. He had a pulse and he was breathing. Wiping her hand across her forehead, she realized it was wet and sticky. It was blood! But whose blood? Was it blood from Sam and Jon? Had Brody been hit? Was she injured? Carly unbuttoned Brody's shirt and discovered he was wearing a Kevlar vest, so she looked for injuries in exposed areas like his face, neck, arms, and legs. No gunshot wounds appeared. He groaned and reached for her.

"Don't move, Brody," she said, still looking for injuries.

"The bullet hit my vest, hard as a fucking sledge hammer. It hurts like hell."

Carly helped him remove his vest, finding a darkening spot near his shoulder. A little higher and the bullet would have found its way to his neck, where the vest didn't cover, which could have killed him. Shuddering at the thought, she pulled him into her arms. They sat on the ground holding each other for a long time.

Finally Brody said, "Carly, it's okay, I'm fine. What about you? There's blood on your face."

"I'm fine. I have to check the others," Carly said, moving toward the two fallen agents next to them. Jon Finnelly was dead; blood had blossomed across his forehead and was drying around the bullet hole. Focusing her attention on Sam Isley, she found he had a very weak pulse and was barely breathing. "He's alive. But we have to get help!"

Brody searched for his cell phone. Finally finding it in his back pocket, he called Dispatch. "Officers down. Jim Ryder has escaped. We need backup. We're behind an old cemetery off State Road 341, just east of Hillsboro. We need help, and fast. Get the medical helicopter from I.U. Health in Lafayette. Get the closest deputies on patrol to close off the road. And put out a fucking BOLO on Ryder. He's heavily armed and dangerous. Driving a newer-model white Suburban."

He ended the call to dispatch and then called Cameron. "Ryder's escaped. Get the copter and come get Carly and me. We have to find him!"

"Are you okay? Is Carly?" Cameron asked.

"We're fine. I want to get us in the air as fast as we can to find that son of a bitch."

"Brody, I'm in Indy meeting with Wayne Griffin. I'm leaving now, but I'm an hour to an hour-and-a-half-away. I'll call Gabe."

"Cam says Brody and Carly are fine, but I need to see for myself. Those two have a bad habit of refusing medical help when they need it," Gabe said to Kaitlyn, who sat in the passenger seat beside him as the helicopter took to the air. He'd just picked up from school and was almost home when he got Cameron's call.

Pulling off the brunette wig Carly loaned her for a disguise, she replied, "They have to be okay. Where's the first aid kit?"

"It's on the seat behind you. I hope the medical copter beats us there. There were three federal agents with them who were shot. Don't know how serious their injuries are."

Soon the helicopter hovered above the cemetery. Four deputies were on the scene, light bars atop their vehicles flashing. Two more deputies had parked to block the road so both helicopters could land safely. The medical helicopter was nowhere in sight.

"There's Brody!" Kaitlyn cried out. Brody stood in the graveyard, waving his hands. Next to him, a man lay near a tombstone. She grabbed the first aid kit from the seat behind her and held it on her lap.

Gabe landed the helicopter on the highway, jumped out, and then joined Kaitlyn to run to his brother.

Reaching Brody, Gabe hugged him hard, then checked for himself to see if his brother had any injuries.

"Will you please stop it? I'm fine. But he's not." Brody pointed to the man beside him who was clearly unconscious, his head bleeding.

"He's wearing a Kevlar vest," said Gabe, as he examined the man.

Brody nodded. "I think Ryder shot him at short range. He may have hit his head on the way down. The impact could also have broken or cracked his ribs. He's still breathing. I just wish that medical helicopter from Lafayette would get here."

"Who is he?"

"Sean Mahoney. He's one of the agents assigned to the case. The other one, Jon Finnelly, didn't make it."

"Where's Carly?" Kaitlyn asked.

"She stayed with the special agent in charge, Sam Isley. He looks like he's hurt pretty bad. Follow the path through the woods. You'll find her. She needs that first aid kit you're holding. Please hurry. Look for a huge sycamore tree. Do you know what they look like?"

"Seriously, Brody? I'm a Hoosier, too. Of course I know what a sycamore tree looks like," Kaitlyn called back, as she entered the woods and followed the path.

Kaitlyn reached Carly, who was sitting on the ground cross-legged, holding an injured man who looked unconscious. The man lying next to him had turned a greenish-blue and was decidedly dead. Carly was covered with blood, making Kaitlyn wonder if she were injured, too, but didn't realize it, thanks to the adrenaline racing through her body.

"Kaitlyn!" Carly cried. "What are you doing here?"

"I came with Gabe in the copter. He's with Brody and an agent named Sean."

"Sean? Oh my God. Did Ryder kill him?" Carly asked, a tear trickling down her cheek. "Sean can't be dead. He and his wife are expecting a baby."

"He's not dead. Ryder's bullet hit his Kevlar vest. He's unconscious, but he's breathing." Kaitlyn sat down near Carly, putting her hand on her shoulder in a comforting gesture and whispered softly, "It's going to be okay, Carly. Are you sure you're not injured? You have a lot of blood on you."

"It's blood spray from Sam and Jon." Carly shook her head. "When Ryder started shooting, Brody got in front of me. He protected me."

"For Brody to lay his life on the line for you, he must love you more than his own life."

"I love Brody in the same way, Kaitlyn. I'd give my life to save his." Carly paused for a second, and then continued. "I don't want to think about not having Brody in my life. I've been such a fool, such a coward. I have something very important to tell him."

"There will be time. Just relax right now."

They heard the distinct roar of a helicopter, its whirling rotors sending trees and leaves into a frantic trembling. Help had arrived.

Ryder ate tuna on crackers and downed a couple of warm beers. Who knew killing federal agents would make him so hungry? He chuckled out loud. He knew he'd hit the sheriff in the chest, but what about his bitch ex-federal agent girlfriend? He'd fire up the old Toyota in a week or so and visit a gas station to find a newspaper. If Carly Stone wasn't dead, he'd find her and make her wish she was. Opening a green metal toolbox, he rifled through the disguise paraphernalia he'd purchased at a costume shop in

Indianapolis. In the toolbox were beards, mustaches, hairpieces, glasses, makeup, and hats that could make him look like a different man every day of the week if he wanted to. He'd travel about in a disguise, driving his old Toyota, and no one would be the wiser.

Opening the duffle bag filled with weapons, he peered inside. He had enough guns and ammunition to hold off an army if he was ever found. Ryder checked to make sure all his food and supplies were exactly where he'd left them, along with the burner cell phones he'd stored in an airtight plastic container. Instead of waiting to go into town, perhaps he'd give his favorite special agent a call to see if she was alive.

Brody, Carly, Gabe and Kaitlyn watched the medical helicopter until it disappeared from view.

"Do you think either of them will live?" Carly asked.

Brody let out a breath. "I think Sean will. He was conscious and talking when they loaded him into the copter."

"What about Sam?"

"Not sure. He's lost a lot of blood. We'll call the hospital later and check on them." Brody wrapped his arms around her. "Right now, I want to find Ryder."

Gabe headed toward the helicopter and fired it up as Kaitlyn, Carly, and Brody piled inside. From the air, they followed U.S. 136 east to Crawfordsville, then back west to Morel, and then east, following State Road 341 all the way to Newtown and back. Then they followed Interstate 74 east all the way to Indianapolis and back. Along the way, the tops of Shawnee County patrol cars, with flashing emergency strobe warning lights, could be seen as deputies searched the area for Ryder.

Brody phoned Cameron, putting him on speaker. "Call the media. I want Ryder's face on every television in the state."

"Will do. I'm at the cemetery and woods with the crime scene techs. Where are you?"

"We're with Gabe in the copter sweeping over the county's roads, highways and Interstate 74, looking for the Suburban."

"Don't you think he would have ditched that beast as soon as he could? Don't forget he was a cop. He knows every method we'll use to find him," said Cameron.

"I don't care what that bastard knows, I'm finding his evil ass," Brody vowed. "Get a list of every foreclosed and empty house in the area. I want deputies to search each one."

"Will do. Got to go. Bryan just arrived."

Brody was just about to end the call when he heard Cameron's voice. "Hey, wait a minute!"

"Yeah?"

"I've got a message from Seth Ziegler for Gabe. Tell him the gun used to shoot at Kaitlyn's house is an AK-47. A list of anyone in the county who owns one will be ready soon. Got one of my detectives working on it. If the Gamers shot at Kaitlyn's house, this list is a good lead."

"What about the necklace Destiny Cooke was wearing?" Gabe asked.

"Wayne Griffin, the detective from Indy, says the necklace belonged to Sharon Maud. He confirmed it with her mother, whose photo was inside the locket."

"Griffin was right," said Brody. "There *is* a connection between the prostitute murders in Indianapolis and the killings of Abby Reece and Destiny Cooke in Shawnee County."

"Find them," whispered Kaitlyn, wiping at a tear rolling down her cheek.

Brody said to Gabe, "Fly over any place you think Ryder might have ditched the Suburban."

"If I were Ryder, I'd push it over a ravine or into the Wabash River." Gabe grimaced. "Let's go to the river first, then I'll fly over the less-traveled country roads."

"I'll text Cam to get some deputies over to the cottages that line the river to find out if anyone saw anything." Brody pulled his cell out of his pocket.

"How many more hours do we have before we lose the light?" Carly asked.

Gabe narrowed his eyes on the equipment panel. "We've got maybe three more hours, but this copter is equipped with heat-seeking equipment that strips away the darkness."

Kaitlyn frowned. "What do you mean?"

"The system senses heat from the ground below, whether it be the heat radiating off sweaty suspects hiding in sheds, or beneath bridges. We're able to pinpoint the exact location on this monitor of all living things, or heat, thousands of feet below." Gabe said pointed to what looked like a small television screen.

"It saves thousands of man-hours, compared to our deputies doing a grid search," Brody chimed in. "It enables us to search an area effectively and quickly. If Ryder is down there on foot, we can direct our ground units to his exact location."

Evan wrote Destiny Cooke's name on a large white

label that he slapped on a plastic bin filled with her clothing and jewelry. He then placed it on top of a stack of bins nearby. They'd already scrubbed the floor with bleach and removed the sheets from the bed.

Glancing at Devan, who was sitting on a folding chair and opening his laptop, he said, "What are you doing?"

"What do you think I'm doing? I'm on the web looking for our next target."

"There's no need for that. I have our next target," Evan stated evenly, and then braced himself for what he knew would be an argument of epic proportions.

"What the fuck are you talking about?"

"Kaitlyn Reece is our next target," Evan said as forcefully as he could.

"No!" Devan shouted, his face reddening with anger. "We talked about this before."

"No, *you* talked about it," Evan insisted.

"What I say goes. Come over here and we'll find another target on Facebook."

"No!" For the first time, Evan went against his brother's wishes. "The target is Kaitlyn Reece!"

"What did you say to me?" Devan put the laptop aside, and rose from the chair, his fingers balled into fists.

"Bring it on! I'm not a kid you can boss around anymore, Devan. I'm as big and strong as you are. I have a say, or I'm out."

Surprised but still angry, Devan shoved his hands in his pockets and glared at his twin. "Why the hell are you so stuck on Kaitlyn Reece?"

"She's dating Gabe Chase. What better way to stick it to the sheriff and the private investigator at the same time?"

"Maybe . . ."

"You heard Dad at dinner last night. People are asking for Sheriff Chase's resignation. They were already angry with him because Ryder was one of his deputies. Our killing Abby Reece and Destiny Cooke has sent them over the edge. One more murder, and he'll be lucky if they don't lynch him."

"You've got a point. Maybe Kaitlyn Reece *should* be our next target."

It was the first time his brother had ever backed down, and Evan was elated. "We've got six hours until curfew. Let's wait until dark, then let the stalking begin."

Evan turned off the van's headlights as they neared Kaitlyn's house. He'd visited her house the day before in time to see a tow truck haul off Gabe's Dodge Ram, which was riddled with gunshots. The shattered windows of the house had already been replaced. There were no physical reminders of the night he shot at the house, but the memory and heady feeling of power would never be erased.

Passing the house, he noted a light on in the front room, but there were no vehicles in the driveway. Was Kaitlyn at home?

"That's her place?"

"Right."

"Where are you going?"

"Up ahead is a dirt road that leads to a cornfield. It runs through a thicket of trees where we can hide the van."

"How the hell do you know that?" Devan asked as he frowned at Evan.

Evan just shrugged his shoulders, turned the vehicle onto the dirt road, and parked when he reached the wooded area.

Leaning against the van, Evan pulled out an expensive pair of night vision binoculars.

"No way. Are those Dad's?"

"Yeah. So what?"

"Do you *want* to get grounded for the rest of your life?"

Ignoring his brother, Evan focused the binoculars on Kaitlyn's house. The curtains were closed, so nothing in the house's interior could be seen. Was she there?

"Let's see if her car is parked in the garage." Evan flicked on his flashlight and headed toward the cornfield in back of the property.

"What is that?" Devan asked, stopping his brother and pointing to something in some brush.

"I don't see anything."

"Give me the flashlight and I'll show you."

Evan handed it to him, and watched Devan move toward the brush, as he pointed the beam of light toward the ground. Soon he picked up a small object, holding it between two fingers.

"It's a bullet casing. Looks like the bullets Dad uses in his AK-47."

Trying to divert his attention, Evan said, "C'mon. Let's see if her car is in the garage."

"You lied to me."

"I don't know what you're talking about. Are you going with me to check out the garage or not?"

"You weren't shooting at rats the night you had Dad's AK-47. You were shooting at her house," Devan said, drilling his index finger into Evan's chest. "Have you completely lost every brain cell you ever had? How can you be so fucking stupid?"

"I'm not stupid!" Evan slapped Devan's hand away from his chest.

"After all the times you lectured me about forensics, quoting from all those investigation television shows you watch, you do this?"

"You don't know what you're talking about."

"This Kaitlyn bitch is dating Gabe Chase, right? You don't think he didn't call his brothers to get her house and this area checked out? Gee, depending on how many times you shot at her house, one of their CSI techs just might have found a bullet casing or two. What do you think, genius?"

CHAPTER TEN

Gabe flew along the Wabash River for miles, finding no sign of the Suburban or Ryder. With about an hour left of light, he searched the less-traveled country roads. The helicopter hovered over State Road 341 and then Gabe focused on the next two-lane side road called Monroe Road.

"Hey, look!" Gabe pointed to a body of water below them. "There's Dead Man Quarry!"

Below them a dozen or so people swam in the water, or were diving off the quarry's edge, dropping straight down into the aquamarine water.

"Why is it called 'Dead Man' Quarry?" Carly asked.

"One summer in the eighties, a college student dived into the old limestone quarry without checking the depth of the water first. Keep in mind, the depth changes based on how much rain we've gotten that particular year. Not much rain that year. He died instantly."

"Hover over it," said Brody. "The quarry would be a good place to dump the Suburban."

"We need divers, and Blake has a whole team of them," said Carly.

"Good idea. Please call Tim Brennan to see if he can loan them to us."

Gabe directed the helicopter further down Monroe Road until the roof of a large house with several out-buildings came into view.

"What's that place?" Carly asked. "It's practically hidden by trees."

"That's the Smith-Cedar House," said Kaitlyn. "It's a historic house that the county wants to buy. I heard about it from a friend of mine who is a librarian and historian."

"Does anyone live there?" asked Carly.

Kaitlyn shook her head. "Not for a long time. It was built in the early 1800s. It used to be a stopping place for runaway slaves. The Smith family provided them food and shelter."

Carly asked Gabe to circle the property, then said, "Look at all of the tall red cedar trees. I bet the house is difficult to see from the road. It's the perfect place for Ryder to hide."

"Maybe," said Brody, obviously discounting the idea. "But considering there are hundreds of empty, foreclosed homes in this area, I don't think it's very likely. But I'll have someone check it out."

Brody's cell phone sounded. Looking at the display, he noted the caller was Lane Hansen.

"Lane. I was just going to call you."

"Oh, yeah?"

"You undoubtedly heard that Ryder escaped. I wonder if you and your dog, Hunter, could help us search for him."

"I'd be glad to do that any day but today. My beautiful wife just gave birth to an eight pound, three ounce baby boy."

"Congratulations!" Brody said. "How is she doing? How's the baby?"

"Both parties are doing fine. We're naming him Tim after Sheriff Brennan, Frankie's uncle. His middle name is Lane."

"Thanks for calling. We could use good news like this today. Can't wait to see the new member of your family."

Brody ended the call and beamed at Carly. "Guess who had a baby?"

Carly applauded. "Did Frankie have a boy? She was convinced she was carrying a boy!"

Brody smiled and nodded.

"Frankie Douglas-Hansen?" Kaitlyn asked Carly.

"Yes, do you know her?"

"Frankie has been my hero and role model since I took her self-defense class. She was in her first trimester during our class, and said she and Lane were hoping for a little boy. I'm so happy for her."

Carly's cell phone vibrated in her pocket. An unfamiliar number popped up on the display.

"Hello."

"So you're alive after all."

"Ryder?" Carly asked, as Brody whipped around in his seat.

"I can't say I'm happy to hear you made it. Such a pity. But that's okay. I like setting goals. And snuffing out your life is a great goal for me to work toward. Believe me, Special Agent Stone. I'll get you. I dream about torturing and raping you. After that, you die, bitch."

Carly waited outside the elementary school where Kaitlyn taught. Driving one of the Shawnee County Sheriff vehicles, she parked in the lane where parents picked up their kids. A caravan of yellow school buses headed out, and she scanned the area for the white van they suspect the Gamers were driving, but didn't see one.

Weeks had gone by, and both Sam and Sean had been released from the hospital. Sean was taking some time off to spend with his pregnant wife, who was hysterical when she'd learned he'd been shot. There were rumors that he might leave his job. Special Agent in Charge Sam Isley was back at work at his headquarters in Indianapolis.

Jim Ryder remained free. Along with the sheriff's deputies, the FBI and U.S. Marshals searched for him without success. There was no sign of Ryder, and many speculated he'd left the state, or maybe even the country. In an episode of *America's Most Wanted,* John Walsh featured Ryder's crimes and escape. With this many law enforcement agencies hunting him, how could he not be found?

Carly wanted him caught before he killed again. It was only a matter of time. Serial killers didn't stop killing until they were caught or they died.

Even though deputies had found nothing when they searched the house, Carly hadn't given up the idea of Ryder using the old Smith-Cedar House on Monroe Road as a hideaway. Kaitlyn met with Constance Willoughby, the county librarian and historian, who had done the most research on the house.

Carly's passenger door opened, and a dark-haired woman slid onto the seat.

"Kaitlyn? I don't believe it. *I* didn't even recognize you in that wig."

"Sorry I'm a little late. I like to walk out with the kids as they head for their buses, so I can blend in a little."

"Good idea. Did you contact your friend at the library?"

"Yes, Mrs. Willoughby gave me a key to the house, a floor plan, and a copy of the land survey."

"Excellent!"

Kaitlyn adjusted her seatbelt and put her briefcase on the floorboard. "She told me there have been rumors for years that there are places in or beneath the house or in the surrounding woods where fugitive slaves hid. The historic society has never found any evidence of that, though."

"Those are the kind of places I'm interested in, areas where Ryder could hide."

"How would Jim Ryder even know about the Smith-

Cedar house?"

"I checked with Cam. Ryder patrolled Shawnee County for years as a deputy. It's very unlikely he would *not* know where the Smith-Cedar House is."

"Well, good. I hope he's there and we nab him."

Carly checked the rearview mirror to see if they were being followed. The nearest car was at least a half-mile away. "Kaitlyn, I'm not sure I'm comfortable taking you with me. What if Ryder *is* hiding there? You're in enough danger from the Gamers. I wouldn't be able to forgive myself if anything happened to you."

Kaitlyn reached for her briefcase, and then pulled out a mean-looking handgun. "I think Ryder is in more danger from *me*. After all, I was trained by Frankie Douglas-Hansen."

Carly took a quick breath of utter astonishment. "Don't underestimate Jim Ryder. I was there when he shot two federal agents and a county sheriff. He is very dangerous."

"There's no need to worry about me. I've been a regular at the sheriff's gun range since Frankie's class. I'm proficient at shooting a handgun, like this Glock G42, and a shotgun. I have a Remington 1100 gas-operated 12 gauge semi-automatic shotgun at home. I really like it. It has a softer kick than most shotguns." She paused for a moment to return her handgun to her briefcase. "I'm a very good shot, if I say so myself. I've got your back, Carly."

"Okay, I'm convinced. Just one more question. Does Gabe know what we're doing?"

Kaitlyn answered her question with a question. "Does Brody?"

"Not so much."

"Let's just say, Gabe might have the idea that we're having a meeting with Mrs. Willoughby, renowned county historian, at the public library."

"Kaitlyn, you're too much," said Carly, smiling as she donned her sunglasses. "You realize Gabe is going to have my head for taking you with me today."

"I won't let him. Besides I'm insisting you take me along. I have cabin fever big-time. In addition, I need some girlfriend time."

"Oh, yeah?"

"Carly, may I ask you a personal question?"

Carly tilted her brow, looking at her uncertainly. "I think so, as long as I have the option of asking you to put it in the vault. In other words, tell no one my answer."

"That goes without saying. What you told me about your friend, Amy, is still in the vault, and will never come out."

Carly turned the vehicle onto U.S. Route 136 and headed east. "Ask away."

"Have you ever been married?"

"No," answered Carly, clearly surprised by the question. "What about you?"

"I came very close to getting married."

"Why didn't you?"

"My groom impregnated one of my bridesmaids. Finding that out at the rehearsal dinner put a real damper on the ceremony."

Giving her passenger a sidelong glance of empathy, Carly said, "I'm sorry, Kaitlyn."

"Don't be. I can honestly say I'm no longer sorry Mitch and I didn't work out."

"Why do you say that?"

"If I'd married Mitch, I wouldn't have found Gabe." Kaitlyn wore a contented and happy expression on her face.

"Do you love him?"

"For longer than you would ever imagine."

Thirty minutes later, Carly parked alongside the old Smith-Cedar house and got out of the vehicle, as did Kaitlyn, who said, "The smell of fresh cedar in the air from these trees is incredible."

With the key to the house in her hand, Carly approached the front, with Kaitlyn close behind her. Reaching the front door, she withdrew her handgun and whispered, "Kaitlyn, keep your weapon pointed to the floor, and don't shoot unless we're in danger, and you absolutely have Ryder in your sight."

Kaitlyn nodded, pointing her Glock down and focusing on the front door as Carly turned the key in the lock.

Carly twisted the door handle to swing the door open. Scanning the entryway, she nodded to Kaitlyn, and moved inside. "Stay here while I clear the downstairs first, then we'll go upstairs."

Carly methodically cleared each of the rooms, then returned to the front entrance of the house. Motioning for Kaitlyn to follow her, they climbed the old stairs to the floor above them. Once they reached the top, Kaitlyn waited for Carly to return after she cleared the rooms on that level.

"All clear," said Carly, as she raced down the stairs.

Jim Ryder busied himself with conducting an inventory in one of the larger rooms that jutted off the tunnel. It was a place he affectionately referred to as "Carly's Room". It was here that Special Agent Stone would feel the slash of his whip across her body as she cried out for mercy. Mercy that he would never deliver. Not if his life depended on it.

Two large dog crates with padlocks were placed against the far wall. Next to them were a couple of plastic bins filled with handcuffs, men's belts, dog collars, two whips, a video camera, a folding tripod, and a couple of bondage and torture magazines he'd moved to his underground hideaway years before.

He admired the leather straps hanging from the ceiling. His penis throbbed with excitement as he imagined a naked Carly Stone dangling from her wrists as he snapped his whip again and again, ignoring her screams and cries for help.

He assembled the tripod and then fastened on the video camera. Rubbing his erection with his hand, he visualized beating and raping her again and again on the dirt floor. She'd come to realize his power over her. Carly would call him "Master."

It was then that he heard a sound. He rushed to the room where above him the trapdoor had been installed long ago. Barely breathing, he listened intently until a floorboard squeaked in protest. He heard voices in the house, mumbled words he could not make out. Someone was in the house! Hurrying to the small room where he kept the duffle bag filled with weapons, he pulled out a handgun, and then returned to stand under the trapdoor, his weapon poised and ready.

Shit, whoever was in the house was going from room-to-room. Who the fuck was up there? Was it the old biddies from the county historical association? If so, he wasn't worried they'd find the trapdoor. They hadn't found it before; why would they find it now?

Was it law enforcement? If it was, how carefully would they search the house?

Standing in the downstairs living room, Carly said, "There are no signs that anyone has been living here. There are fireplaces in most of the rooms. Let's check each of them for loose bricks and other signs it may be hiding some sort of entrance to the area beneath the house."

"Did you see a door to a basement?"

Placing her gun back in the holster at her waist, Carly said, "No. Why?"

"I find it odd that a house built in Indiana, even one over a hundred years old, would not have a basement to keep the family safe in inclement weather, like a tornado."

"Maybe there is an underground storm shelter in the backyard."

"I didn't see a shelter on the survey, but we'll look for one later."

"Besides the fireplaces, let's look closely at the floors. Look for anything that strikes you as odd. Maybe there is a trapdoor. It just makes sense that if the Smith family hid the slaves that came to them for help, the rumors may be true, and they hid them in rooms beneath the house."

"Let's get started."

One by one they checked each room for loose bricks in the fireplace, and examined the flooring for oddities. They had just entered the last room to inspect, when they heard footsteps coming from the front of the house. Both women withdrew their weapons and pressed against the wall on either side of the door. Carly sucked in a breath. The footfalls became louder, as the intruder came down the hall toward the room they were in. A man burst into the room and Carly yelled, "Freeze!"

Holding his hands in the air, an annoyed Brody Chase turned to face her.

Carly shoved her gun back into its holster. "Brody! You scared us to death. What are you doing here?"

"No, what are *you* doing here?"

Just then, Gabe walked into the room, sent Kaitlyn a fierce glare, and stood next to his brother.

"Gabe? You're here, too. Were you following us?" asked Kaitlyn.

"As luck would have it, I was in Brody's office telling him a curious thing I learned in the library where you said you and Carly were meeting with Mrs. Willoughby, librarian and county historian," Gabe began, clearly displeased. "It seems that Mrs. Willoughby left work at noon, and obviously had no meetings scheduled for the afternoon."

Brody interrupted, "Here's the rest of the story, and we're sticking to it. Gabe was in my office worried as to where Kaitlyn might be, when dispatch notified me that one of our deputies had spotted one of our vehicles parked in the driveway of the Smith-Cedar House. The dispatcher called me because the license plate number matched the vehicle that you'd checked out, Carly."

"I see," Carly nodded, her arms crossed defensively.

Brody looked around the room, and then back at Carly. "So what *are* you doing here? Why didn't you tell anyone where you would be?"

"We're checking the house for any signs of Jim Ryder. I still say this is the perfect place for him to hide. Mrs. Willoughby said there have been rumors for years that there are places in or beneath the house or in the surrounding woods where fugitive slaves were hidden by the Smith family."

"No kidding?" Brody's expression held a hint of a grin as he gazed at her. "If you don't mind some help, Gabe and I can go through the house and grounds with you. There is no one who would be more delighted to find Mr. Ryder and slap his ass back in jail than yours truly."

Brody followed Carly out of the room, while Gabe grasped Kaitlyn's hand to hold her back. "Please tell me you realize the danger you are in from the Gamers."

"Of course I do."

"Then why did you tell me a lie about what you were doing today?"

"I have a bad case of cabin fever. I had to get out of hiding, even for just an afternoon, before I went crazy. You had no reason to worry about me. Besides the fact I'm armed," she said as she showed him her Glock. "Carly is a former federal agent. Did you really think she wouldn't know how to protect me?"

Gabe pulled her into his arms. "Sorry, Cat. I know I'm being overprotective, and I can't seem to stop myself. But that doesn't excuse you from lying to me."

Several hours later, the four met at Carly's vehicle. They'd searched every room of the house, examining the fireplaces for loose bricks, and the floors for any indication of a trapdoor, and had found nothing. Next, they'd canvassed the perimeter of the grounds, including the woods, and came up with the same. They were headed toward an old shed on the property to search it when Brody got a call from Bradley Lucas, reminding him he was to give the Commission an update on the Gamer murders in an hour. They left convinced Jim Ryder wasn't on the property, and he probably never had been.

The next day, Gabe sat with Cam in Brody's conference room, munching on a turkey sandwich and chips. Carly entered the room, plopped some file folders on the table, and then retrieved a cardboard lunch box along with a bottle of sweet tea, and then joined them.

"Who else are we expecting?" asked Carly.

Washing his food down with a gulp of tea, Gabe answered, "Wayne Griffin from Indy will be here, along with Robynn Burton from the state police."

It was the first meeting of the Gamers Task Force, and Gabe was impatient to get started. If the postscript on their last email was true, the Gamers were targeting Kaitlyn as their next victim. She continued to dress in disguise, alternating between auburn and raven-colored wigs whenever she appeared in public. Each time he picked her up from school, he canvassed the area looking for a white van. So far, he'd seen nothing. That didn't mean the killers weren't there on foot, or watching from another vehicle. The Gamers weren't afraid of risk, as evident by the way they abducted Destiny Cooke outside the church where her state trooper fiancé waited inside. Gabe had no understanding how anyone could kill another human being for the thrill of it. He hoped Carly would provide more information on the psychology of what she called "thrill killers."

Detective Wayne Griffin entered the room with Brody and slid a plastic evidence bag across the table to Cameron. "Here's the locket for your evidence room. Every time I look at that thing, I think of Sharon Maud's mother when she opened it and saw her own photo inside. The woman broke down, and I couldn't calm her for at least twenty minutes."

"I'm so sorry she had to go through that," said Carly. Her dark eyes were gentle and understanding. She couldn't imagine having the gift of a daughter, only to lose her to a killer.

"Mrs. Maud and Sharon's three small children motivate me to do all I can to help you find these bastards."

It may have been wishful thinking, but Cameron imagined that Robynn Burton's dark green eyes searched for him as she entered the conference room, carrying a black leather briefcase. Her ebony hair pulled back into a long, sleek ponytail, she wore a gray suit that fit her curves like a glove. Her eyes narrowing on his face, Robynn smiled at him, and it was all he could do to hide his immediate arousal. What the hell was wrong with him?

Cameron held out the chair next to him, inhaling her sweet scent as she sat down. After he introduced her to the others, he led her to the food table, where she retrieved a boxed lunch and a bottle of water.

As soon as they sat down, Brody started the meeting. "Welcome to the first meeting of the Gamer Task Force. Our obvious end goal is identification and arrest of the killers of both Abby Reece and Destiny Cooke."

Wayne Griffin leaned forward and interrupted, "In addition, the same killers are linked to the murders of five prostitutes, all of whom frequented truck stops in Indianapolis."

"How did you come to that conclusion?" asked Robynn.

"The shoe found on Abby Reece belonged to one of my five victims, Sara Cassity. The locket placed on Destiny Cooke was owned by my victim Sharon Maud, whose mother had given it to her."

"Any DNA or fingerprints from the killers on these items?" Robynn leaned forward placing her elbows on the table.

"Unfortunately, not with the Indianapolis murders."

"But we were able to lift a print from a piece of the duct tape used on Destiny Cooke," added Cameron. "We ran the print through IAFIS, the FBI's integrated automated fingerprint identifier, but got no hits. Which means this particular perp doesn't have a criminal record. It does match the partial print we found on Abby Reece."

"Don't forget about the white van. I think it is an important link between the prostitute murders and the two in Shawnee County," Gabe quickly added.

Wayne threw his empty lunch box into the trash can and returned to his seat. "We noticed a 2012 Chevrolet 1500 utility van in a couple of our surveillance tapes of the truck stops. On the side of the van was a magnetic sign advertising a bakery. Unfortunately, the bakery listed on the sign had one of their magnetic signs stolen, and we couldn't make out the license plate in the tape."

"That doesn't sound like much of a lead, let alone a

connection," Robynn remarked. There were skeptical lines at the corners of her mouth.

Before Wayne could speak, Gabe pointed out, "I saw the same year and model of van in the surveillance taping of the parking lot of the Hoosier Bar and Grill where Abby Reece was last seen. Two men climbed into the van."

"We talked to the truck stop clerk working that day and showed him the surveillance tape. He remembered two men got out of the van wearing baker's uniforms underneath black hoodies. They came inside and bought Cokes. He didn't offer much of an I.D. He only got a quick look at one of the men. He said the one who paid for their items looked young, maybe even a teenager."

Robynn shook her head. "I'm still not seeing much of a connection."

Cameron pulled two pencil sketches out of one of his folders, but didn't share them with the others yet. "I met with the Hoosier Bar and Grill bartender who was on duty the last night Abby Reece was seen. When I showed him the surveillance tape, he immediately identified the two men heading toward the white van as the two who had fixed their attention on Abby that night. He confirmed they left the bar about thirty minutes prior to Abby."

"That still doesn't—"

"Let me finish," said Cameron to Robynn. "The

bartender also identified the men in baker's uniforms and black hoodies in the truck stop surveillance tape as being the same two men."

Carly pushed a strand of hair out of her eyes and leaned forward in her seat. "What did he guess to be their ages?"

"That's where it gets tricky. I asked the bartender what age he thought the two men were. He said he couldn't tell. He was obviously hedging, and getting more uncomfortable by the second. So I asked him if he carded the men. He was way too defensive when he told me he had."

"Which could mean he thought they were underage, but accepted their identification cards as real anyway."

Robynn pulled the sketch closer with her fingernail. "Are these your sketches of the two men?" Sliding them to the center of the table so the others could see, she turned to Cameron.

"They are the results of the descriptions he gave to our sketch artist."

"You sound skeptical."

"I am, Gabe. I'm not sure I trust that bartender to give the artist accurate impressions."

Carly glanced at the sketches. "Are you thinking he may have given the artist information to age each one?"

"Exactly. He was paranoid about getting caught

serving minors."

"But regardless, does anyone else think the two men look alike?" Carly looked around the table.

"I do." Robynn said and the others nodded in agreement.

"Well, I've got something to add to that." Wayne Griffin pulled a sketch out of his briefcase. "I compared your two drawings to the one our artist made after talking to the truck stop clerk. Keep in mind, the clerk only got a good look at one of the men. See what you think." He carefully positioned his drawing next to Cameron's in the center of the table.

"I wish the perp wasn't wearing the hoodie in your sketch," Gabe examined Wayne's sketch carefully. "We could get a better look at him."

"Wait." Carly pointed to the sketches. "Look at them closely. The bone structure is the same, as is the downward slant of the eyes, and thinness of the lips. See the high cheekbones in both sketches?"

"I agree." Wayne continued to compare the three drawings. "The only difference between the sketches is that in the ones provided by the bartender, the men look slightly older."

Brody looked at Cameron, his mouth thinning with displeasure. "Have one of your detectives visit this bartender, and ask him if he'd like to spend some time in the county jail for causing an unreasonable delay in our investigation by providing our sketch artist with false information. See if he'd like a second chance to work with the sketch artist again."

"Will do," promised Cameron, who began to type a text on his cell.

"Going back to the van," Robynn began. "Do you have anything else that ties the van to the murders here in Shawnee County?"

Searching his file folder for a moment, Wayne withdrew two photographs and slid them across the table to Robynn. "Our crime scene techs were able to cast tire prints from the areas where we found the bodies of Darla Green and Val Staley. As you can see from the two photos, the tire prints are identical. They're Goodyear Tracker 2 all-season tire P245/70R17. These types of tires are commonly used on utility vans."

"May I see those?" Cameron asked as he took out two photos which he placed next to the ones Wayne provided. He turned all four photos around so the others could see them. "As you can see, the tire prints we found at the church parking lot where Destiny Cooke was abducted, and the tire prints discovered near Kaitlyn Reece's home are a perfect match to the ones from Wayne's murders."

"Kaitlyn Reece is dead?" Robynn's eyebrows rose in surprise.

"No." Gabe shook his head. "Her house was shot at by someone with an AK-47 and those are the tire prints we found on a dirt road where I saw a white van fleeing the scene."

"Wouldn't you agree, Detective Burton, that the murders are linked?" asked Brody.

Robynn shrugged. "The tire prints may or may not link the two cases. Is it safe to assume this type of tire is used on other types of vehicles?"

"Unfortunately," Cameron responded. He rose from his seat and headed for the food table, where he poured himself a cup of hot coffee. Returning to the conference table, he asked, "Robynn, do you have any DNA results from the evidence I sent you for the state police crime lab?"

"I have a good friend at the lab who was able to rush your evidence through for me. You sent me the hair that was found on Abby Reece's body. It did not belong to her. You also sent the hair stuck to the duct tape that bound Destiny Cooke's wrists."

"Any DNA found?"

"Yes, each hair you sent was from a different male. The good thing is we now have DNA profiles for two different individuals. The bad thing is we ran them through

CODIS, the FBI's DNA database, and got no hits, so we still don't know who these males are."

"Damn it." Gabe cursed with frustration as he scrubbed his fingers through his hair. "I had really hoped—"

"Wait," Robynn interrupted. "There's more, and it's very interesting."

"You *did* find something?" She had Brody's full attention.

"Realizing that we have two possible killers, my friend ran it again using what is called PCR technology."

"What's that?" Cam lifted an eyebrow.

"PCR technology is DNA analysis that is usually applied to determine genetic family relationship such as maternity, paternity, sibling-ship, etc." Robynn said. "Our two males are siblings. Your killers are brothers."

In his bedroom, Devan worked intently on his laptop.

Evan, sitting on his bed, asked, "What are you doing?"

"I'm looking for another target since your precious Kaitlyn Reece has disappeared like a fucking ghost."

"Can't we give it a little more time?"

"Hell, no. It's been weeks, and I'm sick of trying to trail

someone we can't find. We're focusing someone else." Reading the disappointed expression on his twin's face, Devan added, "Listen, if she turns up, we'll get her. But for now, let's move on. We don't want our favorite sheriff to get lazy, do we?"

"I guess not."

"Come look at this babe."

Evan got off the bed and circled to the back of Devan's chair. "She's beautiful. Who is she?"

"Carly Stone."

"Why does that name sound familiar?"

"The other night at dinner, Dad was talking about her. She's the profiler the sheriff hired last year when they were searching for Jim Ryder."

"That's right. Dad said she is living with the sheriff."

"Which is why I looked her up on the Internet. The photo of her was taken last year when the sheriff did a news conference. She looks like a fucking Barbie doll."

"Better than that, it sounds like the sheriff has feelings for her. Just imagine how he'll react when he discovers her gone. Let the stalking begin. Hello, Carly Stone."

"I think the men who killed the prostitutes in

Indianapolis and the two coeds in Shawnee County are thrill killers who are very organized and careful to pre-plan their crimes. They identify and stalk their victims until they abduct and murder them. They do not necessarily suffer from a mental illness."

Brody grimaced and shook his head. "I have a problem agreeing with that statement. Who in his right mind would do something this evil?"

"I guess we can find out for sure when we catch them," said Gabe.

"Go on, Carly. This is interesting," Robynn urged.

"It is," added Wayne Griffin, who was pouring himself another glass of tea. "I've been waiting a long time to hear this profile."

Carly sipped her iced tea and then continued, "Thrill killers do not get sexual satisfaction from killing their victims. Usually they have nothing against them, and sometimes do not even know their victims. They are motivated by the sheer excitement of the act."

"Like that's not fucking sick," Brody remarked under his breath.

"Remember the Zodiac Killer in the late sixties in the San Francisco Bay area?" Carly began. "He once wrote a letter to the newspapers making a claim that killing gave him the more pleasure than sex. He even said, 'It's better than getting your rocks off with a girl.'"

"Were the Hillside Stranglers, Ken Bianchi, and Angelo Buono, considered 'thrill killers?'" Robynn was curious and intrigued at the same time.

"Yes. They took young women to Buono's home for the sole purpose of torturing and murdering them. Many times, they covered the women's heads with plastic bags until they passed out. Then, after they revived the women, the torture would continue."

Carly went to the whiteboard at the far end of the room to refer to notes she'd written before the meeting.

"We already know our killers are male," said Carly. "They are Caucasian, and in their late teens, as the truck stop clerk and all surveillance tapes have identified them. They are intelligent, good-looking, and charming. Both look harmless enough for our prostitutes to have trusted them to get into their vehicle."

"Besides our suspicions about the Hoosier Bar and Grill bartender, why do you think our killers are in their late teens?" asked Cameron.

"I read the autopsies of the prostitutes who were murdered. Each of them was abducted on a weekend and murdered when school was not in session. Both Abby Reece and Destiny Cooke were abducted on a Friday night," Carly answered. "Robynn, you look like you have a question."

"I do. I remember that most serial killers have a victim preference. For example, Ted Bundy preferred women with long, dark hair. Do you think our killers have a preference?"

"Yes. Though it rarely happens with serial killers, once our predators stopped killing in Indianapolis, they changed their victim selection process. No longer hunting women who work in high-risk occupations such as prostitution, they are now targeting beautiful and accomplished local women. Instead of luring the women into their vehicle with money, they are forcibly abducting their victims. They are no longer dumping their victims in rural areas; they are posing them in public places, where they will be discovered quickly."

"How do you think they are controlling their victims?" asked Wayne.

"Our killers are using Rohypnol, the date rape drug, to control their victims. The drug was found in the blood of several of the prostitutes during autopsy. In addition, Dr. Pittman found the presence of this drug in the bodies of Abby Reece and Destiny Cooke. If we could find out where someone in this area might get that drug, it might be the help we need to find our killers."

CHAPTER ELEVEN

"Good evening. My name is Carly Stone and I am a former federal agent. You may be wondering what I am doing at your second Self-Defense Class for Women here at the Morel Community Center."

Carly smiled at Kaitlyn, who had joined the group, wearing her dark wig disguise, then continued. "Your self-defense leader, Frankie Douglas-Hansen, recently gave birth to a beautiful baby boy. Frankie and baby are fine. Lane and daughter, Ashley, couldn't be happier." Carly paused again as Kaitlyn cheered. Soon the rest of the class joined her. Clearly, Frankie was popular with these women, which made Carly smile. Frankie had become one of her best friends, and she couldn't think of a better role model for the class. "I'll be teaching Frankie's class for a few weeks so she can rest and spend time with her little one."

"For tonight's class, I'll be giving you some ways to defend yourself from an attack."

A bulky woman in the last row raised her hand. "I have

a question. When are we going to discuss hand-to-hand combat? You know, kicking the attacker's ass." Most of the women in the class giggled, and turned around to look at her.

Biting her lip so the chuckle that was bubbling inside her wouldn't erupt, Carly answered her question seriously. "We will go into physical self-defense in class four. But keep in mind, using hand-to-hand combat is not your only line of defense. There are many other ways to keep yourself safe from attackers."

Carly paused for a moment to wait for the giggling to quiet down, then continued, "It may shock you to learn that according to statistics, every two minutes a woman in America is raped, and one out of four will be the victim of a violent crime. Some of you may think that's something that only happens to other people. And that's just the attitude predators want you to have. The more informed and prepared you are, the better the chance you'll be able to avoid an attack or defend yourself, if one should happen. That is what this class is all about."

"Each of you has a handout in front of you. Open it up and go to the back page. I've included six pages of blank paper for you to take notes. I encourage you to do that. This may be the most important class you ever take. The information you learn here will enable you to protect yourself. Taking notes will help you remember what you learn."

A woman sitting next to Kaitlyn raised her hand. Carly recognized her as a waitress from Mollie's café. "I've heard that jerks who attack women look for certain things before they make their move. Is that true?"

"Yes." Carly said nodded her head. "Just like predators in the wild, human predators have a mental process for choosing their victims. One of the things they favor is women wearing a ponytail or braid because it can be easily grabbed. Clothing on women that predators prefer are short skirts, which can be easy for them to remove or push up, or anything with straps, like a camisole, that can be cut."

Carly turned to write on the whiteboard behind her with a black marker. She wrote "Don't look like a victim." Facing the class again, she was pleased to see most of the women taking notes.

"When you are out in public, don't look like a victim. Try to stay in areas with more people, and walk with a purpose, with confidence. Predators go after the weak, so make sure your facial expression says, 'Don't mess with me.'"

On the whiteboard, Carly wrote "Always be aware of your surroundings."

"That means don't allow technology to distract you. One thing I hate to see is a woman jogging, listening to her iPod, seemingly lost in the music. Please don't do this. Pay attention at all times to what is going on around you. Don't talk on your cell or listen to your iPod when you're alone in a public place. Do a three-hundred-and-sixty-degree assessment. Know who is in your immediate vicinity at all times."

The waitress raised her hand to ask another question. "I usually get off work late at night. Would you please talk a bit about car safety?"

"Absolutely," Carly said. "Predators target places where you park your car, during the daytime as well as at night. One thing you should do to proactively protect yourself is to have your keys in your hand." She picked up her own keys. "I like to thread each key between my fingers like this, so my keys become a weapon if needed. Take out your keys and try this."

Carly watched as each woman pulled out her keys and placed a key between each finger like she had. No wonder Frankie liked teaching this class. The women were so eager to learn that it was motivating. The thought that she was giving them ideas and techniques to keep them safe made her feel wonderful.

"Don't unlock your car until you are close to it. If you unlock your car doors from across the parking lot, you risk an attacker hopping inside without you noticing. If you see a van is parked on the driver's side of your car, get in on the passenger side. Once you're inside your car, start driving.

Many women have been attacked by sitting in their car too long and giving a predator a chance to make his move."

"I don't understand how sitting in your car can do that," said a woman in the back row.

"Let me tell you a story about a friend of mine who had a stressful job and two small children that she took to a daycare before work. Arriving every morning at her office building, she'd pull into the parking garage, park, and roll down her window for some fresh air. She'd read her paper for an hour prior to her work shift as she sipped the latte she'd purchased from a Starbucks drive-thru on her route to work. It became her pre-work ritual.

"One morning as she read her paper, she noticed a car pull into a space down the row from her. She didn't think anything of it, because there were many businesses located in the building, with people working different shifts. Without warning, a man appeared at the driver's side of her car. Before she could react and roll up her window, he had her in a choke hold. He strangled her until she was unconscious. By the time, she regained consciousness, she was lying on the back seat of her attacker's car. Luckily for her, the attacker could not get his car started. When he got out and pulled open the hood to check the engine, she climbed into the front seat and locked all the doors. Then she blared the car horn and wouldn't stop even as he cried and begged her to open the door. Soon another car appeared, and her attacker ran from the scene. We were able to arrest him later at his apartment just a couple of miles from the building."

"Does she still do her pre-work ritual?"

"No way," Carly responded. "She still arrives an hour early, but now does her newspaper reading at her desk in her office."

Glancing at the clock, Carly said, "Thank you so much for participating in tonight's class. Next week we will discuss how to identify dangerous and controlling behavior from a predator. See you then."

As the women left the classroom, Kaitlyn stayed behind and helped Carly gather unused handouts.

"Kaitlyn, do you need a ride home? I'm parked in back," said Carly, as she pushed chairs under tables.

"Not tonight. Gabe is waiting for me in the front of the building." She gave Carly a warm hug and left.

Carly didn't realize how dark the parking area would be at night until she exited through the back rear door. The community center was in desperate need of security lights, and surveillance cameras wouldn't hurt. Scanning the lot, she noted a couple of empty vehicles and hurried to her SUV.

With keys in hand, she'd almost made it to her car

when she twisted her ankle in a pot hole, dropped her keys, and tumbled to the ground. Something hard bashed against her head, sending a lightning flash of pain against her eyes.

Grasping her gym bag, she leapt to her feet and swung it to hit her attacker. He deflected the blow and punched her as hard as he could with his fist. Agonizing pain ripped through her face and she was sure her nose and possibly her cheekbone were broken. Blood flooded from her nose. A stun gun appeared out of nowhere, jabbing her on the neck, giving her a brutal jolt. Her entire body started jerking with agony as spasms racked her muscles. Her legs crumpled from under her, and her vision pixeled into a million black squares as she struggled to stay conscious.

Her attacker lifted her easily and dropped her into the trunk of a car. Getting a glimpse of his profile, she strained to focus on his face. Although he wore a fake beard and a ball cap, the face of her attacker was one she'd never forget. Jim Ryder! Carly gasped as sheer black fright swept through her as he slammed the trunk closed and left her in darkness.

"Jesus, Devan. How long have we been waiting? Are you sure Carly Stone is teaching the self-defense class you saw in the paper?" Evan asked, impatiently tapping his fingers on the steering wheel. He unzipped the coveralls that Devan had ordered online with their names embroidered on them.

"Yes, I'm sure." Devan's face reddened and a vein near his eye throbbed noticeably as a hint of his volatile temper made itself known. "I called the community center and asked. Besides, genius, that's her car parked up by the door."

"It's nine o'clock. Shouldn't the class have ended by now?" Evan watched a late-model Toyota pull into the lot and park next to Carly Stone's car. "Fucking great. Just what we need — a witness. Maybe we should abort."

"God, Evan, quit your whining. If the car is still there when she comes out, we'll follow Stone until we can grab her. You know the drill."

Four women emerged from the community center, piled into a Honda Pilot, and then drove out of the parking lot, disappearing once they turned onto the street in front of the building.

Soon a woman in sweats with long, dark hair walked out of the building.

"That's her!" Devan squealed excitedly. "That's Carly Stone!"

A bearded man wearing a ball cap slipped out of the Toyota and ran toward Carly Stone.

"Who in the hell is that?" asked Evan.

"I don't know, but I've seen the guy before. I swear."

"Oh my God," Evan said. "Did you see that? Did you see how hard he hit her? Man, he had to have broken bones with that punch."

"Oh, shit. He's got a stun gun. She's toast."

They watched as the man picked up Carly, throwing her over his shoulder, and carrying her body fireman style to his Toyota.

"He's putting Carly Stone in his trunk. What the hell?" gasped Evan. "Who is that guy? What do we do?"

Devan studied the man in the ball cap as he picked up Carly Stone's gym bag and threw it into the back seat of his car. "You're not going to believe this, but that's Jim Ryder."

"That's such bullshit, Devan. Why would a man who is being hunted by every law enforcement agency known to man risk his safety to drive into Morel? Everyone in this county knows what Ryder looks like, as does the rest of the nation's television news viewers."

He shot a heated glare at his brother, his hand clenched into a fist. "The beard is fake and he's trying to cover his face with the ball cap. I'm telling you, that's Jim Ryder."

"He's backing up the Toyota. What do we do?"

"Follow him, Evan. Carly Stone is *our* target. He's past news. This is our Game, and we make the rules. Jim Ryder has no place in the Game. Who in the hell does he think he is messing with our next target? Start the van and get behind him. Let's see where he's headed."

"How was self-defense class?" Gabe asked after he kissed Kaitlyn soundly on the lips.

"I think I have a new hero. Carly is amazing. She has such good stories about what women can do to save themselves in dangerous situations."

He drove the truck out of town, continually looking in the rear-view mirror to make sure they weren't being followed. Soon he turned onto a two-lane highway toward home.

Suddenly Kaitlyn screamed. A rusting old Ford truck had stopped and was idling in their lane. Gabe slammed on the brakes, sending the truck into a tailspin in the middle of the road, and finally stopped inches before the onset of a deep ravine on the other side. Cursing, Gabe checked on Kaitlyn. "Are you okay, Cat?"

"Yes," she gasped, her heart racing. "What kind of idiot parks his truck on the road like that?"

Gabe leapt out of his truck just in time to see the old Ford truck racing down the road.

Getting back into his truck, Gabe said, "I should chase

him down and kick his ass." Shoving the gear into reverse, he backed the truck onto the road.

"No! Stop!" Kaitlyn shouted. "There is a box in the middle of the road. He put something in the road." She started to get out of the truck, but Gabe grabbed her arm.

"It may be a trick. The driver may have put that box in the road to stop us and is circling back. Stay in the truck and lock the doors. I'll move the box."

Getting out of the truck, Gabe saw the lights of an oncoming vehicle. He sprinted toward the box, praying he could reach it before it was hit and possibly caused an accident. Going too fast to stop, the car raced past the box and Gabe, its horn blaring into the night.

Once Gabe got closer to the box, he realized it was a white cardboard box with a lid, the kind of box computer paper was packed in. Inching closer, he heard a yelp, then whimpering. He pulled off the lid and looked inside to find a puppy, which was wagging his tail as if to say "glad you found me." Running his hand down the silky fur of the puppy's back, he said, "Who in the hell would leave you in the middle of the road like this?"

Picking up the puppy, he kicked the box to the side of the road and hurried toward the truck. Getting inside, he flicked on the interior light as he held its warm body to his chest, and felt the brown puppy's legs for injuries. When he touched its back leg, the puppy yelped with pain. The bastard who hurt this puppy was lucky to have gotten away.

Mouth open, her eyes wide with surprise, Kaitlyn said, "This puppy was in the box? Who could be so cruel and evil as to leave a helpless puppy in the middle of a two-lane road at night in a box? If we hadn't stopped. . ." She shuddered at the thought of the animal's fate had they not come along.

"Honey, hold it so I can drive. Be careful. I think his or her right back leg is broken."

Kaitlyn opened her arms, accepting the whimpering puppy from Gabe, stroking its soft fur as she cuddled it.

Gabe pulled out his cell and punched in a number. "Hello. This is Gabe Chase. How late are you going to be open? Can you wait for me to get there? I'm maybe twenty minutes away. I have an injured puppy. Thank you." He ended the call and looked at Kaitlyn.

"I know a vet not far from here. Charlotte was good friends with my mom. She is closing for the day, but is willing to wait for us."

A light was still glowing in the front window of the small, one-story building that housed Charlotte's Vet Clinic. Gabe followed Kaitlyn as she rushed into the reception area with the tiny puppy in her arms.

Hearing them arrive, Charlotte, a petite woman in her fifties with a shock of white hair, came into the waiting area to greet them. Hugging Gabe, she said, "It's so good to see you. What a handsome man you've become. And who is this beautiful young lady?"

"Charlotte, this is Kaitlyn Reece. The puppy she's holding may have a broken leg."

"Let's get our patient into this exam room so I can take a look."

Following her into the exam room, Kaitlyn lay the puppy on the aluminum table, keeping her hand on its back so it wouldn't fall to the floor. The puppy gazed up at her with a flicker of adoration in its dark eyes.

"Good-looking puppy," said Charlotte, as she stroked its head and looked her over. "Looks like this little girl is a chocolate Lab." Gently lifting the puppy, she carefully examined each of its legs. It shrieked with pain as she probed one of its hind legs.

"Is it broken?" Gabe asked.

"Sure is. I'm going to have to get an x-ray before I can do anything else," Charlotte glanced at the two of them. "Who does the puppy belong to?"

"Me!" Gabe and Kaitlyn said in unison, then looked at each other with surprise.

Laughing softly, Charlotte carried the puppy to the treatment area in the back of the building, leaving Gabe and Kaitlyn alone.

Gabe was the first to speak. "I didn't know you were an animal lover."

"And I didn't know *you* were," Kaitlyn returned. "Listen I know I am in no situation to adopt a puppy. My head tells me I can't even live in my own home because it's too dangerous. I wouldn't want her to be in danger with me. But my heart tells me that I already love her."

"Since I want her, too, there are a couple of things we could do," Gabe began, pulling a coin out of his pocket. "We could flip a coin for her. Or we could adopt her together. Of course, if we did that, we'd be making a lifetime commitment to the puppy."

"And to each other," interrupted Kaitlyn.

"That's a serious step. Are you ready for that kind of commitment, Cat?"

"Are you?"

"Honey, I've been ready since the second grade."

She roped her arms around his neck, feeling his warm breath fanning her face seconds before his lips touched hers. God, she adored this man. Weaving her fingers into his thick hair, she deepened the kiss as he folded his muscular arms around her waist.

"Excuse me," Charlotte cleared her throat and placed the puppy back on the examining table. "She has a minor fracture, so I'm going to put a cast on her leg and she'll be good to go. I forgot to ask you. What's her name?"

Before Gabe could think of a name, Kaitlyn called out, "Godiva! She's a chocolate Lab, and we named her after my favorite chocolate."

Evan stayed two cars behind Ryder's Toyota as he headed east on U.S. Route 136. "I hope he stops soon. We're low on gas."

"Just stay behind him. If he doesn't stop the Toyota soon, we'll run him off the road if we have to."

"Think she's alive?"

"Who?"

"Carly Stone."

"Why wouldn't she be?"

"Her body really looked limp when he dropped her into the trunk," said Evan.

"I have no idea how the hell you get such good grades. How many times have we used a stun gun on a target? And how limp are they after the electric shock?"

"Shut up, Devan. What if he poked her too many times with it? What if she hit her head when he dropped her into the trunk?"

"What if I sprout wings and fly out of the van? She's okay, Evan. If she's not, then Ryder goes down, and we collect the $20,000 reward money. Actually, that's not such a bad idea. I say we do both."

"Are you completely crazy?"

"Crazy as a fox. We incapacitate Ryder, then wrap his mouth, wrists and ankles with duct tape, just like we do with our targets. Once we get him into the back of the van, you inject him with Rohypnol."

"You're kidding. Right?"

"No, I'm not. Once Ryder is taken care of, we get Carly Stone out of the trunk and do the same with her. Then we take Stone to the storage unit and secure her to the bed. We drive to the sheriff's office and turn Ryder over to them. Collect the reward. Easy."

Frowning, Brody looked at his cell phone. There were no calls or texts from Carly. He'd been waiting at least thirty minutes at the new Morel Steakhouse, where they had agreed to meet after her class.

Punching her number into his cell, he let it ring until

her voicemail came on. "Carly, give me a call. I'm at the steakhouse."

The more he thought about it, the more concerned he became. It was out of character for her to be this late. It also wasn't like Carly to not answer her phone. He threw a ten dollar bill on the table for his drink, and strode to the restaurant exit door. Once he reached his SUV, he jumped inside and drove to the community center where Carly was scheduled to teach Frankie Hansen's self-defense class.

Driving into the parking lot in back of the community center, he immediately noticed Carly's car parked near the back door. Flooding the area with light from his headlights, he got out of his vehicle and headed to the back door, thinking Carly may have stayed late with a student. Both doors were locked. He pounded on the glass, but no one came to the door.

Brody was heading back to his SUV when he spotted something glistening on the ground near Carly's car. Picking up Carly's car keys, he noticed the gravel was in disarray as if a scuffle had ensued near her car. Bending down, he plucked a couple of pieces of gravel up. Holding them in the light in the palm of his hand, his heart froze as he noticed small drops of blood.

Rushing to his vehicle, he pulled out his cell phone and called Gabe.

"Are you with Kaitlyn?"

"Yes, she's sitting right next to me. What's wrong, Brody?"

"Put me on speaker." He paused for a moment, and then continued. "I'm at the community center. Carly's car is parked in back, but she's not here."

"Oh no," Kaitlyn said fearfully. "Carly asked me if I needed a ride. I turned her down because Gabe was waiting for me in front of the building."

"What time was that?"

"It was about nine-fifteen," Kaitlyn replied.

Brody sent a text to Cameron, and then called him. "Cam, Carly is missing. She did a class at the community center, but it ended at nine. Her car is in the parking lot, and there are signs of a struggle."

"What can I do to help?"

"I just sent you her cell phone number. Her cell has GPS. Track her and tell me where she is."

"Will do. I need a few minutes. I'll call you back."

Brody ended the call, leaned back against his seat, and took a deep breath to calm himself. Carly cannot be missing. She cannot. What will I do if anything happens to her?

His mind went back to the first time he saw her swimming nude in her Florida swimming pool. He knew then he had to have her. Then later when they made love in the Honeymoon Cottage, he realized he needed her in his life.

His cell vibrated. "Cam?"

"Got a location. Just got a ping off the cell tower where U.S. Route 41, U.S. Route 136, and Interstate 74 intersect. It's near Veedersburg.

"Leaving now. Stay with her. Let me know if there is a change in direction."

Flipping on the light bar and siren, Brody floored the accelerator and raced out of the parking lot.

Carly willed her arms and legs to move. She felt drained, as if she were recovering from a bad case of the flu. Wiping the blood from under her nose, she assessed her injuries. On fire, her face painfully throbbed with each beat of her heart, and she was certain her nose was broken. One of her eyes was swollen shut, and she strained to see in the inky darkness of the trunk. She inhaled a mix of rust, oil and gasoline. The trunk was filthy, and the heat had her body slick with sweat.

All that meant nothing now. She had to find a way to get out of Ryder's trunk. Running her hands across the back of the trunk, she didn't stop until she felt the inside of the latch. Wiping the sweat out of her eyes with the back of her hand, she searched for the glow-in-the-dark trunk-release lever mounted in all cars since 2002. It was usually installed near the trunk latch, but she couldn't find it there. Nearly crying out loud with frustration, she realized Ryder's car must be older than a 2002 model. Just her luck. Who was she kidding? The car was probably going more than fifty miles-per-hour. What good would opening the trunk do her now? She wasn't desperate enough to jump out of a car going that fast.

She lay still for a moment and monitored her breathing. Biting her lip until it hurt, she reminded herself that breathing naturally was the key to her survival. Hyperventilating meant death.

Closing her eyes, Carly slowed her breathing, and prayed to God that He would help her survive so she could see Brody again. How could she have been such an idiot to put him off? She'd marry Brody in a second if she could just escape the certain death Ryder promised her.

Brody clicked the button for speaker and then placed his cell phone on the console of his SUV. "I'm almost to Veedersburg, Cam. Where is she on the GPS?"

"Got a ping from the cell tower just outside Veedersburg. They're still heading East on U.S. Route 136. The car she's in has passed the U.S. 41 and 136 intersection."

Frustrated and panicking, Brody pounded the steering wheel with his fists. "That intersection is at least three miles up the road. What if I'm too late?"

"Don't talk like that, Brody. The vehicle is still moving. The bastard can't hurt her and drive at the same time."

Pressing the accelerator to the floor, he increased his speed to sixty-five miles-per-hour, which was careless and dangerous on the two-lane highway. He didn't care. If he didn't get to Carly in time, nothing in his life would matter. "You talk like you think it's Ryder who has her."

"Who else hates her as much as he does? He as much as promised to come back for her."

"What if it's the Gamers and they have her in the back of their white van? One of them could be driving, while the other one in the back could be doing who knows what to her?" His gut clenched with one of his intuitions that never foretold anything good.

"Brody, please calm down. You can't think like that. I sent patrols out in the car's vicinity. You may see one of them soon. I've got them coming at the car in both directions on 136."

"How are the deputies going to be able to tell which

vehicle she's in?"

"They're looking for a car with stolen license plates, or one going unusually fast or slow," said Cam. "You should see Gabe soon. He and Kaitlyn are in the chopper flying over U.S. Route 136."

Brody's heart slammed against his chest. "Dammit, Cam. Tell him not to get too far ahead of me. If Ryder sees the copter, he might do something stupid. Same goes for the Gamers."

"Gabe knows that. Come on, Brody. Calm down. Look up. Do you see the helicopter?"

A long pause followed, and then Brody said, "There it is. I see the lights. He's right over my SUV. Cam, I'm disconnecting the call. I just thought of something and need to call Gabe."

Pressing a couple of buttons on his cell, he soon heard Gabe's voice as he answered.

"Brody, how fast are you going? Slow the hell down. You can't drive that fast on a two-lane highway! Please, Brody. Slow down, there's a curve ahead!"

Brody slammed on the brakes and the SUV nearly fishtailed as he approached the curve. He rode it out until the road straightened, then pressed on the accelerator again.

His heart now slamming against his chest, and

breathless, he said, "Gabe, I have a question about your thermal imaging equipment. I think Ryder may have Carly in the trunk of his car. There's no way he'd allow her to sit in front with him if she's conscious. Is your thermal imaging equipment able to detect a body in a car's trunk if you were flying overhead?"

"I wouldn't be able to see something distinct like the outline of a body, but the system would pick up heat coming from the trunk area if the person is alive." Realizing what he'd just indicated, Gabe said, "I'm so sorry. That came out wrong. Carly is *not* dead. Do you hear me? There is no way she's not alive. She's a former federal agent who knows how to protect herself."

"Forget it. Just fly ahead and keep in touch with Cam. He's tracking her with GPS. Get close enough to the cars on the highway to focus on their trunks. If Ryder has Carly, I think that's where she'd be. Don't get too low or stay low for long, Gabe. I don't want Ryder to spot you and do something stupid that might endanger Carly."

"Will do."

With lights swirling and siren blaring, Brody's tires squealed as he took the turn at Veedersburg to get to the U.S. Route 41 and 136 intersection.

"Carly, dear. How are you doing back there in the

trunk?" Ryder called out.

Her body stiffening at the sound of his voice, she gritted her teeth and said nothing.

"We'll be home soon. What plans I have for you. I'm getting more excited by the minute."

"Go straight to hell, Ryder!" Carly shouted, fiery anger burning through her veins.

"Now, Carly, is that any way to talk to me?" Ryder said, her reaction amusing him. "I bet you're curious as to what events I have planned for you. First, in the special room I named after you, I'm going to strip you naked. Next, I'll hang you from leather straps and use my whip on you until you bleed and beg for mercy. And then, Special Agent Stone, that's when the real fun begins."

Knowing she needed a clear head, Carly fought back the anger and focused on what she needed to do to escape. Sweeping her fingers past the latch, she focused on a plastic corner panel covering the back side of the brake lights. She might be hesitant to jump out of the trunk of a moving car, but she had no problem pushing out the brake lights. She'd wave her hand through it to gain the attention of any cars behind her, or better yet, get Ryder's car pulled over by the police for a faulty brake or tail light.

Twisting her body, she kicked at the panel until she heard the plastic crack, and then turned around so she could reach it again. Wedging her fingers inside, she pulled until the panel came off, and then pushed it aside. Ripping the wires out, she kicked the lights through so that they fell off the vehicle and bounced on the highway. Beams of light streamed through the hole, piercing the darkness inside the trunk. There was someone driving behind Ryder's car. Carly stuck her hand out through the hole, waving frantically to get the attention of the motorist behind them.

"I mean it, Evan. Slow the hell down! Back off before Ryder sees us behind him and gets suspicious."

Devan ripped off his painter's cap and threw it on the console. Running the back of his hand across his damp brow, he partially unzipped the painter's coverall he was wearing.

"Sorry. I zoned out for a minute. Didn't realize how close I was to his car. I'm not used to driving so slow." Evan pulled off his painter's cap, too, and wished they'd had the van's air conditioner fixed. Their father had been hounding them to fix it for a week. He rolled down his window for some fresh air.

"Ryder's driving the speed limit. The last thing he needs is to draw attention to himself."

"Did you see that?"

"What?"

"The plastic cover on his back lights just flew off." Evan began laughing. "Look! Carly Stone is waving her hand through the hole where the brake light used to be!"

"Brody!" Gabe said excitedly. "I think I found her. Just hovered over what looks like a Toyota or Mazda. There is heat emanating from the trunk. There's definitely someone locked inside. Besides the white van behind it, the car is the only one on the road for miles."

"Stay with the car, but do what you can to make sure Ryder doesn't notice you."

"No problem. The car's approaching the 136 and 341 intersection in Hillsboro."

"Let me know if it turns."

"It's turning and is now heading north on U.S. Route 341."

"Okay, thanks."

"Wait a minute. The van is turning to go in the same direction."

"Got it. Keep an eye on both vehicles."

Turning the van onto 341 to follow Ryder, Evan said,

"Damn him. Where is he going? Look how low our gas gauge is."

"He's been missing for weeks. Ryder must have a hideout. How else could he have avoided capture for so long? Keep following him until he either slows down, or we run out of gas."

"Devan, if he doesn't do something soon to give us an opening—"

"Okay, okay. Let me think." Several minutes passed before Devan said, "I've got two ideas."

"Let's hear them, and make it fast."

"We could ram his car with the van—"

"No way," interrupted Evan. "He could spin out and land upside-down in a ditch. Isn't that what happened to Joey Dickson last year when he totaled his brand-new Accord?"

"I forgot about that. Some idiot was tailgating his car and didn't see Joey slowing down for a turn. Slammed right into him. Poor Joey spent a month in the hospital."

"Not such a good idea to ram Ryder's car if we want our target alive. Besides, law enforcement might not pay the entire $20,000 reward if we deliver Ryder and he's dead."

"So the reward is now sounding good to you, Evan?"

"Oh, yeah. Let's use the money to buy a Corvette. I'm

sick of this van."

"A Corvette? Hell, yes. A red one."

Evan thought for a second. "How about a souped-up Dodge Ram?"

"Yeah, Rams are cool. But what about a Jeep Wrangler with the works? We could take it off-roading."

Shooting a smile to Devan, he said, "You had me at off-roading!"

"Look out! Ryder's turning!"

Slamming on the brakes, Evan said, "I missed the turn. Sorry about that." He swung the van into a U-turn, and then back-tracked until he turned onto Monroe Road. He quickly caught up with Ryder's car.

Evan's heart beat wildly. "What's the second idea you had before we got distracted?"

"We blink the high-beams at him until he pulls over. On the pretense of telling him his brake lights are out, I walk up to his driver-side window and jab him with the stun gun. Lights out. You help me drag him, and then we shove him into the back of the van. Hello, Rohypnol injection, and good night, Jim Ryder. Next stop, county sheriff office."

"I like it," said Evan. "After we get Ryder settled in, we get Special Agent Stone out of the trunk, and give her a taste of the stun gun with a Rohypnol chaser, too."

"Brody, Ryder just turned onto Monroe Road. He's almost to the quarry."

"Okay. Be there soon."

"Remember that white van I told you about. It missed the turn to Monroe Road and is doing a U-turn."

"What?"

"Yeah, now the van is turning onto Monroe Road, too."

"This is too much of a coincidence. That van is following Ryder. It's the fucking Gamers. I just know it is!"

"Why would they be chasing after Ryder? Doesn't make sense."

Brody's mind raced. There was a connection between the Gamers and Jim Ryder. What was it? He remembered one of the interviews Carly had with Ryder. "Gabe, Ryder told Carly that the Gamers had slipped a note to him during his trial."

"The Gamers attended Ryder's trial? Is there a risk they won't take?"

"Ryder said they were trying to impress him with their murders."

"So you think they were tailing Ryder to and from the community center?"

"That doesn't make much sense, does it? How could they have found Ryder's hideout when our deputies, the FBI and U.S. Marshals couldn't find it?"

"No, it doesn't gel."

Kaitlyn turned in her seat beside Gabe and spoke loud enough for Brody to hear. "What if the Gamers didn't tail Ryder to the community center? What if they were already there, waiting?"

"How would they know Ryder would be at the community center in Morel? Why wait for him there?" asked Brody.

"Oh, my God," said Kaitlyn. "The Gamers weren't waiting for Ryder. They found out Carly was teaching her class there. They were waiting for Carly!"

"I don't know," Brody said doubtfully.

"I think Cat's right," Gabe gasped. "The white van is now close to Ryder's car, almost touching his bumper. Their headlights are on bright and flashing wildly. It looks like they're trying to get him to pull over."

Slamming on the accelerator, Brody's SUV thrust ahead. His need to keep Carly safe overrode every reasonable thought. He had to get to her before it was too late.

Evan flicked on the van's bright headlights and then started flashing them on and off. This went on for several minutes. "What do I do now? He's not pulling over."

"Get closer. Get so close to the bastard that you're practically touching his bumper."

Cutting the distance between the two vehicles, Evan continued to flash the high beams. Soon Ryder slowed down and pulled off the road.

Devan reached under his seat and pulled out his stun gun. "Time for Ryder to find out who's boss." Turning off the van's interior light, he eased out of the passenger seat.

Evan climbed into the back of the van, grabbed his Morel High School athletic bag, and pulled out a syringe. Slipping it into his back pocket, he then carefully withdrew his father's prized "Dirty Harry" Smith & Wesson 44 Magnum and climbed out through the back door. By the time he reached the front of the van, Devan was at the rear of Ryder's car, and walking nonchalantly toward the driver-side window.

"Hey, buddy!" Devan called out. Reaching the window, he leaned inside and said, "Did you know your brake—"

"Do you know who you're dealing with? You little prick!" Ryder shouted.

An explosion burst before Devan's eyes as agonizing pain pierced through his brain. A second shot impaled him.

Blood burst out of his chest, and spread across his white coveralls. Devan fell to the ground as darkness overcame him.

Now at the rear of Ryder's car, Evan froze, his heart slamming against his ribs and his knees shaking. He opened his mouth to scream Devan's name, but nothing came out. He crept to the passenger side of the car, aimed his father's handgun, and shot Jim Ryder until he ran out of bullets, until Ryder was bloodied unrecognizably, slumped against the steering wheel.

Racing around the car, Evan reached his twin and sank to his knees, sick and shaken. He pulled Devan into his arms, rocking him back and forth, willing the lifeless body of his brother to be alive. It was then he saw the flashing lights of a vehicle speeding toward him. Above him were the glittering lights of a helicopter, its search light beaming to the ground, illuminating everything in its range. There was no time to get Devan *or* Carly into the van. Gently lowering Devan's body to the ground, he sprinted to the van, turned on the ignition, and hurtled the vehicle onto the road.

"Brody, be careful. Something's happened. There is a body lying on the road!" Cupping the phone so Brody couldn't hear him, he whispered to Kaitlyn, "What was Carly wearing tonight at class?"

"She had on a pair of sweats with a zipped hoodie. She said she'd owned the outfit since her training at Quantico."

"What color?"

"White. Both pieces were white."

Gabe felt the blood drain from his face. "No. That can't be Carly's body in the road. Please, God, no."

Up ahead Brody could see the tail lights of Ryder's car. It was parked on the side of the road.

"Gabe, where's the van?"

"I think the driver saw the lights of the helicopter and took off, heading north on Monroe Road."

"Call Cam for backup. Have him get all deputies in the area to find the van."

Rolling to a stop, Brody pushed the gear into park, but left the engine running, along with his bright headlights. He could see Ryder's dark silhouette in the driver seat. With the blades of the helicopter roaring overhead, Brody pulled his gun out of its holster, grabbed his flashlight, and climbed out of the SUV. In a low, crouched position, he hurried to the back of Ryder's car, stopped, and then sneaked a quick look around the vehicle. On the road next to the driver's door lay a body dressed in white. Aiming his flashlight in one hand, and his gun in the other, Brody crept closer. Blood completely covered the face, and soaked the chest area of the clothing, forming a widening dark pool on the pavement. Carly? His heart froze.

Aiming the beam of his flashlight into the car's interior, he saw a man wearing a ball cap in the driver's seat. "Freeze!" Brody shouted. "Don't move a muscle, Ryder!"

A wild thumping sounded from within the trunk. "Help me!" Keeping his gun and flashlight aimed, Brody backed up. "Carly? Baby, is that you?"

"Brody, I'm in the trunk. Please be careful. I heard gunshots."

"Just hold on. I'll get you out of there."

Inching toward the driver's door, Brody said, "Put your hands out the window, Ryder. Do it now. I will not hesitate to shoot you."

There was no movement.

Brody stopped at the back door and aimed his flashlight inside. He could now see that the body of the man inside was slumped against the steering wheel, either unconscious or dead. Jerking open the driver's door, he yanked the handgun out of Ryder's clenched hand, then pressed his fingers on his wrist to get a pulse. There was none. Covered with blood, his body riddled with bullets, Jim Ryder was dead. Reaching across his body, Brody pulled the keys out of the ignition, raced to the back of the car, and opened the trunk. Carly lay inside in a fetal position, sobbing hysterically.

"I'm here, Carly. You're safe." Brody gently lifted her out of the trunk and held her trembling body as she cried.

"I thought I'd never see you again," she sobbed. "He was going to kill me."

"It's over, baby," he said with a sigh of relief. "Jim Ryder isn't going to hurt you or anyone else ever again."

CHAPTER TWELVE

Evan had just finished pumping gas into the van when he heard police sirens in the distance. Jumping into the vehicle, he circled the building until he could park the van behind it. Two county sheriff vehicles raced past.

Closing his eyes, he rested his head against the steering wheel and tried to ignore the ache that had settled just behind his heart. Wailing hysterically in pain and anger, he visualized his twin's body lying on the highway. A pang of remorse shot through him. How could he have left Devan there all alone? He needed his brother, and didn't know if he could continue living without him. The only person who had ever loved him was gone.

Gazing at his father's gun on the passenger seat, he wondered if he had the guts to point it to his temple and pull the trigger. Of the two, Devan was the one with the guts. He could do anything, no matter how unpleasant, without blinking an eye.

Evan gritted his teeth as anger poured through him,

boiling his blood, and clouding his brain. Sheriff Brody Chase and anyone he cared for would pay for his brother's death. He had nothing to lose. Evan had already lost the most important person in his life. He'd make sure the Chase family felt the knifing pain of loss.

With the sleeve of her terrycloth robe, Carly wiped steam from the bathroom mirror.

As soon as they'd returned from the hospital, she'd told Brody she needed some alone time. She'd stepped into a hot shower and emerged thirty minutes later. Had she washed away the Ryder nightmare? Not completely. But it was a start.

"Carly, are you okay?" Brody tapped on the bathroom door.

"Honey, I'm fine. I'm back in the home I love, with the man I adore. How could I not be fine?"

"Just checking. You need to lie down soon. I've got an ice pack downstairs ready for your nose, like the doc recommended."

"How about a glass of wine?"

"No can do. You heard the doc," Brody chastised. "No alcohol."

A smile creased her face but quickly disappeared as she

gazed into the mirror. Tinges of purplish-blue appeared beneath both eyes and the right side of her face, where Ryder had punched her. One of her eyes was swollen shut, and the doctor confirmed her nose was broken. She resembled a young woman she'd had to arrest for prostitution in a human trafficking case. The woman had been beaten by one of her traffickers as an example to the rest of the women, who might be thinking of escape.

Looking around the bathroom, Carly realized she'd forgotten a nightshirt. Aching all over, she yearned for something soft against her skin. Opening the door to the bedroom, she eyed Brody's dresser. There was nothing softer than one of Brody's undershirts. Pulling open a drawer, she fingered through the neatly stacked pile, searching for the oldest and softest shirt. She touched something and placed it in the palm of her hand. It was a black velvet jewelry box. Inside was a ring, an exquisite circle of glittering diamonds.

Hearing Brody's footfalls on the stairs, she clicked the box shut, and put it under his pillow. She climbed into bed, and waited for him. Soon he entered the room, holding an ice pack and a tall glass of water.

Brody's face brightened at the sight of her. Placing the items on the nightstand, he settled down on the bed. "I have this fantasy of playing doctor with you, but having you actually injured isn't exactly what I had in mind."

His boldly handsome face smiled warmly down at her, as he lightly fingered a loose tendril of hair on her cheek. Carly reached out and clutched his hand.

Nervously licking her lips, she cleared her throat. "Mr. Chase, I have something to say to you and please don't interrupt me. I need to get this out — all of it."

His eyebrows rose inquiringly, but Brody said nothing. Carly squeezed his hand and continued, "I've never felt like I was part of a family before. When I was growing up, in the midst of our parents' divorce, it was just Blake and me. Thanks to you, I have the family and love I've always wanted. Everything that's happened has made me realize how much I love you, Brody. I've never felt this way about any man. I want you, your babies, and this wonderful life."

Slipping the black jewelry box from beneath his pillow, she handed it to him. "Marry me, Brody."

Gazing at the box in his hand, he opened it. "The jeweler told me this is called an eternity ring." Lovingly and gently, he kissed her lips. "That's what I want with you, Carly. An eternity."

Evan blinked several times as his eyes adjusted to the dim light in the room. He lay on the same bed where he'd watched his brother kill Abby Reece and Destiny Cooke. Glancing at the rows of plastic storage bins, he thought of the lethal games he and his brother had played for the past several years. They'd had a good run, and the cops had no clue.

He'd gotten little sleep. When Evan wasn't reliving the nightmare of Devan's death, he lay awake plotting how he would avenge his twin by slicing into the Chase family until they bled.

After he'd left the convenience store the previous night, he'd taken little-traveled country roads until he reached Morel, and then he'd headed to his father's storage unit business on the outskirts of town. Hiding the van behind the building, he unlocked the unit where he and his brother were supposed to be storing their athletic equipment. It was a lie the old man had bought, like usual, and soon the unit became the place where they imprisoned and murdered their targets. It now was a hiding place until Evan came up with a concrete plan to avenge his twin's death. He couldn't go home. How could he? Soon his parents would be notified that one of their sons was dead. He couldn't watch them grieve, knowing he'd left Devan behind, bleeding in the road like an animal struck by a car.

Lying on a pillow, staring at the ceiling, Evan ran the options through his head. What would hurt the Chase family? Maybe he should have taken the time to get Carly Stone out of Ryder's trunk. But she was never *his* pick for a target anyway. Kaitlyn Reece was his obsession. Why were they unable to find her? He'd warned Devan not to add that postscript at the end of their last email to Gabe Chase. It was crazy to hint that Kaitlyn was their next target. Doing so gave Chase time to tuck her away in a place where he and Devan couldn't find her.

Where could Kaitlyn be hiding? He and Devan had spent hours watching her home. But she wasn't there. Her VW wasn't even in the garage. Maybe he'd made a serious mistake by firing the AK-47 at her house. That and the hint in the email was more than enough reason for her to go into hiding. But where?

Though they'd kept an eye on Gabe Chase's office, he couldn't be sure Kaitlyn wasn't hiding inside. Then there was the Chase property outside Morel. He vowed to find her, and he'd start looking immediately.

Evan climbed out of bed, exited the storage unit, and headed toward the van.

Although he was hesitant to bother Brody after the nightmarish events the day before, Cam knocked on the door of the Honeymoon Cottage with one hand, and held a manila folder in the other. Brody soon opened the door, his hair ruffled by sleep, holding a cup of hot coffee.

"Sorry to bother you. But I didn't think this could wait."

"No problem." He handed the hot coffee to his brother. "Let me get another cup. I'll meet you at the picnic table. Carly's sleeping and I don't want to wake her."

Soon Brody sat across from Cameron, his face beaming with joy.

Studying him for a moment, Cameron said, "Has something happened I should know about? You look awfully happy this morning considering the night you and Carly had."

"I'm getting married."

"Oh man, that's the best news I've had in a long time. How did you get Carly to say 'yes?'"

"She asked me."

"No way."

"Yes, she did, and I couldn't accept fast enough," Brody laughed. "Now tell me what's in that folder."

"I've got two reports. One is the list of county residents who own AK-47s, like the one used to shoot at Kaitlyn's house, and the other is an inventory of county owners of 2012 Chevrolet 1500 white utility vans, like the one we think the Gamers are driving."

"I knew you had your guys working on these lists. Did you find anything that jumps out at you?"

"Yes." Cameron nodded his head. "We did a comparison of the two lists and one name appears on both."

"Whose name?" Brody asked.

"Bradley Lucas."

Brody jerked as he absorbed the stunning news, and nearly dropped his cup of coffee. "There's got to be a mistake. Is there another man in the county named Bradley Lucas?"

"We checked. There's only one Bradley Lucas, and it's the president of the county commission, who owns a construction business and a half-dozen smaller ones in Shawnee County. It's *our* Bradley Lucas."

Brody's cell phone vibrated in his back pocket. Retrieving it, he glanced at the display. "You are not going to believe this. Guess who's calling?" He punched the Answer button.

"Good morning, Mr. Lucas. How may I be of assistance?"

"My boys are missing!" Lucas said, his terrified voice laced with panic. "My wife just checked their beds and they haven't been slept in."

"Are you sure they didn't spend the night with one of their friends?"

"Hell, yes I'm sure. Do you think I'd be calling you if I

thought they were with one of their friends? We've called every kid we could think of, and no one has seen either one of them."

"I can hear in your voice that you're upset. Try to calm down. I'm sure this is something innocent and they're both okay."

"Bullshit! I know my sons. They're good boys. They never miss curfew, and they call if they're running late. There's no way Devan and Evan would ever stay out all night, unless something had happened to them."

"Do you have photos of them you can email to me? I'll put out a BOLO. What were they driving last night?"

"They're using one of my Chevrolet 1500 utility vans from my construction business. It's a 2012, and it's white. I'll send you the license plate number, along with the photos."

Brody ended the call and said to Cameron, "He just reported the Lucas twins missing. They were last seen driving a white Chevy utility van." He heard someone call his name, and then spotted Bryan Pittman hurrying across the lawn toward the picnic table.

"That body you found next to Ryder's car last night —" Bryan started, as his chest heaved from the run.

"You couldn't have conducted an autopsy this fast. What are you vying for, some kind of coroner record?"

Cameron interrupted.

"Funny guy," he said, rolling his eyes. "Seriously, I have a preliminary identification of the body. It's Devan Lucas, Bradley's kid."

"How do you know?" asked Brody.

"He had a fake driver's license in his pocket with his photo on it."

"Sweet Jesus," Brody shook his head and glanced at his brother.

Bryan held up his hand. "That's not all. The kid was wearing white coveralls, like the kind worn by house painters. Didn't you tell me the Gamers might be wearing uniforms, like those worn by bakers, to make their victims feel safe? Why not a house painter uniform?"

"Shit, Bryan, Devan Lucas was only sixteen- or seventeen-years-old."

His brow creased in concentration, Cameron said, "Don't forget we have eye witnesses who said our suspects are young. Carly pointed out in her profile that the Gamers may be as young as teenagers."

"I'm having a hard time believing Devan Lucas is involved in our killings. I've watched his brother and him grow up."

"Consider this," Cameron began. "Detective Burton's

DNA analysis reported our suspects are brothers. I don't think that it's a coincidence that Devan Lucas has a brother, and the two are close as thieves. C'mon, Brody, put it together."

"Here's one more thing," added Bryan. "Devan died clutching a stun gun in his right hand."

Brody heard a ping from his cell, indicating he'd received an email. Bradley Lucas had sent photographs of his two sons. Brody quickly forwarded the message to Cameron. "Put out a BOLO on Evan Lucas, last seen driving a 2012 white Chevy utility van. The license plate number is in Bradley's email. Tell the deputies to use caution when approaching the van, and consider Evan armed and dangerous."

Kaitlyn smiled as she headed for the mailbox at the end of the long lane. It was an incredible day, the air brisk enough for a light jacket, but not cold enough for a winter coat. Yellow, red, and orange leaves fell from trees on both sides of the driveway, and skittered across the road, drifting in the ditches. Geese honked as they flew overhead, and she heard Gabe in the backyard, wielding an axe to chop firewood for a promised romantic evening, spending time together in front of one of the fireplaces in the main house.

Reaching the mailbox, she shoved her mother's

birthday card inside then noticed a van stopping near her. A handsome boy leaned his head out the window and called out, "Hello there. Can you give me directions?"

Kaitlyn shook her head, and had begun to walk back to the house, when she realized the boy was out of the van and walking behind her. "Aren't you Miss Reece? You teach at Morel Elementary, don't you? Wait a minute. My little sister Tiffany is in your class."

Kaitlyn had turned to tell him that she had three little girls named Tiffany in her class, when he struck her with something on her neck that sent a vicious electrical current racing through her body like a freight train, causing her muscles to spasm and making her legs useless. The boy caught her as she collapsed, threw her over his shoulder, and rushed back to the van where he shoved her in the back. Climbing inside, he pulled a syringe out of a gym bag, along with a roll of duct tape.

"Don't try to move, Kaitlyn," the boy said, and then laughed. "As if you could."

He heard the motor of an oncoming car. He leapt out of the back, slammed the doors, and raced to the front of the van, where he jumped in and sped down the road.

Dwight Goodman was driving down the highway on his way to the state park where he and his date, Jenny

Hartley, would have a picnic. It was his first date with Jenny. In fact, it was his first date with anyone. Sneaking a glance at Jenny, he smiled. She was the prettiest girl in the freshman class, and getting a date with her was like winning the lottery. His stomach growled, and he prayed Jenny had not heard. He was starving. His mom had packed the picnic baskets with her special chicken salad with cranberries and pecans, waffle-cut carrots with ranch dip, a loaf of fresh French bread, a jug of iced tea, and two slices of what she called her to-die-for-dark-chocolate-cheesecake.

He was driving behind a van, when Jenny let out a shriek that sounded like his grandma's cat after she'd rocked on its tail.

"Look! Someone in that van is kicking at the glass in the back door. It's a woman. She's pounding on the glass with her fists now."

Dwight adjusted his glasses and saw that Jenny was telling the truth. Someone was trying to get out of that van. Fishing his cell phone out of his jeans' pocket, he pressed the buttons for 9-1-1 with his thumb, and then put it to his ear.

"What is your emergency?" asked the dispatcher.

"I think I'm reporting a possible kidnapping," said Dwight.

"What do you mean you think? You're either reporting

a kidnapping or you aren't."

"Tell her about the woman," Jenny whispered as she tapped his arm with her finger.

"There's a woman in the back of a van who's kicking at the glass in the back door. I think she's trying to escape."

"What van?"

"The van that I'm driving behind."

"Can you describe the van, son?"

"Sure. The van is a Chevy. It's white and fairly new. Maybe a 2011 or 2012."

Dwight could hear the rustle of paper in the background until the dispatcher put him on hold. Soon she returned with urgency in her voice, "Sir, would you please tell me your location?"

"We're on U.S. Route 136, and we're half-way between Veedersburg and Morel."

"Thank you. Now would you please tell me the make, model and color of the vehicle you're driving?"

"My dad loaned me his truck. It's a brand-new, black Dodge Ram. He's only had it a week."

Dwight heard someone whisper to the dispatcher. "Are you close enough to the van to get the license plate number?"

"Oh, I can read it." As soon as he read the number to the dispatcher, her voice changed from urgent to fear.

"What did you say your name was?"

"I didn't say. But my name is Dwight Goodman."

"Dwight, I need for you to slow down and put some distance between your vehicle and the van ahead of you."

"I'm sorry, but I can't do that. The lady just kicked out the glass and she's waving her arms at us. We have to help her."

Gabe swung at the last log, breaking it in two with his axe. Glancing at the cord of wood behind him, he decided they had enough wood for the fireplace that night. In fact, he'd cut enough wood to keep the fireplace roaring for many nights to come. As he wiped the beads of sweat from his brow, he realized Kaitlyn hadn't returned from the mailbox.

"Kaitlyn," he called out. When he got no answer, he went to the driveway and looked down the long lane to the mailbox. When he didn't see Kaitlyn, he entered the house through the kitchen door.

He called her name as he checked the rooms in the lower level of the house, but didn't find her. Upstairs, he did the same, but Kaitlyn wasn't to be found. Flying down the stairs, taking the steps two at a time, he reached the floor below, then raced out of the house toward the Honeymoon Cottage, where he saw Bryan and his two brothers sitting at the picnic table by the lake. He sprinted to them, panic rising in him like a NASA rocket. "Have you seen Kaitlyn?"

All three men shook their heads.

"What's wrong, Gabe?" asked Brody.

"Kaitlyn's gone. She walked to the mailbox and hasn't returned. I've looked in every room of the house. She's gone!"

Suddenly, Cameron's cell phone sounded. He talked for a short time and then put it on speaker. "Ellen, Sheriff Chase is here. Would you please repeat what you just told me?"

"I said I just got a call from a Dwight Goodman who is driving behind a white van that has a license plate number matching the one in the BOLO you just put out. The kid says there's a woman trapped in back of the van and she kicked out one of the glass windows in the rear door and is waving frantically for help."

"Where is the van?" asked Brody.

"Dwight says they're halfway between Veedersburg and Morel on 136," Ellen said. "The problem is I asked the kid to slow down and put some distance between his truck and the van, and he won't do it. He's determined to help her."

"You tell that kid to back off before he gets himself killed," Brody shouted. "Give all deputies in the area the location of that van now!"

To Gabe, he said, "Evan Lucas is driving that van. We think he's one of the Gamers. There's a good chance that the woman waving for help is Kaitlyn. Get the helicopter in the air. I'm staying here with Carly."

Angrily, Evan pounded the steering wheel. The effect of the stun gun was wearing off and Kaitlyn was moving her arms and legs. He'd panicked when he saw the truck heading toward them, and had dropped the syringe, along with the duct tape. That meant there was nothing to hold Kaitlyn down, and he couldn't leave the driver seat because the truck was still tailing them. What would Devan do? A visual of his brother's bloody body on the road sprung into his head. The pain of the memory knifed through him, leaving him breathless, tears blurring his vision. He needed his twin. Devan would know what to do.

He glanced in the rearview mirror. Sitting up, Kaitlyn was rubbing her arms and legs. "Just relax, Kaitlyn. Be good back there and I won't hurt you."

Whirling around to face him, she met his eyes in the mirror. "Who are you?"

"My name is Jon," he lied. "My little sister, Tiffany, is

in your class at Morel Elementary. She's in the hospital with a broken leg and wouldn't stop crying until I promised to bring her favorite teacher to her. That's where we're headed — to the hospital."

Kaitlyn rubbed her neck. "What did you hit me with? Why did you hurt me?"

"I didn't want to hurt you, but I knew how disappointed Tiffany would be if I didn't bring you to the hospital to see her."

Seeing the athletic bag, she dragged it to her and looked inside. "I don't know what your name is, but you don't have a sister named Tiffany. What you *do* have is a bag with a stun gun, syringe, drug vials, and duct tape." Kaitlyn pressed the stun gun to his neck. "I'm now in control, you sick freak. If you think I don't know how to use this baby, just try me."

"Listen, I already told you. I won't hurt you."

"Too bad I can't make the same promise," Kaitlyn shot him a glare in the mirror, and then glanced at the weapon in her hand. "Isn't this the Deadly Tech Model 5 with the rechargeable flashlight? Nice choice. If I recall, it packs a powerful punch of 19 million volts."

"What? How did you know that?"

"If you make one wrong move, you're going to get the same kind of up-close-and-personal experience you gave me of what 19 million volts feels like. Understand?"

"You're not going to do anything to me, bitch. Have you forgotten who's driving? Shoot me with that thing and we both could die."

"Thanks for reminding me." Nervous sweat slicked her body. "Now slowly and safely press on the brakes and stop this van."

The van hit a pothole in the road, sending it airborne for a second. Kaitlyn fell backward, slamming her head against the floor, sending the stun gun flying into the front compartment of the van and landing on the passenger seat. Instantly, Evan secured the weapon. "Now who's in control?"

Kaitlyn rubbed the back of her head, and considered the contents of the Morel High School athletic bag. Using the syringe was a good defensive tactic, but he would know she wouldn't be able to inject him. The last thing she needed was a driver incapacitated at the wheel. What the hell could she do with the duct tape?

Twisting herself around, she immediately noticed two large windows mounted in the rear door of the van. Crawling closer to the windows, she balanced herself and peered out. There was a truck behind the van. Delighted, she kicked one of the windows until the glass shattered. Then Kaitlyn stuck her arms out the window, waving wildly at the driver of the truck.

"Stop it!" Evan screamed.

Kaitlyn turned in time to see Evan pull something from the glove box. Her heart froze when she saw the fierce-looking gun in his hand. With one hand on the steering wheel, he stretched his arm and pointed the gun at her chest.

"How about I stop you permanently, bitch? Devan would approve of my shooting you. If he were here, you would undoubtedly already be dead."

The calm in his eyes was more frightening than if he'd shouted the threat at her.

Heart pounding, knees shaking, her thoughts racing, Kaitlyn fought for control. Biting her lip, she thought of Frankie's self-defense class. Although Frankie didn't recommend the technique unless it was an extreme emergency, she'd taught her class how to jump from a moving vehicle. It was to be a last-ditch effort, if they'd been abducted. Frankie had emphasized serious injury and even death could occur from leaping from a moving vehicle. Kaitlyn racked her brain for Frankie's instructions, opened both doors at the rear of the van, and then motioned for the truck behind them to back off.

"What the hell are you doing? Do you *want* to get shot?" Evan shouted.

Once the truck slowed down, she moved her body to

an angle so she could aim toward the soft grass at the side of the road. Kaitlyn jumped, tucked her body into a ball, her chin to her chest, and prepared to roll. Hitting the ground with her shoulder, she rolled across the grass into a ditch. The air whooshed out of her as if she'd been sucker punched, the pain so severe she could scarcely breathe. But she was alive. Lifting her head, she saw the black truck had pulled off the road, and a teenaged boy and girl were running toward her. In the distance, a police helicopter hugged the highway. Gabe?

Evan stared in the rearview mirror in disbelief. The crazy bitch had jumped. Just as he watched her roll into a ditch, he saw the helicopter heading toward him, along with a sheriff patrol car. He floored the accelerator, catapulting the van down the highway. He'd reached seventy-miles-per-hour when he saw the deer leap in front of him. Evan slammed on the brakes, making the van do a sickening whirl, spinning until it rolled and rolled, banging his head against the ceiling and then the window, until a heavy darkness overcame him.

Two patrol cars blocked traffic, while another raced in pursuit of the white van. Gabe lowered the helicopter to a landing, and leapt out. He was followed by Cameron, along with Bryan, who clutched his black medical bag. They hurried to the body in the ditch they'd spotted from the air.

When Gabe reached Kaitlyn, a young boy was near her body talking on his cell phone, while a girl stroked Kaitlyn's arm as she talked to her soothingly.

"I'm here, Cat." Gabe tried to keep the hitch of emotion out of his voice.

"I just knew that was you in the helicopter," Kaitlyn said softly, moaning in pain when he touched her.

"Where does it hurt?"

"Everywhere, but mostly up here." She pointed to her arm.

Bryan arrived. "Move aside so I can look at my patient." He bent down and examined Kaitlyn, who cried out when he prodded her upper arm. "Looks like her shoulder is broken. We need to get her to a hospital, Gabe. She's going to need surgery."

A loud and fiery explosion pierced the blue sky, and a dark cloud of smoke arose from the highway in the distance.

"What happened, Cam?" asked Gabe.

Ending his call, Cam placed his cell phone in his pocket. "Before the deputy in pursuit could even reach the white van, it spun out of control and flipped several times, until it burst into flames. It's too hot for the deputy to get too close to the vehicle, but he doesn't think the driver made it."

Cam's cell phone sounded. It was Brody.

"Hey, I was just going to call you. I've got some bad news."

"What happened? Is it Kaitlyn? Did she get hurt?"

"Except for a possible broken shoulder, Kaitlyn is fine. She jumped from the back of the van." Cameron paused. "It's Evan. He just wrecked the van and it exploded into flames. There's little chance he lived through it."

"I'm sorry to hear that."

"Bradley Lucas not only has to cope with the fact that his sons were serial killers, but now they are both dead."

"He just called. He looked for the boys at the storage business he owns outside of town. He'd given them a unit to store their athletic gear. Bradley discovered a bed inside the storage unit, along with plastic bins labeled with each of our victim's names. There were other bins, too, and he didn't recognize the names, but I did. They're the murdered Indianapolis prostitutes. Each bin contained personal items belonging to each victim."

"Bradley has never been one of my favorite people," Cameron said. "But I truly feel sorry for the guy. Do you want me to visit his wife and him with the news?"

"No, I'm going to handle that myself. Thanks, Cam."

Several weeks later, Gabe carried Godiva up the stairs, headed for Kaitlyn's suite. Halting in her doorframe, he looked at the stack of clothing on her bed. She stood near a dresser, her broken shoulder healing nicely, thanks to a white collar on her neck connected to a white cuff, supporting the weight of her arm. Gently, he placed the chocolate Lab puppy on the floor. Spying her yellow tennis ball, she crawled under Kaitlyn's bed to fetch it.

Gabe eyed Kaitlyn. "What are you doing? The doctor told you to rest."

"That was six weeks ago, and I'm tired of resting. It's time I moved back into my house." Sighing, she pulled open the first drawer of the dresser, and then tossed some T-shirts onto the bed.

"Why?"

"Well, one reason to move is the school board. The members are notoriously conservative, which has resulted in three female teachers being fired in the past few years for living with their boyfriends. The board claimed they were bad role models for their students because they were living in sin."

"You're kidding."

"No, I'm not. Besides, both Evan and Devan Lucas are dead. It's no longer dangerous for me to live alone. I have

Godiva to protect me."

"Godiva is still a puppy," Gabe protested.

"She can bark, can't she?"

"I wanted to wait until the right time to do this, but I guess now's that time."

"What are you talking about?"

Gabe plucked something out of his pocket, and held in the palm of his hand the 1976 Pontiac Firebird Matchbox car he'd given Kaitlyn years before.

Taking the toy car from him, she held it a second before noticing something was inside. Opening the tiny door with the nail of her index finger, she pulled out a folded white piece of paper that she quickly unfolded. In black ink were written the words "Marry me".

Joy bubbled in her laugh and shone in her eyes as she wrapped one arm around his neck. "Tell me you're serious, Gabe. You really want to marry me?"

Careful not to hurt her shoulder, he put his arms around her waist, and squeezed her affectionately.

"I've loved you since the first time I saw you on the Morel Elementary School playground. Please marry me, Cat. I can't bear to think of not having you in my life." Pausing for a second, he added, "Besides do you want Godiva growing up in a broken home? She needs both of her parents."

ABOUT THE AUTHOR

USA Today Bestselling Author, Alexa Grace's journey started in March 2011 when the Sr. Director of Training & Development position she'd held for thirteen years was eliminated. A door closed but another one opened. She finally had the time to pursue her childhood dream of writing books. Her focus is now on writing riveting romantic suspense novels.

Alexa Grace is consistently listed in top twenty of Amazon's Top 100 Most Popular Authors in the categories Romantic Suspense and Police Procedural.

In 2013, she was named one of the top 100 Indie authors by Kindle Review. A chapter is devoted to her in the book *Interview with Indie Authors* by C. Ridgway and T. Ridgway.

Her books *Deadly Offerings*, *Deadly Deception*, and *Deadly Relations* have consistently been listed in e-retailer's Top 100 Bestselling Romantic Suspense and Police Procedural Books.

Deadly Holiday, published in November 2012, is her holiday-themed romantic suspense novella, featuring all her Deadly Series characters.

Alexa's book *Deadly Relations* is included in the bestselling book set *The Perfect Ten book set* along with Dianna Love, Norah Wilson, Nancy Naigle, Andrienne Giordano, Misty Evans, Sandy Blair, Mary Buckham, Tonya Kappes and Micah Caipa.

Profile of Evil, the first book of the Profile Trilogy was published in May 2013. *Profile of Terror* is released in 2014 and *Profile of Fear* will be published in 2015.

Alexa earned two degrees from Indiana State University and currently lives in Florida. She's a member of Romance Writers of America and Sisters in Crime.

Her writing support team includes five Miniature Schnauzers, three of which are rescues and daughter, Melissa.. As a writer, she is fueled by Starbucks lattes, chocolate and emails from readers.

You can visit her at - http://www.alexa-grace.net/
Subscribe to her newsletter at - http://eepurl.com/sJ-Df
Friend her on Facebook -
https://www.facebook.com/AuthorAlexaGrace
Tweet her - @AlexaGrace2

BOOKS BY ALEXA GRACE

Deadly Offerings

Deadly Deception

Deadly Relations

Deadly Holiday

Profile of Evil

Profile of Terror

CPSIA information can be obtained
at www.ICGtesting.com
Printed in the USA
LVOW07s2257140517
534528LV00009B/394/P